Harry & Ruth

by

Howard Owen

THE PERMANENT PRESS
SAG HARBOR, NY 11963

Library of Congress Cataloging-in-Publication Data

Owen, Howard
Harry and Ruth / by Howard Owen
p. cm.
ISBN 1-57962-066-3
1.World War, 1939,1945--Fiction. I. Title.
PS3565.W552H37 2000
813'.54--dc21 99-034819
CIP

THE PERMANENT PRESS
4170 Noyac Road
Sag Harbor, NY 11963

To Max Gartenberg, whose guidance and tenacity kept *Harry and Ruth* afloat.

Grateful appreciation to Bob Bledsoe, Sue Durden, Max Gartenberg, Bev Orndorff, Jeff Schapiro and Phyllis Van Neste for their expertise in various aspects of human endeavor. Thanks to Martin and Judith Shepard for editing, guidance and friendship. And, as always, thanks to Karen, for everything.

ONE

HARRY STEIN SITS on his front porch, the morning breeze tickling the crap that he's claiming for hair these days. He's waiting for Bob the Driver.

Bob the Driver used to be a pharmaceutical salesman. He and his wife retired to Safe Harbor almost 10 years ago; nine years ago, Bob realized he could not live without work.

Now, he drives people between the airport and the eastern end of Long Island's south fork. Harry's only problem with Bob the Driver is that he drives the way Harry imagines he used to work — full tilt.

Harry and Bob used to play tennis and drink together. Today, though, Harry is happy to be his passenger. The airport in Islip is not as close as it used to be.

Harry gets up and checks the front door again. He's had everything turned off. He's given away half a freezer of food to the Naughtons next door. He's told them, God help him, that their teenage son can drive the Camry once in a while "to keep the tires from going flat."

Harry dozes for a few seconds in the warm sun, and Bob the Driver wakes him up with a series of short blasts from the station wagon's horn as he roars up the driveway.

"Hey, you old goat," Bob yells. "I thought you were dead. That'd really piss me off, 'cause then you wouldn't pay me." Bob's hard, playful laugh makes Harry smile.

Bob brings the wagon to such an abrupt halt in the sandy yard that dust rises higher than his head as he jumps out and stomps around to the porch. Before Harry can get to his feet, his old friend has grabbed the two largest suitcases. Harry tries to help, bringing the smallest one, but Bob orders him to "just stay there, dammit," talking to him like a kid, really.

Harry does as he is told, though; he does that a lot lately. All that he is allowed to carry to Bob the Driver's car is his own diminished body.

These days, Harry accepts a lot of sympathy, even from guys like Bob the Driver, a guy he used to wear out on the tennis courts. But at least Bob remembers him when.

It's the other ones, when he ventures out from home, who he wishes, just once, could have seen Harry Stein in his prime — tall, slim but not skinny, jet-black hair, dark, smooth complexion, piercing brown eyes. These days, it hurts him to come across pictures from his youth. Wearing his floppy, old-man's cap, his pants bagging as if they were handed down by a larger, healthier man, he knows he never again will be either flashy or dependable.

"Ready to go?" Bob the Driver asks, starting the car and jerking away already.

Harry nods, frantically searching for the seatbelt.

"Hank!" Her voice from a second-floor window encourages a dog two houses away to start barking. "Do you have that little red suitcase I packed last night?"

Ruth is still giving everything one last look: lights, locks, thermostat, hair. Hank has already taken the car to the garage and had everything possible checked. Now, distracted from his search for the flashlight he's sure is back there, somewhere, under all the luggage, he emerges and looks up.

"It's in the trunk, Momma. It must be. Everything else we own is."

She tells him she'll be there "in a minute." Hank stands up straight, stretches and leans against the car. The sun is warm, and it is — give or take a barking dog — quiet.

Finally, understanding that this trip might never start if he lets his mother continue checking and rechecking the already-checked, he sighs and goes upstairs.

It's already 9 a.m., and Hank hopes to reach Sugar Beach by bedtime. He is (everyone in Saraw knows) a demon driver, capable of sitting behind a steering wheel for six hours at a time, taking a 15-minute break, then driving another six.

Hank would just as soon stay here. He loves fall in the low country. The days are as crisp and blue as the new shirt he bought for the trip; the nights are cool enough for sweaters.

Behind the house, past Ruth's pumpkin patch, the cornfields have been plowed under, awaiting spring, and six boys are playing a game of tag football in a wide backyard full of still-green grass. It's a Saturday, and Hank thinks he should be fishing, or maybe painting the old shed, a college football game or a stock car race on the radio. Florida will seem like stepping back into summer.

He climbs the stairs slowly, one step at a time. On the second floor, Ruth is going from room to room. She stops at a door, hands on her hips, stands still for a few seconds, then moves on. There are six bedrooms upstairs, and Hank overtakes her at the last one.

"It's gonna be dark soon," he says.

"I know I'm forgetting something, but I can't think of what it is. I hoped it would jump out at me."

Hank assures her that anything she's forgotten probably can be bought in Florida. Finally, she surrenders. She makes sure the stove is turned off, gives the faucet in the kitchen a final twist and at last walks out the front door, which she locks and deadbolts.

Hank says he'll drive first. He doesn't add that he will also drive last and always, if he has his way. His mother, for all her accomplishments, is not what he considers interstate rated.

It's the last day of September, and they'll be back by the 5th, the day after Ruth's birthday. "Assuming," she says, "we can all get along for five days."

On the way out of town, Hank drives by Mercy's so that Ruth can leave the house key. Mercy walks out to the car, telling them to "stay put," then taking the key and wishing them a safe trip. She kisses Hank on the cheek, then walks around and gives Ruth a long hug through the window.

"Say hey to everybody," she tells her cousin and oldest friend.

They share a smile, a secret one that seems to take in all those years, all those letters.

TWO

ONCE THEY GET past the Hamptons and onto the expressway, Bob the Driver stops talking for as much as five minutes at a time. Harry looks out the window at the pines and sand, and for a moment he is back in Saraw.

Lately, Harry's mind has a mind of its own. It wanders whenever and wherever it wants, sometimes into areas Harry would as soon leave unexplored.

Even the good times Harry would as soon leave alone some days. He is taunted by their goodness.

Much of the time, where his mind takes him is into the realm of Ruth.

He saved her first letter, and then he saved the second one and the others that followed while he was still stationed at Camp Warren. Harry did not consider himself a pack rat, indeed thought of himself as an unsentimental man, a light traveler, but he never stopped saving.

In the first letter she ever wrote him, she called him "Dear Harry Stein."

She was Saraw High School salutatorian ("but I should have been valedictorian") the June before and had no plans beyond working for her grandfather and eventually going to a small Presbyterian girls school. "By then," she wrote, "you all probably will have already given the Germans and Japs a good licking and come back home . . ."

Of course, it didn't start with letters.

That September afternoon, another would-be officer in his company, a boy from a steel town in western Pennsylvania with the lowest hairline Harry had ever seen, said he'd met this girl. Harry had driven his second-hand Ford down to Camp Warren and parked it off base, and Larry Olkewicz told him he would get him a date in exchange for a ride to and from Saraw "just down the road."

Harry could read road maps. He knew Saraw was 20 sometimes-paved miles away, but he was homesick and bored, so he went along. He didn't know he was going to a Presbyterian social until Olkewicz directed him to park in the grass next to the wooden, low-steepled church. The humid air smelled like sawdust.

"Olkewicz," he said, "are you aware that I'm not Presbyterian? That I'm not Protestant? Not even Christian? These people might lynch me."

"Take it easy, Jewboy," Olkewicz said, already getting out of the car and combing back his slick straight hair. "They don't care down here. As long as you ain't colored, we're OK. Shoot, they'll get all excited, probably think you want to convert."

Harry sighed, turned off the ignition and followed Olkewicz in.

They walked into what was referred to as the fellowship hall, although there was little fellowship going on, as far as Harry could see. Homely country girls standing in little groups, giggling as if they'd never been in public before. Deacons and Sunday-school teachers doubling as chaperones. Grapefruit punch. And what appeared to be about half of Camp Warren.

Olkewicz, it developed, had not exactly lined up a date, for either of them. He'd heard an enlisted man say that this Presbyterian church on the other side of the county was having a social for the soldiers at Camp Warren. There were at least five other such patriotic events the same night in a 20-mile radius. Olkewicz just happened to have heard about this one.

Harry has not, for most of his existence, been very philosophical, not a man to look always in the rearview mirror, but he wonders often what his life would have been like without the clumsy subterfuge of Larry Olkewicz.

The hall smelled of varnished wood and mildewed hymnals. Harry had been in a few Protestant churches; one in Richmond passed him off as a gentile for the betterment of its basketball team. His father almost had a stroke when he learned that his only son was seen belting out "What a Friend We Have in Jesus" at Cokesbury Methodist.

"You couldn't at least have played for the Episcopalians?!" he yelled at Harry.

But country Presbyterians. Harry figured they could smell a Jew.

He did not feel mistreated, though. It helped that Olkewicz and a few other new soldiers who seemed not to have spent much time indoors were so obnoxious that Harry looked good in comparison by just standing still, not starting fights or picking his nose.

And Harry did look good. His hair was so black it was almost blue, and being outdoors in the hot dregs of Southern summer had enhanced his tan. He was lean as a rail. His eyes always seemed to be supporting a smile. In addition, he and Olkewicz were among the few men present who were in officers' training, and their uniforms were magnets. Even Olkewicz couldn't avoid latching on to a curly-haired blonde who needed braces and who spent the rest of the evening trying to either pronounce or spell his name while he spent the rest of the evening trying to get her to slip outside to Harry's car.

The social would end by 9. Before then, two separate pairs of girls approached Harry Stein nervously and tried to make small talk. He was polite enough; he had not ruled out the occasional date, even if he was engaged. It did seem to him, though, that it would take a girl at least half as attractive as his lovely Gloria Tannebaum to make him stray.

One of the matrons came over.

"And where are you-all from?" she said, sweetly.

He told her Richmond, which seemed to please her.

"And are you a Presbyterian?" she asked, her voice full of hope.

"No, ma'am; I'm a Methodist."

She seemed to let herself believe this, and they talked for a while. It was after 8:30, and his only goal was to round up his passenger and return to camp.

He almost missed her.

She said later that she hadn't meant to come at all, that she and her cousin Mercy had gone to a dance at the beach and were headed home. Ruth saw that the social was still in progress and had Mercy let her out at the church, no more than 200 yards from her house.

Harry was walking out the front door, bound for his car.

But then, stopping in the shadows to light a Lucky Strike, he heard a car whine to a stop. Two girls were talking. He couldn't even hear what they were saying, but something about the inflection, the accent, the nuances of one of the voices struck a chord. It wasn't much, just enough to make him stop and wonder. Who knows why Harry didn't go on? Was he reminded of the future Richmond debutante who kept him aroused his junior year in high school? Did she sound like the girl who stole his heart in fifth grade? Was it something he heard from the womb? Fate? Luck?

Even now, Harry could not tell you.

A door slammed and the car moved on. Then, as the engine noise faded, he heard a tinkling sound, like bells. He had moved to one side, farther out of the light. Leaning on a white pillar that still smelled of its last coat of paint, he watched as she came into view.

Maybe it was some property of the church light that hit her as she walked toward it in the night-wet grass, making her Gibson-girl face look flush and slightly damp, almost as if she had a skim of dew on her, too. Maybe it was the confident way she walked, striding enough to make the bracelet on her left wrist jingle. Maybe it was the tune she was whistling: "Deep in the Heart of Texas." It was very popular that year. When she got to the boom-boom-boom-boom part, she would shake her wrist four times.

She reached that part the second time as she was walking up the front steps. Without thinking, Harry clapped four times and then croaked out (he was not a singer), "deep in the heart of Texas."

She hadn't seen him until then, and she gave a small, violent jump, as if she had the hiccups. Harry stepped out of the shadows.

"You nearly scared me to death," she said. "Didn't anybody ever teach you not to lurk? I hate it when people lurk."

She didn't look scared to Harry. She looked capable. And beautiful. She had hazel eyes that seemed at least three-dimensional, dirty-blonde hair that tumbled down to her shoulders, full, expressive eyebrows that danced up and down when she talked. She was wearing a white dress with straps that might have earned her a sharp look or a warning from some deacon's wife had she walked inside the church hall that night.

Harry apologized and introduced himself, holding out his hand. Hers was warm to the touch. He tried to disguise the fact that he wanted to fall to his knees and kiss that hand, and the wrist, and the elbow, and the soft skin of her upper arm, and her shoulder, eventually stopping when a couple of elders dragged him off her.

"Harry Stein," she said, arching one of those eyebrows and sizing him up. "There are some Steins in Newport. They own Stein's Men's Store. The Jews own just about all the clothing stores in . . ."

She stopped and shook her head.

"I beg your pardon," she said. She was blushing. "I'm just assuming you're Jewish. And even if you were Jewish, it wouldn't matter. I mean . . . Please tell me to shut up before I dig myself in any deeper."

"If I told you to shut up," Harry said, "I wouldn't have the pleasure of hearing you any more. Say anything you want. Just talk."

He told her she sounded mellifluous, which made her laugh.

She was tan and witty and sensual. When she talked, she would put her right hand behind her head, rub her neck and close her eyes as if she were giving herself an immense amount of pleasure.

She had that voice some Southern girls had, back in Richmond, sweet and feminine, while at the same time hinting strongly of desire and abandon. Harry was sure, lying on his bunk in the barracks that night, that he never had been so affected by another human being. And it would be part of the bittersweet mystery of his life that he never could have told you exactly why.

He asked her if she would like a cigarette. She declined.

They moved into the shadows again. A few other couples had slipped out, but Harry and Ruth were unseen. They talked quietly, about the war and weather, and his eyes never left her.

At one point, she frowned.

"You're making me nervous," she said. "You're looking at me like you want to have me for dinner."

"I have X-ray vision," he told her, taking a last drag and dropping the cigarette to the concrete porch.

He had used that particular line often, back home. It tended to pleasantly discombobulate women, if they liked him to start with. Ruth Crowder, though, stared him down, looking him over from top to bottom, and said, "So do I."

This time, Harry blushed, and laughed.

He began asking her questions, about herself and her rough-edged little town, stalling for time, trying to drink in as much of her as he could. They stayed right there, Harry leaning against the pillar, Ruth standing two feet away. When she wasn't rubbing her neck, she kept her hands folded in front of her, the way, he supposed at the time, her mother had taught her, but she answered straight, with none of the country backwardness of the other girls.

He asked her what she was doing in a place like Saraw, and she told him that she considered Saraw, North Carolina, plenty good enough for her. He doubted that, but he kept his doubts to himself.

Far too soon for Harry's liking, it was 9:30, and the deacons were walking around the grounds, rousting everyone and trying to prevent sacrilege.

He asked Ruth if he could see her again, and she said yes. She said it casually, as if it didn't mean that much. They agreed to meet at White Oak Beach, on the boardwalk by the dance hall, the next Friday night.

Harry shook her hand, and then, unable to restrain himself from touching her somewhere with his lips, he leaned down and kissed her on the forehead. It was warm and a little damp. She had brought the scent of the ocean back with her.

He forced himself to step back, afraid of doing anything that might scare her away. She looked up, surprised but not angry, not skittish. She blew him a kiss.

That's when Harry took out a piece of paper and a pen and wrote down his address at camp, then handed it to her. "Write me," he said, and it sounded like a plea.

"I'm going to see you Friday night," she said, smiling and shaking her head.

"Write me," he said again. "Tell me everything you can think of about yourself. I want to know everything."

"I don't have that much time. . . . OK, Harry Stein. I'll write you, then. I just hope it gets there before I see you again."

And she turned and left, jingling as she disappeared into the darkness.

By the time Harry got back to the car, the girl with bad teeth was leaving. She seemed offended.

Olkewicz had a reddish mark on the side of his face.

"Can't we give you a ride?" he asked, undiscouraged.

The girl did not look back.

"Jeez," Olkewicz whined, "I wish you coulda waited a little longer, Stein. I almost had her going."

Harry Stein said nothing, and they departed in what he thought was silence. About halfway back to camp, his traveling companion thought to ask him how his evening had gone.

Pretty well, Harry said, all things considered.

"I thought so," Olkewicz said. "You've been whistling ever since we left that damn church."

THREE

On a warm fall night, the sixth of October, Harry Stein and Ruth Crowder went to White Oak Beach, where they'd had their first actual date. They parked a hundred yards past the last inhabited houses and went over the dunes to the water.

Ruth preferred to stay along the boardwalk, where the ocean was only background noise and a cool, salty breeze. But there might not be a night this perfect again until spring, and she did want to please Harry Stein, so she wore her bathing suit underneath her dress.

At Virginia Beach, where Harry went as a child, it might already be too late for swimming, but here, it was perfect. The water was cooling more slowly than the air; it felt warmer than it would some days in July. Farther off into the darkness, a Tommy Dorsey tune was playing.

Harry went rushing in, as he always did, diving head-first into a wave. When he surfaced and looked back, Ruth was still standing where he'd left her, going no farther than the very tip of the tide's boundary. She reminded Harry of a little girl at the ocean for the first time, fearful every time the water crept up to her. She was so beautiful in the white one-piece bathing suit. For the rest of his life, string bikinis and clothing-optional beaches notwithstanding, no girl on any beach would stir him so. She had the kind of tan that she accepted as her birthright, merely for living that far south and being young. On that night, in that place, he thought perfection had temporarily been achieved.

The spell lasted a few seconds. Then, dragging her into the water seemed like the only thing to do. But when Harry came out, grinning his intentions, stooped in front of her and lifted her over his shoulder, then started walking back into the water, she went suddenly and completely berserk. Before Harry could put her down, she had managed to give him what would turn into a rather impressive black eye.

"I can't swim!" she kept screaming, and by the time he

put her down, she was crying so hard she could barely catch her breath.

Harry knew people who couldn't swim. In Richmond, no summer passed without some luckless child diving into the river on a dare and never again touching dry land. He himself learned in stages, with his father's hand growing lighter and lighter every time they tried at a lake or the pool. One day, the water was holding him and he was moving forward, all of 20 feet.

"See, Harry," his father had said, putting a sunburned arm around him while he used the other to keep his cigar from getting wet, "now you can swim. Now you're a big boy." Old Harry had even smiled.

"Can't swim" did not properly describe Ruth's relationship with water, though. Harry was just beginning to fully understand that she feared it the way other children feared fire.

In a letter the next day, Ruth apologized, and tried to explain.

"More than anything else," she wrote, "I remember the day of the big hurricane, the one in 1928. You see, it hit on October 6. I should have told you about it before, but it gets treated like some deep, dark secret around here. We don't talk about it among ourselves, even on October 6. When I was a little girl, I would ask my grandparents about it, or one of my aunts, and they'd shut up tight. If you asked Uncle Matty, he'd start to cry. After a while, I stopped asking.

"That day, I remember my grandfather arguing with Momma and Daddy, trying to keep them from going to the beach. It was windy, but the sun was shining, and I was crying because they wouldn't take me with them. After they left, Grandma let me `help' her make biscuits, and by the time we were finished, late that morning, it had gotten very dark. Granddaddy wouldn't come away from the window. He was looking toward the ocean. . ."

Before he fell in love with Ruth Crowder, before he became immersed in a girl and a family and a place to which only a war could have led him, Harry was unfamiliar with the concept of family secrets.

Among the Steins, there were no secrets, no subtext. Until the day she died, Harry's mother was liable, at any family gathering, to launch into a monologue about what exactly went wrong between Harry and Gloria, with aunts and uncles and cousins freely volunteering their opinions, pro-Harry and con.

The Crowders, though, not only could keep a secret, they had trouble letting go of one — provided it was important enough. With the trivial ones, they have proved themselves, even at this late date, to be completely untrustworthy.

The party for Ruth's 70th birthday, meant to be a surprise, had no chance whatsoever of remaining one. Her younger son, Paul, must have known that when he enlisted Hank's aid in luring her down to Florida under the guise of an ordinary week at the beach. It took Ruth all of five minutes to worm the truth from Hank. But she still agreed, somewhat hesitantly, to go.

"Paul," she wrote to her younger son, "thank you for thinking of me, but I just don't like surprises. I have never gained much pleasure from them."

Three weeks after they met, Harry told Ruth about failing to get into law school, and about his lukewarm plans to try again after the war. He told her not to tell anyone else. Three weeks later, he stopped at the small general store in Saraw, beside the river, to buy cigarettes. The store owner, a man who (Harry thought) didn't even know his name, said, in his most conspiratorial tone, "Don't worry, son. You'll get into that lawyers' college next time for sure."

With the important and central mysteries, though, such as the story of Belle and Theron Crowder and The One in '28, information was not so easily obtained. Some of this reticence might have grown from an inability or unwillingness to deal with trouble and heartache, a fear of the uncomfortable. Or it might have had its seeds in the belief that knowledge is power, that if you know the old, old stories and no one else does, you have something of value, something not to be given away to every meddlesome stranger.

Once, when Harry expressed his theories on Crowder secrets in a letter, Ruth wrote him back that all it was, was good manners. Sometimes, though, it was maddening to her as well. What would the South be, she asked Harry once in another letter, without its idiosyncracies? He wrote back: Sane.

Harry did, though, before the spring of 1943 took him away, hear most of the story of Belle and Theron and the One in '28.

Theron Crowder IV was a handsome man. He had a brooding, unflinching, angular look, even in the wedding picture, not hungry-seeming like some underfed tenant farmer but more the haughty, high-cheekboned look of the country patrician, king of an undemanding hill. He was the last of three children, born in 1902 into what passed for a well-to-do family in a small North Carolina town. His father owned the lumber mill and turpentine works that were the only reason the Saraw and Wallace Railroad, all 34 miles of it, was built. Timber was shipped from the forests farther inland to the mill. Lumber and supplies went back up the same way, or down the Saraw River, before it silted over. Young Theron's father, whom everyone called T.D., was a stubborn man when Harry knew him. In his prime, before The One in '28, his inflexibility was his strength.

Theron IV had two older sisters, Charlotte and Jane, and it is still accepted dogma among older Saraw residents who remember the stories that he was "spoiled rotten." (Harry has a theory: There are approximately six times as many boys whose siblings are all older sisters as there are girls with all older brothers, or at least there were at that time and in that place. The husbands made their wives keep having babies until they either died or produced something on which a Roman numeral could be hung.)

The Crowders were the only family in Saraw living in a brick house. They wanted their son to marry well, and so Theron IV's acceptable gene pool in the town of his birth was limited. Because he was warned not to, and because of how he was, he fell in love with Belle Culbreth. In the surviving photographs, she could be Ruth's twin.

Belle was the best-looking girl in town. She was the youngest of nine children who lived with their mother and occasional men alongside Turpentine Creek, among other families of subsistence farmers and sawmill workers whose rickety pine houses were connected to each other and their respective privies by winding dirt paths where copperheads liked to sun. Some of Belle's siblings had "Father: Unknown" by their names at the county courthouse. ("Don't you dare mention this to anyone," Ruth warned when she finally admitted that fact to Harry.)

Belle Culbreth was said to be "wild as a buck." When she was 16, she went for a ride with her boyfriend, who stopped long enough on the way to the beach to rob a store at gunpoint. He was caught, and he claimed that Belle was the one who had planned it all and urged him on, but the jury believed her, and only the boy went to prison.

What Ruth herself knew, she came to know in drips and drabs; nobody in her family told a truly important story straight on. The ones worth remembering came from the periphery, from the corner of your eye and ear, pearls thrown aside casually in the middle of a conversation about pie recipes or gallbladder surgery.

Her grandparents were horrified when young Theron told them he was marrying Belle Culbreth. Besides the social chasm, they were both 17, just out of high school.

But Theron was wild, too. Before he was 16, around the time that Belle was (by the most charitable interpretation) a spectator and passenger in an armed robbery, he had tried to enlist in the Army during the waning days of World War I. After he was rejected because of his age, he got into a fight with two soldiers on the courthouse square in Newport and came home with a broken nose.

They were, Ruth's Aunt Charlotte would say, two of a kind, for better or for worse. They eloped.

Theron's parents tried to get the marriage annulled. T.D. threatened, then pleaded. He sent Theron's beloved older sisters to cry on the Culbreths' doorstep. Sudie, Theron's mother, shut herself in her room for two weeks, threatening to die. Finally, though, she sent for Theron and Belle and told them they could have a roof over their heads, no doubt a finer roof than was covering their shack along Turpentine Creek.

T.D., when he accepted reality and tried to cut his losses, did his wife one better. He told the newlyweds that he would build them a brand-new house, fine as any in Saraw, on the birth of their first male child.

It is an indicator of the stubbornness of Belle and Theron that they waited six years to have their first and only child, a girl they named Ruth McNair Crowder. Belle nearly died giving birth and was told she couldn't have any more children. T.D. waited three more years, obviously believing that the promise of a new house would cause Belle to will herself pregnant, whatever the physical barriers.

"I'm pretty sure," Ruth wrote Harry once, "that Momma didn't really want to have children. Oh, she was a good enough mother, as best I can remember, but it wasn't what she was cut out to be."

What Ruth can remember: her mother singing "Yes, We Have No Bananas" to make her laugh; the way her father's breath smelled when he'd kiss her good night, a taste she later learned was a mixture of tobacco and bourbon; falling down the stairs at her grandparents' and her mother rushing her to the hospital in Newport for stitches, then taking her to Pearson's Drug Store afterward for her first vanilla milkshake; her father carrying her on his shoulders through springtime fields, running down the furrows while she squealed in fear and delight.

And, of course, the day itself.

Finally, in 1928, T.D. brought in a crew and had the workers start on the long-promised house. Theron and Belle had lived with him and Sudie and the others for nine years already, and it is possible that he was driven by a desire for space and privacy and peace in his own house.

The footings were dug in June. By October, the house was three-fourths ready.

Fourteen years later, Harry still could see where those footings were. After the hurricane, T.D. Crowder had the same crew tear the house down and haul away the lumber and bricks.

In 1928, Theron and Belle were 26. Theron was helping run the mill, working six days most weeks, but he and Belle still had some of the wild streak that made them the life of the party and the despair of the Crowders. Only two years before, they had been arrested in Newport for "public lewdness in a motor vehicle," which was being driven by Theron at the time.

That fall, they must have been at least somewhat content with their lives. They and their daughter would be moving into the finest house in town — a two-story brick Colonial — by Christmas. Theron's future was secure if not dazzling in its possibilities. They were said to have been the center of young married life in Saraw; if the Crowders never quite accepted Belle as their daughter, she apparently was liked well enough by her husband's peers in Saraw and Newport.

The storm came on a Wednesday. Some of Belle and Theron's friends talked them into driving to White Oak Beach for the day. Another couple was already vacationing at a cottage there, and they talked their friends into joining them for a hurricane party. It had been done before: Everyone would sit on the porch, drink and stare down an ocean. One time, two years earlier, the waves had completely surrounded the party cottage, cutting it off from the mainland. But the water receded in a few minutes, and everyone had a story to tell.

Theron had an almost-new model-T. He told his father he was taking the day off, and he and Belle both laughed at T.D.'s threats and warnings.

The old maps and the history books show how the big storms sculpted the Carolina coast, and continue to do so.

A large percentage of Atlantic hurricanes head straight for the part of North Carolina that juts into harm's way. Then, they swerve, borne out to sea by the Gulf Stream, dealing a glancing blow to a few beach towns, sometimes plowing into Long Island or the New England coast, or limping, old and broken, into the North Atlantic. Sometimes, one will hit the coast head-on, washing a few abandoned cottages out to sea. Even those, though, almost invariably weaken as they make landfall. Even those tend to hover a bit, almost stopping, before finally lumbering landward.

Once every few decades, though, seldom enough to breed carelessness, there is a storm like The One in '28.

Technically, White Oak Beach is an island. From Newport, the river is on one side and the ocean on the other. Fast-food restaurants and the cheap cottages of those not able to get closer to the sea line the six-lane road all the way to the end. At the five-mile mark, the road goes over a slight rise and the water is visible on both sides, several hundred yards away. Just before the beach itself, the distance closes until the land is bisected by a channel 200 yards across.

The channel is younger than Ruth. It is not man-made.

Theron and Belle took a bottle of whiskey with them that Wednesday, bought from a bootlegger on the beach highway who later remembered them because Theron had thrown the bottle's cap away as they drove off.

There were six other couples, all from Saraw, at the cottage that day. Most of the rest had, like Theron and Belle, driven there that morning, looking for a little excitement.

This was before much was known about hurricanes, beyond the empirical wisdom of the survivors. No one bothered to name them. Even less was known about storm surges. Still, everyone knew something was coming. Hardly a soul was left at the beach by the time Theron and Belle got there; all that remained were a few dozen partiers at a handful of houses. The cottages almost all had names; the one where Ruth's parents spent their last morning was the Sink 'r' Swim, because it was owned by the Sink family that lived just two blocks from the Crowders, and, Ruth thinks when she considers such imponderables, because perhaps Someone has a sense of humor: Neither Theron nor Belle could swim at all.

Around 10, the sky became twilight dark, with a greenish tint. The storm wasn't supposed to hit until early afternoon, so it was presumed, according to one survivor, that the revelers had a couple of hours to drink and dance before deciding whether to ride it out.

From later reports, three bad things happened with no warning:

The storm, already rolling along at close to 110 miles per hour, suddenly strengthened, to what was later estimated to be about 140.

Also, it originally was on a path that would have brushed the coast around White Oak Beach with gale-to-small-hurricane-force winds. About 9 that morning, though, it inexplicably took what was later called a hard left turn.

When it turned, it also accelerated, from 5 miles an hour forward speed to an estimated 20-25. It roared into the cape just south of White Oak Beach like a bull charging a matador.

Even all that might not have doomed Theron and Belle except for a fourth item. Above the equator, hurricanes blow counter-clockwise. Thus, to the west of the storm's eye, the force of the wind is lessened by the extent of the storm's forward motion. A 140-mile-per hour storm, moving 25 miles per hour forward, might only have winds of 115 miles an hour, the forward motion acting against the storm winds coming around from the north.

East of the storm, the opposite is true. The forward speed of the hurricane is added to the wind speed.

The hard left turn put White Oak Beach east of the storm. Winds were estimated later to have exceeded 160 miles per hour.

There was no radio to warn them, and they didn't believe the sky. They jeered at the other vacationers and partiers as they fled.

When the storm hit, the dozen partiers at the Sink `r' Swim would be on their own.

Six of them, rebuked as cowards, bailed out before the ocean cut the channel that would make White Oak Beach an island for the rest of the century. By the time the others realized the extent of their folly and bad luck, they were trapped.

A storm-surge wave that one survivor said was at least 15 feet high hit the beach and washed several cottages off their foundations, including the one in which Theron and Belle were marooned. They were now hanging on to the walls of a house chest-deep in water.

The only thing standing that looked as if it might survive the storm was the White Oak Beach water tower, only a short block away. As the water temporarily receded and the wind came howling in ever harder, the remaining six tried to reach it. They were halfway there, a survivor said, hanging on to each other, when another wave separated them, and they had to swim.

Four of them reached the water tower, which somehow did not collapse. They climbed up as high as they could and used their belts and other clothing to lash themselves to the stairs on the back side, facing land.

They could see Theron and Belle down below. They had gotten as far as a yaupon tree that stood like a gnarled old man in the middle of a vacant lot. Theron was helping Belle up to the highest point that would hold her when the next large wave hit. The four hanging on to the tower didn't see it coming, because they were facing away from the sea, but they were 30 feet above the ground, and the water that roared in was no more than 10 feet from their perch.

Theron and Belle weren't washed away. The yaupon tree perversely snared them, hanging them up in its limbs, spearing them there, while they struggled to get free, screaming for help and choking on seawater. Then the tree disappeared beneath a solid wall of ocean.

It was some time, nobody knew exactly how long, before the water receded enough for the other four to see Theron and Belle, their clothes torn away, their bodies stuck like kites in the yaupon tree. That was what dominated the survivors' view for the next three hours, whenever they ventured to open their eyes.

When the winds finally subsided, the four in the tower climbed down and saw that they had chosen the only structure still standing for five blocks. The men walked through the still waist-deep water over to the tree; none of the four was wearing anything except rags by now. They were able to untangle Theron and Belle's bodies and carry them over to a brick pumphouse. One of the women found a tablecloth snagged on a piece of wood and covered them. A survivor told Ruth, years later, that their faces and bodies had been sandblasted as smooth as if they were babies.

FOUR

Bob the Driver wakes Harry with a question.

"So, your sister killing the fatted calf for you down there?"

"Maybe the fatted tofu. Freda and Artie eat a little healthier than I do."

"Fatted tofu," Bob barks out a laugh. "Guess that's kosher."

Harry has regained, if nothing else, some of his appetite. For that he's grateful. The last time he visited Freda, he and Artie went out for a pork barbecue sandwich at one of his old favorite places.

His sister asked him, when they got back, as politely as she could manage, if he didn't think a man with the big toe of his left foot in the grave ought to try to walk the straight and narrow just a little bit.

No, he told her. He didn't think God would approve of such hypocrisy. Harry believes, as much as he believes anything, that Harry Stein will have to stand on his record, barbecue and all. The idea of undoing 70 years of wrongs with a single moment of remorse seems too easy to him.

"God forbid," he told Freda, "that I should be forgiven so easily."

Bob gets him to the Islip airport with an hour to spare. Harry used to think nothing of rushing up here 20 minutes before the flight took off. Now, on top of everything else, he's anxious, nervous.

His old friend carries most of the bags to the gate and makes sure Harry is checked and on his way south.

"Now, you make sure he gets to the right gate in Baltimore," Bob admonishes the ticket clerk, to Harry's great embarrassment. He starts to protest, to say something sharp, when Bob the Driver grabs him and gives him a painful but sincere hug.

"You take care of yourself," he says. "You and I have got some goddamn tennis to play, come spring."

And then Bob the Driver is gone, hurrying out the door. Harry watches him get back in the station wagon and sit there for a few seconds before he hurtles off into traffic, almost clipping a shuttle bus.

Harry likes the little USAir Express flights. The propellers make such a racket that he is almost always lulled to sleep. Somehow, the small cabin, the dull vibrating roar going up and down like a metallic chant in his ears, seems cozier, safer than the big planes do, a womb of noise.

He has a window seat, and once he gets comfortable, even before the plane begins to taxi, he is asleep.

Soon, Harry is in the middle of the same cruel dream he's been having since the fall of 1944. Sometimes it will go away for years and then he'll have it four sweat-drenched nights in a row, for no reason.

Lately, it has been on him again, hard.

All the variations have the same basic thread, and they all owe their existence to one single minute a thousand years ago.

In the dream, as it happened in life, Lieutenant Harry Stein is with a platoon of men crossing a small river a few kilometers east of Verdun. It is no more than a creek, a tributary that feeds the Meuse. The banks are lined with poplars, and the only houses and farm buildings in sight have been deserted for two days.

Harry and a sergeant even younger than he, are side by side, at the end of the irregular line wading in three feet of water, chilled by the fall wind, their rifles held overhead. The men are wary and silent, but they are not really afraid, not foul-your-pants afraid; there are no Germans within five miles, they know.

Sergeant Stevens is from Maryland, a square-headed, blond farm boy who says little unless he has been drinking, a vice he has taken up in the holes and trenches of northern France. He is on Harry's side, for some reason, and Harry knows that this is important. Just before it happens, Harry and the sergeant agree that this would be a day better spent hunting quail back home.

They all know light travels faster than sound. They have seen it before. Still, Harry is surprised for the split second between Stevens' sudden lurch and the tut-tut-tut from a barn more than a hundred yards away.

The water turns red, fading to pink. Stevens is moving forward, leaving his trail in the water. The other men rush in random terror for the safety of land and trees, no more than 50 feet away. The bullets barely disturb the water at all.

Stevens stumbles, then falls. Harry catches him around the waist and tries to go forward. When that fails, he bends low, beneath the water line, and tries to lift him. As he raises upward, staggering under the weight, a sudden convulsion tells Harry the sergeant has been hit again, and they both fall into the creek. Harry gulps a mouthful of water and thinks he can taste the other man's blood.

Harry tries again, as the sniper continues to fire at them. He sees two more of his men hit. One falls into the water, blood streaming from his head. The other, shot between the hip and knee, is helped to safety by two friends.

Harry feels a stinging in his right arm. He makes one last, hurried effort, and then he lets the sergeant's body slide slowly down his as he follows the other men out of the water and through the line of poplars. He has to pull hard to escape Stevens' grasp, and this second above all the others will stay with him forever. He hears Stevens moan behind him, once, as he flees. He expects to be shot every step of the way; he has never known such fear.

When he looks back, the sergeant is nowhere to be seen. It is then that he sees that he himself is wounded. It is not a serious injury, and Harry will be back with his men soon, in truth more quickly than he would have preferred.

Gradually, he comes to understand that the other men either did not see his surrender of Stevens or do not choose to judge him. The incident is never spoken of except obliquely. Harry's men do not turn on him, but no one tells him that he did his best, either. On good days he can convince himself that he did what he could.

On bad days, he has the dream.

This time, he looks back. Stevens, whose first name — Eldridge — Harry knew only from rosters and dog tags, is sitting up in the water. He is laughing, beckoning Harry back through the bullets. Stevens is bleeding from his mouth, and there are holes in his chest, yet he still laughs.

"C'mon, in, Harry," he yells. "The water's fine. It doesn't hurt."

Harry tries to get away, but the current carries him back toward the sergeant, and finally he crashes straight into the blood-soaked, laughing man, who embraces him.

"Is he OK?" Harry hears someone ask, and he thinks he must be in a hospital, somewhere behind the lines. Someone else, a woman, answers, after a pause, "I think so. He's been asleep since before we took off."

And then Harry realizes that he's waking up, that it's just the dream. He can't believe, after all this time, that his brain can trick him so, can send him back to that day. Why, he wonders, don't the good days become the stuff of dreams?

He is covered in sweat, but he keeps his eyes closed, embarrassed that his seatmate and the stewardess have seen this. He feigns sleep until they are descending toward the Baltimore airport.

Hank and Ruth cross into Georgia around 4. Outside Savannah, Hank finally pulls over and lets his mother drive for a while. She has asked three times. It's still light, and they both know it's preferable that she not have her turn on the interstate after sunset.

Ruth is pleased to see that Hank can actually doze off for a few minutes. He is the master of the 20-minute nap, and by the time they reach Jacksonville, he seems rested and ready for the final stretch, across the Florida panhandle to Sugar Beach.

With Hank back behind the wheel, they sail along between 75 and 80 miles an hour, westward into the sun. Ruth's mind wanders; she's as tired from her hour of driving as Hank is from all his.

“I wonder if Naomi is there yet,” he says, ending a long silence. Ruth and he, long used to living in the same house, can go a day comfortably without talking, but she has been too quiet today, too much inside herself.

Hank passes a long line of trucks and a billboard advertising alligators, boiled peanuts and fireworks.

Ruth found out, as soon as she called Paul to thank him for the surprise party, that her daughter would be coming, too. She wonders what inducements or threats it took to get her there, and she hopes all that effort isn’t for naught.

“Oh, I don’t know,” Ruth replies, trying to sound casual. “I think she was supposed to get there around 6.”

“Well, then, I suppose she will be there when we get there, unless I can figure some way to shift this Lincoln into warp speed.”

“You seem to be trying.”

She’s doing a tap dance on the console with her fingernails. Hank reaches over and puts his hand on hers.

“It’ll be OK, Momma,” he tells her. She sighs, shakes her head and tells him to pay attention to the road.

“Wonder if Thomas and the kids are coming, too.”

“You know as well as I do,” she answers, and looks away.

There are many things Ruth would change if she could. Naomi and her family’s last visit to Saraw is near the top of the list.

It was Christmas of 1992.

Actually, it was the first week in December, but Ruth was just thrilled that her daughter’s family was coming at all. She was filled with the Christmas spirit as she had not been in years. She and Naomi had not been close, not the way they once had been, for some time, but Ruth had hopes.

Grace was in college and Gary was a senior in high school that year. When they were in Saraw, they and their father would go for long drives, no doubt (Ruth imagined) counting the hours until time for the flight back to Denver. Thomas grew up in North Carolina, but he had said, at a family dinner a few years before, after a few glasses of a good Bordeaux, that if he never saw the state again, it would be too soon, and Hank had suggested that nobody had built a fence around it, that there were still flights out. Thomas thanked God for that, falling into his high-pitched cackle that Ruth always found irritating.

Then came the Christmas of '92. They all seemed to be on edge, a half-step off, misunderstood and misunderstanding. Hank tried to be gone whenever Thomas was around.

Naomi and her family were in Saraw from Wednesday to Saturday. On Friday, the last full day, the others were outside playing a sloppy game of pickup basketball. Ruth, Naomi and Thomas were at the breakfast table, talking, with a cable news show on in the background. A story came on about a gay rights parade in San Francisco. Ruth, a little too quickly, picked up the remote control and clicked the TV off.

Naomi looked at her for a second, then asked her, a little sharply, "Anything wrong, Mother?"

Ruth wondered later how she had missed it.

"No, nothing's wrong." And then she said, "I just can't bear to watch all that, that mess. It gives me a cold chill. How can people do that?"

Ruth had never considered Gary's sexual orientation. He was a nice boy, very thoughtful, a little quiet. She never picked up on it at all. Otherwise, she would never have said anything. Surely they must know that.

Naomi seemed to take it as a blow to the heart, an outright attack on her only son. She lectured Ruth at length about tolerance and the myth that one has any control over sexual preference.

Ruth, her feelings hurt, brought the Old Testament into it, going deeper than she meant to. Thomas half-heartedly joined the fray on his wife's side.

"It's just a breakdown of the family," Ruth said, "all this homosexuality is part of the whole thing."

"The breakdown of the family!" Naomi bit off the words. "How can you lecture anybody, especially me, on the breakdown of the family? If this family was a car, they'd have junked it for parts 20 years ago."

And she left Ruth sitting there with her mouth open, too stunned to cry right away. They avoided each other as much as possible for the rest of the day.

The next morning, Ruth was supposed to make breakfast for them before they left. They had a 10:30 flight.

The departing car woke Hank before 7. Ruth was still asleep, so he went downstairs. Naomi left a note, as cold as the cement steps where he read it, about trying to get an earlier flight back, as if there were more than one flight a day leaving Newport for Denver.

He had to break the news to Ruth, and that's when he told her what everyone else seemed to know already.

She tried to deny it at first, then realized what she had said. How, she wondered then, still wonders now, can I be so stupid sometimes? On Christmas Day, she had to be persuaded even to open presents, and then she regretted spoiling things for everyone else.

She wrote a long letter to Naomi, trying to patch things up without actually saying that she knew her grandson was gay. Naomi didn't write back for four months, and her letter made no reference to Ruth's.

How, Ruth asks herself, can you expect it to be any different? If it hadn't been Gary, it would have been something else. With her and Naomi, it's always something, a million small somethings spawned by the one Large Something that turned everything upside-down.

When the plane lands at Baltimore, Harry tries to carry his own luggage and almost falls. Two airport workers take the large bags to the lobby, where Harry is placed near the departure gate. He's surprised they don't put a name tag on him so he doesn't get lost.

In less than half an hour, he's on another, similar plane, and soon they're droning toward Richmond. He nods in and out of sleep, but the dream doesn't come back.

At the Richmond airport, he goes through the same ordeal of having to have his bags toted into the lobby. Here, at least, is family. Freda and Artie are waiting, first ones he sees inside the building. They approach him gingerly, it seems to Harry, as if he might break. He hasn't seen them in a while. Maybe he's not looking so good.

"You seem better," his sister says, and he thanks her for that, for trying.

"Yeah," Artie is nodding his head like a large dog. "Better."

"Better than what?" Harry can't resist saying, and they laugh, relieved to see that somewhere in there is old, wise-ass Harry Stein, not gone yet. At least it keeps them from exchanging The Look.

When he sees The Look, the one used by those mutually considering the plight of people like him, he wants to shout, "I'm a man, dammit! I've done amazing things! With another break or two, they'd have named schools after me!" But these days, what he mostly wants to do is nap.

There is a two-mile causeway leading from the mainland to Sugar Beach, which is a large sand bar packed solid with cottages and condominiums. When Paul and Tran bought their cottage, the beach was inhabited by only a dozen older places and one motel. Now, though, there are few vacant lots left.

Ruth has been here twice before. The beach is beautiful, but she privately prefers the Atlantic to the Gulf. She likes a strong salt breeze in the air, and she likes to hear the waves crashing in the distance. She is proud that she has learned to at least tolerate great bodies of water, at a safe distance.

Ruth has dozed off on the final stretch, but she wakes up when the car stops and frantically checks herself in the visor mirror.

"Don't worry, Momma," Hank tells her. "You look pretty."

She gives him an impatient look, but she does smile.

Paul, Tran and their children come out to welcome them. Hank and Paul carry the large pieces of luggage in. Ruth brings the pecan pies.

"Thanks for driving," she tells Hank.

"If it wasn't for my fear of flying," he says, waving away her words, "you could have been here in an airplane a long time ago."

Up the steps to the cottage they go, Paul taking Ruth's elbow. Naomi is waiting on the landing.

She is still an attractive woman. Three years haven't changed that. She has retained her athlete's body. Her hair is still dark and is pulled back so severely that her mother worries it might give her headaches, and she is suffering from a slight overdose of makeup and lipstick. But she is, at 52, still pretty. Ruth can still see, through it all, the little girl who once was her best companion.

Ruth and Naomi say hello and exchange a hug, skin barely touching skin. Ruth finds she is afraid of her own daughter, afraid of squeezing too hard and scaring her away.

Tran comes up with the children, Leigh and Stephen, who embrace their grandmother. Ruth looks around.

"Where are Thomas and Grace and Gary?"

"Oh, they couldn't come," Naomi says. "Thomas couldn't get away from work, and Grace and Gary couldn't miss classes."

Ruth nods.

"Well, I'm glad you're here," she says to her daughter. "It's been a long time."

Naomi doesn't reply, except for a look. She turns and goes back into the house, and the rest follow.

FIVE

When Ruth became aware that Harry was saving every letter, she wanted him to burn them all.

"I can't bear to think of you or, God forbid, someone else reading all that nonsense I wrote when I was a girl," she wrote.

He told her he would burn one of hers for every one she burned of his.

Sometimes now, she will go to the big black trunk and read one of the hundreds of pieces of paper that came to her over the years. And sometimes, Harry reads thc ones Ruth wrote to him.

As much as anyone can, they relive their youth (and much of their adulthood), and they have come to understand what the letters did, and what they were.

"I feel as if I have met my soul mate," Ruth wrote Harry the week after Thanksgiving that first year. "I know it cannot last. Don't worry. You have been truthful with me, about your girl back in Richmond. I do not feel deceived."

Harry fed a hunger Ruth had known for much of her young life, a hunger she had come to fear might be her natural state. In her world, it was considered sinful for a woman to want to devour life. She saw the way her grandmother and aunts and cousins laughed with their hands covering their faces, how they ate less and drank less than the men, how they deferred to them in conversation. And the boys she had dated would admit to no thoughts that transcended the literal, day-to-day business of living.

Harry Stein was the first boy or man with whom she could sit and talk about ideas and ambition.

"I feel as if I have been waiting all these 17 years for something to happen," she wrote him, "for someone to come along and show me that there is more to the world, someone who isn't afraid to ask why, or to take off his clothes and run into the waves head-first."

Ruth knew, even at 17, that she had been spoiled by kind, overcompensating grandparents, aunts and uncles. At that time, their little lane was full of Crowders, and all of them, after her parents died, seemed to close ranks around the new orphan and try to ensure that she never had a reason to cry. But still there was a void.

When Harry told her that he had sometimes felt he was born at the wrong place or the wrong time, she wrote, "that was when I felt you and I were one. It seems, at times, as if I were some adopted baby they found in Kinlaw's Hell and brought home. Even cousin Mercy, who's my age exactly, doesn't understand what I'm talking about sometimes. Mercy doesn't see why anybody would want to move to a place where no one knew them. She says she would die if she had to do that.

"Sometimes, although I don't even tell Mercy, I feel I'll die if I can't."

Harry called her a child, on one of those chilly nights in the parlor. He said it light-heartedly, but she dug her nails into his wrist and told him, "I am as grown as you, maybe more, and you know it."

Once, after she had been caught skipping school, she overheard her grandfather tell Charlotte that it was the Culbreth in her. But she knew that none of her mother's family had ever been able even to get away from Turpentine Creek, where no house yet had indoor plumbing. Whatever was in her, she knew, it was more than a severe case of Culbreth.

The Crowders lived on the dead-end lane off Polk Avenue, which still connects at both ends to the main highway bisecting the town. It is now officially Main Street for its short promenade through Saraw but is still the Beach Road to most of the town's residents.

Saraw in 1942 reminded Harry of some of the Virginia villages that he and his father passed through a decade earlier, when Harry was allowed to accompany him on business trips, places where the edges of the wilderness could be seen from any store or house.

Saraw, though, was rougher, more raw, more full of life. The previous summer, an alligator had been trapped within the town limits. The next spring, a bear would wander onto Polk Avenue, where one of Ruth's uncles would shoot it. Everything smelled of fresh-cut lumber; the swamp water behind the Crowders' home was reddish-brown. Of the four types of poisonous snakes found in the United States, all could be found within ten miles of the Crowders' back door.

Between Ruth's grandparents' home and the swamp, serving as the boundary to Kinlaw's Hell, was the Saraw and Wallace Railroad, the Sam and Willie. The right-of-way is still there, a flat rise above the Venus's-flytraps, pitcher plants and standing water on the other side. The state has turned it into a linear park, and it is possible to walk it, along the swamp's boundary, for 20 miles. The view changes little, and the copperheads are fond of its warm bare earth on cool days.

In 1942, though, the tracks were still there, and the train came and went once a day, six days a week. On Saturdays at the Crowders', the background noise was the shifting and braking of the S&W's only engine bullying flatcars of timber onto and off of sidetracks.

Saraw, in its unfinished state and on the edge of a wild world considerably larger and more powerful than itself, was fond of the supernatural.

There was rumored to be a creature deep in Kinlaw's Hell that roared and squalled like a panther, and any number of men claimed they had seen its yellow eyes while following the rail bed home from the bootlegger's down by the river late at night.

There was the Bolton house, downstream from the bridge, haunted by a man who murdered his wife and children with a butcher knife.

And there were the Saraw Lights.

Ruth showed them to Harry one November evening. She told her grandparents and the rest where she was taking him, and he could tell that they weren't pleased, but to Harry's amazement, they didn't forbid it. There was a new moon, and she took along a lantern and a blanket. It had been particularly warm that day, and the ground was wet with dew.

They walked toward the swamp, and he helped her up the four-foot climb to the tracks. Gradually, his eyes adjusted to the dark.

"You're not going to feed me to the tiger, are you?" he asked her.

"Panther."

They walked along a few steps, and then she stopped and put the lantern out.

"All right," she said. "Now look straight down the tracks. Just keep staring until you see it."

He stared intently for a long minute.

"I can't see a damn thing," he told her. By then, he'd been outside long enough to make out the slightly darker outlines of distant pines.

"Keep looking. I can see them. You're supposed to be the one with the great eyes."

Finally, he did, too.

Two tiny, yellow-white points of light, far, far away, twinkled, faded, twinkled again. They seemed to move slightly from side to side. Harry had to hold his head at exactly the right angle, between blind spots, to keep them in his vision.

"That's amazing. What is it, a car?"

"There isn't a road crossing for ten miles."

"What, then?"

"Well," she said after a pause, "there are a lot of people around here who'll tell you that's Theron and Belle Culbreth."

There are several notable ghost lights in North Carolina, and the story tends to be approximately the same: a tragic accident, a lost soul trying to find its way home. In this case, the swamp gas or whatever other phenomenon caused the apparition was alleged to be the ghosts of Theron and Belle Crowder, trying to get back to Saraw.

People swore that the lights had never been there before 1928.

"Aren't they coming from the wrong direction?" Harry asked.

"Hush," Ruth said. "This isn't something I show to just any boy."

He was going to say something else when he noticed that her body, next to his, was shaking. She was crying silently.

"I'm sorry," he said, and bent down to kiss her.

"I'm a lot better than I used to be about it," she said, sniffling a little. "In grade school, they used to tease me. They said my momma and daddy were ghosts. Sometimes, I believed they were, too.

"One afternoon, Aunt Charlotte caught me half a mile down the track. I had packed a sandwich in a brown paper bag. I told her I was going to see my momma and daddy."

They had the blanket around them. Harry's right arm rested on her shoulder, and he could feel the warm curve of her right breast. To this point, they had only petted. She always stopped him, and he always let her. Harry had known several girls since the first time, when he was 15 and, on a dare, paid for the services of a black woman of some notoriety who took him for half-price, "since you's such a baby." For months he lived in fear of his penis falling off.

He didn't try very hard with Ruth, certainly not as hard as he wanted to. It was wrong enough, he knew already, that he was trying at all, that he didn't just do the clean, cold thing he couldn't bring himself to do. It was doubly wrong at this instant. Nonetheless, he did try.

This time, she didn't stop him. And Harry didn't stop himself.

They set the blanket out on the grass beside the tracks, and they lay upon it. After all the unsnapping and unzipping that preceded such surreptitious sex in 1942, after a certain amount of stroking on his part and permission on hers, he rolled over on top of her.

Ruth's head was actually resting on one of the rails as they drove into each other with missionary zeal. Harry was prepared and careful; he always tried to be. It was, he didn't understand until afterward, the first time he had had sex with a girl he loved. Gloria Tannebaum was saving herself.

The thing he remembers most now: Ruth kept watching him, training her hazel eyes right on him, and even though there wasn't a moon, they were shining. When they rolled back in her head and he could only see the whites of them, it was the most erotic thing he had ever witnessed to that point. If he had cared not a whit for her, the lust she invoked at that moment would have been enough.

What Ruth remembers most: She had never before had an orgasm, didn't even know what one was. She was afraid that she was having a seizure, or a stroke like the one that had crippled her Uncle Carter the month before. She feared she would die there in shame, with her head resting on one of the rails of the Saraw and Wallace Railroad and her underpants around her ankles. She had been with only one other boy.

All through November and into the winter they would slip away whenever they could, making love in a cheap boarding house near the beach, in Harry's car, even once in Ruth's own bedroom, still smelling of powdery childhood. More than the sex, they both remembered, through all the years, the kissing, how it went on for hours as they lay there in the dark with the radio on.

One unusually warm early December day, a year and a day after Pearl Harbor, they went for a picnic in Kinlaw's Hell. Harry rowed the little boat wherever Ruth told him to and hoped she remembered the way home. The Spanish moss slapped against his face; there was just enough black water underneath to keep them afloat. In addition to the bears and ghosts, Ruth had shown Harry the plants in Kinlaw's Hell that eat insects. He knew he could live there his entire life and not know which channel was a dead end and which one led to a creek. Even Ruth was sure of only a few of the watery paths, and she was careful not to stray.

Ruth said she liked the swamp better in the winter, even as cold as it got, because there weren't any spiders and snakes around.

She found a hummock out in the middle that was dry and no more than three feet above the water around it, and that's where they spread their blanket and had their picnic, with each other for dessert. It was there that Ruth told Harry that she loved him, and he told her that he loved her, too. He'd known this almost from the beginning, but he resisted saying it until she did, because he had nothing to offer, and because he was afraid.

He had returned to Richmond once on leave since he'd met Ruth. He and Gloria spent as much time as they could in the three days they had, and it was more apparent than ever that both the Steins and the Tannebaums were amenable to a quick and very non-traditional wedding before Harry shipped out, which probably would happen in late January or early February.

With Gloria, in the setting where they had first danced together and first kissed, among their old friends, in the well-to-do homes of their comfortable neighborhood, he saw Ruth Crowder almost as an illusion, other-worldly as the Saraw Lights, something that had briefly startled and confused him but was seen more clearly in the harsh daylight of Richmond's brick reality.

Harry cared deeply for Gloria Tannebaum, who had gone to Mount Holyoke while he was at Princeton. They were seen as special in their community, among the few to achieve such a lofty academic berth in the larger world. They had known each other all their lives but never dated until they were accidentally thrown together at a college mixer. Afterward, there had been no good reason not to follow the smooth path to where they were now, their friends and families nodding with approval from the wings.

Harry's father had been a salesman before he took a chance and started his own clothing store, then branched out, starting two more men's clothiers in Richmond and one each in Lynchburg and Charlottesville. He became comfortable enough to send his son to an Ivy League school. Harry does not remember ever wanting to go to Princeton, except that it was his father's dream. Old Harry wanted him to be a lawyer.

Max Tannebaum was a lawyer already, a generation ahead of the Steins, but he was not as well off as Old Harry.

When Harry got back to Camp Warren, he resolved to see Ruth one more time, to do the brave, hard thing and end it. Even before he saw her face, he knew he couldn't. She was standing there at the train station, looking the wrong way, at soldiers exiting the next car. Just the tilt of her head, the way she stood on tiptoes so as not to miss anyone, the cut of her hair and the memory of the way it had smelled when he kissed her goodbye before he left — these alone were enough to stop him, to convince him that no matter how real Gloria Tannebaum was, this was more real. He called her name and she ran into his arms, and he never told her goodbye until he had to.

Sometimes, Harry can't help but look back.

If he had married Ruth, his parents and the Tannebaums would've gotten over it; he's sure of that now. Gloria would have married some other nice Jewish boy who would have become a lawyer like her father. They would have lived happily ever after, all of them.

It didn't seem that easy in 1942, though. It was much easier to go with the majority vote.

All Harry could think of was his third cousin, Stuart Schapiro, who was nine years older. He fell in love with a gentile girl from Petersburg, and they dated for nine years before his parents would let them marry. There was always a Stuart Schapiro argument at family gatherings, with a younger cousin taking Stuart's case, in absentia, and an older aunt or uncle screaming that such a thing could never be allowed to happen.

Harry could rationalize by telling himself, truthfully, that the Crowders would not be popping any buttons over Ruth marrying a Jew, either. But he knew in his heart that

Ruth had a way with her family, that she did what she made up her mind to do, that her surrogate parents never seemed to put their feet completely down when it came to Ruth.

Ruth writes her willfulness off to the conditions of her childhood. She might not have turned out better if her parents had lived, but she knows it would have been different.

The day they drowned, she remembers her grandfather coming back home, and then his brothers Harwood and Fred helping him out of the truck and walking him up to the front steps the way they sometimes had to when they all had been drinking. The front yard was full of felled trees and broken limbs.

When he got inside, he blurted it out, as if he had to say it quickly or not at all: "Theron and Belle are gone." Ruth's grandmother fell back into her chair and began screaming. Ruth asked "Gone where?" and it was up to her Aunt Charlotte to take her into the back sitting room and explain, although it only became clear to her gradually, in terrible flashes large and small — seeing their salvaged but unreal faces at the funeral home, waiting for her mother to come read her a story, the realization that there were two less Crowders walking to their church the next Sunday. Gradually, two steps forward, one step back, the pain came, then receded and hardened.

She slept with her grandparents for two years after that, before they finally got her back to her own room. They bought her a pony. They humored her so much, buying her any candy or treat she wanted, that she was plump for the first and only time in her life when she started school.

When Harry first met them, T.D.'s sister Goldie was well into her 60s, recently widowed, and Charlotte and Jane were in their mid-40s. Charlotte had never married. Jane's husband had died in 1921, of the flu. Neither was as attractive as Ruth, but they were both pretty, pleasant women. Jane told her, when she was 7 or 8, that there was only one man out there for every woman, and she had lost hers.

The Crowder house's other resident was Uncle Matty. Uncle Matty was T.D.'s brother, eight years his junior. He was in his mid-60s when Harry met him, but his simple nature made him seem younger. He was an accomplished furniture-maker, he was dependable, and he was as loyal as a German shepherd. Since he was six feet, six inches tall and had T.D.'s dark, dangerous looks, he could be an imposing figure to those who didn't know him, but he would never harm anyone unless he felt he or his family was threatened.

Harry was treated well by the six older Crowders. When he wasn't there, though, they tried to gently warn Ruth against getting too deeply involved with someone "not of your religion." She never told them that they had nothing to worry about, that the elegant Harry Stein was not about to marry some little country Presbyterian girl. She allayed their fears mainly by telling them that she was playing the field. She would go out occasionally with some boy from town, and she claimed she dated other soldiers whom she met at the various dances and socials that some church or civic group was always having that winter.

But Ruth had no other prospects; she wasn't looking for any. It seemed to her and Harry that they had lived the same lives in very different worlds. They were both their class salutatorians, laughed at the same jokes, had the same doubts about the existence of God that few, especially before and during the war, voiced. They never talked about it much, but they had the same physical needs, the same sexual timing and appetites. They had been together no more than a month when they started noticing how often they had the same thoughts at the same time.

I was kidnapped from a good Presbyterian home, Harry would tell her, and forced to live a life without barbecue or bacon, a life of circumscription and circumcision. Pity me, Ruth would say, born to a wealthy Jewish family and spirited away by Protestant gypsies, sold to a family that forced me to learn all the books of the New Testament, to dress Christmas trees and boil Easter eggs.

The weeks and months passed quickly, between the warm September night they met and that freezing, frantic

February day at the train station in Newport, when they promised to write and to love and to remember.

It had all happened so fast. Harry remembers being more or less force-marched to his destiny — the hurried, excited news that his platoon was moving out, the call home, the instant wedding plans that seemed to suck him into their vortex. Until that weekend, he had switched his mind from one future to the other, lying in the barracks and staring at the pale ceiling in the dark, never letting go of either option, not really. Now, suddenly, he realized he was more ready for war than for this split. He couldn't move and was thus moved by others.

Harry didn't really deceive Ruth. She knew he was engaged. But she didn't know that, within 48 hours, he would be married.

And she didn't really withhold the truth, either. Hanging on to him that cheerless day, she only suspected, and she wasn't sure yet whether to fear or hope.

SIX

EVERYONE IS TALKING at once around the dining-table cold cuts, and Hank feels dizzy, as if the words were spinning him around. When Naomi slips outside, he soon follows her, unnoticed. He craves the quiet and cool as much as the rare chance to talk with his older sister.

When he closes the sliding-glass door, Naomi jumps, short and quick as if she's just run across a carpet and touched metal.

"Oh," she says, "it's you."

It is strange to Hank, an athlete himself once, that someone of Naomi's caliber could be so nervous. How, he wonders, did she bear the strain of competition at that level? The least unexpected movement seems to unhinge her. Maybe the hair-trigger reflexes were an aid to a swimmer, maybe they got her into the water a hundredth of a second before anyone else. And the jumpiness hasn't just happened. Hank can barely remember her not being like this, although she's gotten a little worse. She seems, even to Hank, like one large exposed nerve.

"Sorry. I didn't mean to scare you."

She's dropped some of her cigarettes out of the package. The brand advertises on billboards all around Saraw and Newport: A young woman, carefree, perky and athletic, cavorts above large green letters that say "Slim and cool."

Naomi is slim, and she is cool. With her dark hair pulled back and the makeup and arched eyebrows, she looks as if frost might form on her forehead. To Hank, no rock himself, she seems to fluctuate between flustered and frozen.

"That's OK. It's been a long day," she says as he tries to help her pick up the rest of the cigarettes but mainly succeeds in bumping her head with his. "Any day that involves changing planes in the Atlanta airport is a long day. And that thing we've got in Denver — don't get me started."

But she does get started, talking at great length and with

great heat about the foibles of a distant airport into which Hank will never fly. He shakes his head sympathetically.

She stops to take another drag. She's leaning against the deck railing. Behind her, the Gulf is whispering in the dark, sending up waves too short to matter. There is barely enough wind for them to smell the salt.

Hank asks about Thomas and Grace and Gary. They're fine, she says. Thomas Ferrell III is raking it in. Grace is doing well in law school. Gary's trying to find himself.

Naomi and Tom met when she was the semi-famous Naomi Crowder and he was in law school. She went all the way across the country to UCLA to fall in love with another North Carolinian, Ruth said at the time. Although Naomi would graduate from law school, too, Thomas Ferrell's skills as a corporate lawyer created a world in which she didn't have to practice for long, and she didn't.

Hank and Naomi talk for a while, catching up.

Finally, he can't help himself.

"So," he says, "are you and Momma going to play well together?"

She gives out a short burst of laughter; such mirth as there is doesn't come anywhere near her eyes. Smoke floats out of her mouth.

"Hell, Hank. You know her better than I do. Do you think we can play well together?"

"You know she loves you, Naomi. You know she'd rather cut her tongue out than upset you."

Naomi stubs the butt out on the deck's bourbon rail and flips it into the sand below.

"Her tongue, huh? Then why does it always work out that way, Hank? Huh?"

She turns away from him, toward the Gulf.

"Want to go for a walk?" he asks. He's tired, but he's been cooped up in a car all day and would like to take big, long steps along the beach, stretch out and talk with his sister.

"Uh, no. I don't think so, Hank. I'm really tired. Maybe later. I think I'm going to turn in." She walks toward the door, then turns, as an afterthought, and says, "It was nice talking with you, though. And don't worry, we'll be fine. We'll play well together."

And she graces him with a smile, the first one he's seen from his sister in some time.

Ruth has been watching from inside, half engaged in conversation with Paul and Tran as she wonders what her other two children are talking about. Me, probably, she's thinking. She hopes that, if nothing else comes of this visit, she will at some point be alone on a quiet deck with Naomi Crowder Ferrell, just the two of them.

Back inside, Naomi moves toward her mother, who has turned momentarily to the table. She reaches to put her arm around Ruth's shoulder, amazed at what an awkward, unnatural thing this seems to be. At that moment, Ruth leans over to pick up a deviled egg. Upon being touched, she looks up and reaches, too quickly, to put her arm around her daughter's waist. They wind up in an ungainly, uncomfortable knot, side by side with arms patting each other's shoulders for a few long seconds before Naomi moves away.

Like two cats in a room full of rocking chairs, Hank thinks, watching from outside.

The weight of the day lands on Harry suddenly, with a force that makes standing a task. He can barely keep his eyes open.

"Harry," Freda says, "do you need to sit down?"

You don't look so good, he can almost hear her thinking. But they don't say things like that to Harry these days.

Artie takes his elbow, more gently than Bob the Driver and just as depressingly. Artie Marks, for God's sake. Harry used to babysit for Artie Marks.

Harry's guest room is the good one, away from the street, facing the carriageway behind Freda and Artie's brick Victorian house on Monument Avenue. It has a nice, high ceiling. It is chilly, though, and Harry hurries into his old-man's pajamas and works his way under the covers. He looks up at that ceiling for a few seconds. It seems so far away, and so blue, that it might be sky. Before he can reach over to turn out the bedside light, he is asleep.

"Harry," Freda says. "Wake up, Harry. Wake up."

She looks worried.

It takes a few seconds for him to regain full consciousness.

"What? What was I . . . Was I talking in my sleep?"

"Yelling would be more like it."

She looks down at him, frowning.

"You kept saying you're sorry, that you tried."

Harry is silent. Maybe he should share this dream with someone other than Ruth, but he doesn't know if he's up to it. Freda gets him a glass of water.

Now Harry's wide awake. It's 2:30 a.m., he's in pain, and experience tells him there is little use in trying to go back to sleep. He knows he'll just toss and turn, then do a facedown in his breakfast cornflakes.

"Harry?"

"What?"

"Does it scare you? It shouldn't, you know."

He realizes his face is wet. It is difficult for him to explain even to his sister that it isn't the future that makes him sad; it is the past.

She puts her hand on his head. Her smell reminds Harry of Freda as a little girl, tagging along after her big brother. Amazing, he thinks, how that basic scent, that basic Freda-ness, hasn't changed. He wishes he could say the same for himself, but even though he's heard that a person can't smell his own stink, he can tell that his night sweats are the odor of decay, of rot.

He decides to go ahead and tell her about the dream, without revealing its source.

"Oh, Harry," smoothing his dwindling hair as if he were a child, "it's only a dream. There isn't anything to dreams but dreams. You dream about what you think about."

He knows she's probably right, but as he has more or less accepted The End and its smirking, scythe-wielding inevitability, all things great and small have become portents. This acceptance did not come easily or quickly; it just came, until one day he woke up and could swallow it. What Harry would like to tell everyone: You think you have accepted death? You think you're a big boy or girl now, well aware that you won't live forever? Just wait. Wait until you make the victory tour, going around one last time to visit everybody you don't think you're ever going to see again.

When Harry appeared unexpectedly two months ago on the doorstep of the former Gloria Tannebaum Stein, mother of his children, forgiver of so much, he found that neither of them had the words to tie it all up neatly. They had their nervous cup of coffee. They talked, with her present husband in the next room, about the good times, pretending the bad never existed. Finally, silently, they agreed to not voice regret, to not curse fate or second-guess. To just get on with it. To compare notes on "the kids" and let it go at that.

When Harry left, telling Gloria that he could walk himself to the car (she didn't protest very much), his "See you later" sounded like a curse.

He knows he may as well get up. There is no sense in lying here in his own sweat, sleep moving farther and farther away.

He takes his pain pills and waves off his sister's half-hearted offer to accompany him. She goes back to her and Artie's bedroom while Harry, in his bathrobe and slippers, walks down the hall, stopping to give his aching bladder some relief. He continues into the living room, stubbing his toe on a chair and almost relishing some new, cleaner kind of pain.

It's chilly in the living room, the only illumination a streetlight shining through the bay window, but Harry has always had great night vision. He feels it kept him alive in France and Germany; his men tried to stay close by him when they were on the move after dark and before light, even after Stevens was lost. Some of his superior officers mistook this for devotion, but the men knew that, if anyone was going to see something move that wasn't supposed to move in those cold, murderous woods, it would be Lieutenant Harry Stein.

There's a recliner over in the corner, and there's a wool blanket lying on the couch beside it. Harry manages to ease himself into Artie's favorite chair, covers himself to the chin and lies there looking out into the darkness. After five minutes, he can see every detail of the room.

This new position, half sitting and half lying, somehow suits him. He gives the blanket a yank and reclines there, unable to sleep just yet (although the pain has lessened some) but glad to just lie still and see things.

Being still is something that has come late to Harry. One of the great, abiding forces of his adult life has been the fidgety sense that he was missing something, somewhere. Sometimes it worked for him, sometimes it didn't. Law school, he soon knew, would be too boring, but his energy level was a large part of the making of a young stockbroker. Going full tilt all day, always looking for the edge, never satisfied, then sometimes partying half the night with clients and other brokers — the restlessness defined his life and was the blame and credit for much that happened to it.

Gloria was a good sport for a long time, Harry sees clearly now, willing to forget a lot for a man she loved, a man who swore he loved her, a man with a future.

Part of it, he knew, was that nothing ever seemed as glamorous as a bar in the money district of a city, with everybody full of energy, everybody late in the afternoon just as they once were after a big game in high school, all full of themselves — look at me: I just made some schmuck $10,000 because I am the smartest, quickest guy who ever read the *Wall Street Journal.*

It wasn't a drinking problem, not in the sense of being unable to stop, not in the sense of drunk-driving citations or scenes in public places. Harry could stop. Harry could hold it. What Harry knew he had — and how could he tell Gloria this? — was an excitement problem.

He came to understand, slowly and painfully, that something was missing, that the past would be with him, would not recede.

Sometime before sunrise, Harry does drift off to sleep. At times like this, he is seldom granted unconsciousness until he abandons hope of achieving it. Then, it sandbags him. Later, he wakes up flat on his back, snoring.

This time, though, his slumber is interrupted by the voices of Freda and Artie. They are in the kitchen, down the hall, trying to quietly get Sunday breakfast going. Harry hears Artie curse softly, as if he's just spilled orange juice or dropped the toast.

Harry is undiscovered. They haven't gone into the living room yet, and he left his bedroom door closed. From where he sits, he can hear them well enough.

". . . That's all I know." Freda's voice. "He's pretty close to the vest, you know. Maybe I should call Ruth."

As he hears Artie walking toward the living room, Harry feigns sleep.

"Maybe he should . . ." Harry hears his brother-in-law stop in midsentence. Then there's a long pause before Artie Marks tiptoes back to the kitchen and says something Harry's ears can't pick up. Before long, he can hear, feel Freda walking softly toward him, then stopping and whispering to Artie, "Look at him," the way you might point out a child or a dog in unguarded repose. He feels the blanket being pulled to his chin.

Freda and Artie go back to the kitchen. Harry squints one eye open to see that they are out of sight, then shifts position slightly. In seconds, he is asleep again.

The next thing he knows, they're waking him.

"Hey, Harry," Artie says. "Want some breakfast?"

"Sure. Yeah, thanks."

"What's the matter? Is that guest bed too hard for you?"

"Nah. Sometimes I just need to move around, find another spot. Sneak up on the sandman."

Harry yawns. He smells french toast and bagels and cream cheese. He is, he realizes, hungry.

They go back into the kitchen, and Harry untangles himself and shuffles back to his bedroom, where he tries to comb his sad hair and brushes his teeth.

When he comes back out, finding them in the breakfast nook overlooking a yard full of birdfeeders and hardwoods, Freda looks at him and frowns.

"Are you OK?"

"Sure. Slept like a baby."

Freda knows he's lying. He appreciates that she doesn't cry, and he's glad he will only be making a short visit. He wanted to see Freda again, although they no longer seem to have much to talk about. He guesses he did it because he felt he ought to.

Old age, son of a bitch that it is, is not without its consolations, thinks Harry Stein. People care, more than he reckons they should. He revels in the balm of that care; he would not forfeit an ounce of it, no matter how ill-gotten.

SEVEN

RUTH STILL REMEMBERS most of what she wrote to Harry Stein that March day in 1943.

She tells herself that she tried not to make it sound pitiful, and that she tried not to make him feel guilty, although a larger part of her than she would admit wanted him to go AWOL, renounce all other encumbrances, to women and family and armies, and rush back to her side, tears streaming from his cheeks, vowing never to leave again.

"It seems a good time to write (if there is a good time to write someone who never writes back)," she began, then begged his forgiveness (but didn't throw the paper away and start again). She knew he might already have been shipped overseas. "At least, Harry," she wrote, "let me know you are alive."

She saw no point in telling him before he left. She despised girls who traded on weakness.

"What we did," she wrote, "we did for my pleasure as well as yours. I knew it was foolish. (It makes me blush to think of some censor somewhere reading this, but it must be told.)"

She did tell him, though. She could not bear to do otherwise.

"You are the first to know (assuming this letter reaches you in a timely manner)," she wrote. "I wasn't sure when you left, didn't want to be sure, I suppose. Now, there can be no doubt. Soon, I will have to tell my grandparents and the rest. Of course you are the father. Do not panic. (You do not seem the panicky kind. Neither am I. Do not think that I am running around like a chicken with my head chopped off.) I claim no hold on you. You had your life planned for you before you ever came to Saraw, before that September night a thousand years ago. When we said goodbye, at that awful train station, I meant goodbye. But we also said we would write, that we would 'stay in touch,' whatever that means."

Ruth had already had three weeks to swallow the sometimes sobering, sometimes dizzying truth growing inside her. She was certain, at 17, that she had seen the one perfect complement leave her life on a northbound troop train. She had convinced herself, to stop the pain, that she would never, ever see Harry Stein again.

But still she wrote; she had to do something. And she did have a plan.

"I think," she wrote that March, "we both know that we have met the Other Half, the half that would make the sum of us better than the parts. I know your family would never forgive you. I know you would break the heart of that girl back in Richmond. I know all that, and perhaps what I'm about to do is just my way of keeping a piece of you in my arms . . ."

Ruth wouldn't know for another three weeks, when she finally received a letter from Harry, that he and Gloria had already married. They did it quickly on Harry's two-day pass to Richmond before his unit was shipped to Texas for desert training that would never be used.

"Why didn't you tell me?" he wrote in that first letter to her, the one he had put off for weeks. "We could have done something." But he wondered what, and a small, selfish part of him hoped she would take care of this, that it would somehow, magically take care of itself. He had met a girl he might love more than any other, ever, but life was long. He would, by dint of will, get over it.

"Why didn't you tell ME?" she wrote back, three days later. But she knew it was inevitable that Harry would marry the girl everyone expected him to. It was only a question of when.

Harry has come to believe that every life has a defining moment when a person does either what is right or what is expedient, but he wonders how many have faced such a well-marked intersection and taken such a wrong turn as he did in that dark second winter of the war.

If Ruth had told him in February that she was pregnant, would he have done the right and honorable thing? He has always wanted to believe he was not the kind of man who would have let a 17-year-old orphan in a small North Carolina town endure the pain and humiliation that logically would follow, had he known all the facts.

He knows the range of possible answers:

He might have looked for an abortionist, not an easy or safe route.

He might have, with some thought, taken her across the South Carolina state line for a quick marriage that they would have quietly ended, long distance, without Gloria or the Tannebaums or the Steins ever knowing, just to give the baby its father's last name.

Less likely, he might have done the thing he thought of doing a hundred times before he and Ruth parted at the train station, the thing you could look back on at the end of a long and eventful life and say, "When everything mattered, everyone told me I must not do this, but I knew in my heart I should, and so I did." That is, he might have chanced the loss of his birth family and most of his friends and become a stranger in a strange land, the Jew who married the Crowder girl after he knocked her up.

He and Ruth both know, without ever expressing it, that the Harry Stein who lived in early 1943 would either have run away or, worse, stayed with regrets.

And so you have the riddle of Harry's life. He could have chosen one of two potentially very pleasant futures.

One would have been with the one girl he remained sure (when he was sure of little else) would complete him. He knows that, if he could only have gone off and lived his life with Ruth, braced against the scorn of his whole community back in Richmond, knowing that his parents bore the brunt of all that disapproval, it would have been a good life. He can see that now. They would have had friends, they would have had money. They would have been forgiven, in time. They would have had, even failing all that, each other.

Or he could marry Gloria, whom he had loved and liked for three years, and settle into the bosom of his family and hers, forgetting that he had ever known a girl named Ruth Crowder.

Either choice, though, required the chooser to forgo remorse, to forget the other path.

After a honeymoon weekend spent mostly with family and seldom alone, Harry and Gloria saw each other once more, in June, before his unit shipped out for England. He would spend a year there, in what seemed to Harry like an adult, black-comedy version of the summer camps of his youth, preparing for the vague something, the Plan that would save the world. They knew they could die, as much as young men ever believe such a thing, and it made their sorties into London, the courting and fighting in village pubs, all the more intense.

Harry was true to Gloria, though, in the flesh. He laughed at the stories of other officers, equally married, who came back to their base bragging of trysts in third-floor London walkups, with air-raid sirens going off in the distance, of drunken fistfights made comic by war's shadow.

But he did cheat. The letters, once he worked up the nerve to write Ruth back after he knew her secret, never stopped. For a while, he would write Gloria every time he wrote Ruth, but he realized he had more to say to the girl he left than the woman he had married. Before long, he'd taken the path of least resistance and was writing Gloria twice a week, out of guilt, and Ruth four times a week, because six or seven would have been unseemly.

In April, Ruth wrote that everyone knew she was pregnant, and that it would no longer be possible for Harry to send letters to her grandparents' address. No one knew who the father was, and no one, save Cousin Mercy, was going to know, if she could help it.

He was to send future letters to Mercy, who would tell her parents that she had met a soldier at Camp Warren who was crazy about her. It was meant to be a temporary solution, but Cousin Mercy never married. For many decades, people in Saraw were convinced that Mercy Crowder had a secret beau, who wrote her first from Army posts and then from Richmond, then later from Washington and Long Island. So the letters never stopped.

Mercy, generous and energetic, was never overly attracted to any of Saraw's young men. After her siblings moved out, she stayed on and took care of her parents. She dated occasionally, but never very seriously. Once, she told Ruth that she couldn't imagine a man as good as her father.

Ruth's grandfather concocted the plan to save his family's honor. Ruth had made it clear that she would have the baby, that she would keep the baby, and if they wanted to put her out in the cold, she would manage.

By May, T.D. Crowder had enlisted a cousin who was a judge. This judge arranged to produce a marriage license, back-dated to February. Ruth McNair Crowder had secretly married Randall Phelps on Feb. 14, 1943. Randall Phelps had then shipped out to North Africa in April, from where he wrote back and said he had changed his mind, that he didn't want to be married any more. The judge, with T.D.'s help, invented a bridegroom and granted him a divorce on the same day. If anyone believed it, it was because Ruth had her secrets. If something like this could happen, it would happen to someone like Ruth. She hadn't brought Harry Stein to any more church socials or dances in Saraw itself. People knew she was dating other boys as well. She was known to go to dances in Newport and meet other young men (although a cursory investigation would have revealed that most of them were named Harry Stein.)

Ruth had no intention of taking some fictional last name for either herself or her baby, and the family said Ruth wasn't going to honor that sorry Randall Phelps by giving the child his name. If he wanted that baby to be a Phelps, they said, he could just come back and be a proper husband.

Ruth feared on occasion that one or the other of her grandparents had actually convinced themselves that Randall Phelps existed.

"The best I can tell," Ruth wrote to Harry, "the departed Randall Phelps was a blond-haired Baptist womanizer from

Ohio with a slight limp in his left leg, although Aunt Charlotte slipped up and said right leg the other day. He likes to play cards, and before the war he worked in a hardware store. He smokes Camels. It gets very confusing to Uncle Matty, who said the other day he wished I'd married 'that pretty dark-haired boy' instead of 'that damn Randall Phelps.' If Granddaddy hasn't made the delinquent Mr. Phelps real to anyone else, he has apparently made him real to Matty. I rather fear for the safety of any stranger he might come across with the name of Randall or Phelps."

Despite T.D. Crowder's efforts, there was embarrassment enough when Ruth had a daughter on September 12. Even with the backdated marriage certificate, only seven months had passed since Valentine's Day. And Ruth only fed the rumors with her silence. She stopped going to church, and in July she quit her job at the lumber yard. The other Crowders living next door on either side, T.D.'s brothers and their families, more or less stopped talking to her, although they closed ranks and didn't talk about her, either.

Each grandparent assured her that her willful behavior would bring about the death of the other, and that she would pay for her sins on Judgment Day. Charlotte and Jane were kinder, and Matty only harbored a grudge against the Randall Phelps he couldn't quite remember, but whom he was ready to travel to England, by car if necessary, to kill.

When T.D.'s sister Goldie, then in her 69th year, died from pneumonia the following winter, Ruth's heedlessness was considered to be a contributing cause.

It was not Ruth's intention to make her family suffer, but she wasn't going to have an abortion, and she wasn't going to give the baby up. She did her crying mostly in private. By the time she told them all, in April, she had reached her own crossroads. For a week, when it was still her secret — hers and Harry's — she imagined herself not going to college, not moving to a big city, not living the life she could if she traveled alone. And she knew, after a week, that she could forgo all that. She just wanted the baby.

She narrated the various phases of her pregnancy for Harry, even as Gloria was filling him in on the week's social highlights in Richmond. It was not fair, Harry told himself, to think Gloria frivolous for this. He was sure she could be heroic, too, if circumstances had forced her to be.

If the Crowders suspected Harry was the father, they never said so outright, burying any suspicions under the ruse T.D. and the judge had invented. Ruth continued to withhold the father's name, and no one ever again mentioned the name of Harry Stein in the Crowder household.

Harry worried more about Ruth than about himself. Boredom and anxiety attacks were the imminent dangers. They would drill for hours at a time, trying to lose themselves in minutiae. They would hear of the Allied victories in North Africa and Sicily, and then the Italian mainland. The Italians surrendered by early September, and, trying to be tough outside so they might build up some calluses where it mattered, the college boys and store clerks and farmers complained bitterly about the lack of Krauts to kill.

Once in a while, though, Harry would turn a corner and there would be a young man, his age, just looking up into the sky, clearly wondering if he could do whatever had to be done.

Outwardly, Harry was impatient to kill. Inwardly, he couldn't always stop himself from thinking of what death the Nazis would reserve for a captured soldier who was also a Jew.

Usually, Harry saved Ruth's letter for last. This day, it took all his discipline not to tear it open while he was still among the anxious men hoping to be remembered. He knew her due date was near. He was stationed near Tiverton, in the southwest of England, when the letter came at last, the same day as one from Gloria.

It was her handwriting, on the envelope.

"Dearest Harry," she wrote. "I (or we, I suppose, if you want to be precise) have a daughter. She weighs five pounds, eight ounces. Not so big, but then Grandma says I was no larger than that.

"The naming is all up to me, it seems, so I have named her Naomi. Naomi Jane Crowder. Ruth and Naomi, in the Bible (your part of it, Harry), were such good friends, and I know that this little girl and I are going to be just like that. With one true parent, I must be her friend.

"Oh, Harry. I wish you could know how good it feels, here holding her. It's as if I finally have a family. Some people would tell you I have been raised by six parents, but it isn't the same. There is a feeling, really just a memory of a feeling I can barely recall, of being in my father's arms or snuggling in bed with my mother, when she would let me, that all this has brought back. It isn't much family, by some standards, but it, or she, is my family.

"She looks like you. I don't tell anyone that, of course, and there is a certain amount of whispering about the baby being born with a full head of jet-black hair, since, as we all know, Randall Phelps was blond. Some day, maybe when she is 16, the two of us will take the train to Richmond and find where you work. We'll sit at a soda fountain across the street, and when you come out of your big building, I'll know it's you. And I'll point you out to Naomi. Maybe I will tell her you're her daddy, or maybe I'll just tell her there's a handsome man I used to know, but I don't want him to see me now."

Harry's tent was facing a large open area, and soldiers were always walking back and forth; it was as if a never-ending parade was going past, people bound to save the world, somehow.

Harry Stein put his head down and really knew, for the first time, what he had done.

He started sending the money that day. Ruth never asked him to.

He wrote to Freda, in care of Mrs. Cameron's boarding house. She was five years younger, but even when he was in junior high, skipping the occasional day of school, swimming the dangerous currents of the James River with his friends, he could trust Freda not to tell.

He instructed the paymaster to send a certain amount to his sister every payday. At first, it was only 10 dollars a month, which Freda would forward to North Carolina. He explained about Ruth, although no more than he had to.

At first, Freda thought Harry was being "shaken down," as she expressed it to him, but she always sent the money south, to Miss Mercy Crowder of Saraw, N.C. And she never breathed a word about it to anyone until after she married Artie Marks. Old Harry and Ella never knew about Ruth Crowder, or their first grandchild.

Harry's other gift, beyond ink on paper and the ten dollars a month that later grew to fifteen, then twenty and beyond, was the kind of advice only a person of will and vision could use.

A friend from Princeton had come through Richmond in the spring of 1942, not long before Harry enlisted. They had lunch at a diner downtown. Bobby Weinberg had become a stockbroker, and he was filled with the gospel of the dollar.

Bobby Weinberg took a paper napkin and a pencil and filled up row after row with numbers, showing Harry what it meant to invest while you were young. With the Depression only lately beaten back by war's prosperity, Harry had little use for such advice. No one trusted the stock market, and Harry had youth's contempt for thrift.

But Bobby did get his attention with one deceptively hard fact: If you invested a certain amount of money between 18 and 29, he said, you would have more money at 65 than if you started at 29 and invested until you were 65. This Harry could understand. He didn't do anything about it, having not yet developed either the need for or the love of money that drove Bobby Weinberg.

It seemed a good thing to tell Ruth about, though.

"I know you need money for many things right now, but if you can spare anything of what you earn or what I send," he began, then told her what Bobby Weinberg had said.

In her next letter, Ruth thanked Harry for the advice. She had worked it out on the office adding machine, and Bobby Weinberg was right. She appreciated the inevitability of numbers. She never mentioned it again, just kept thanking Harry for the money that she didn't spend.

Harry's fall and winter and spring passed in the damp of England, while the day itself was hinted at, then rumored, then expected, and then finally there. On June 6, he was far enough back to avoid the worst. Several men who served with him died, on Omaha Beach and in the hedgerow hell that would haunt him worse than D-Day itself. They seldom seemed to have a plan that could fully withstand the reality of German artillery, but somehow enough of them would survive and make it from Point A to Point B. War, as Harry saw it, required belief in a strategy coupled with the knowledge that it would, at some point, have to be utterly, hopelessly abandoned.

Harry Stein's luck seemed always to hold, though. He was only shot the one time, he didn't step on a land mine, he didn't freeze to death or even lose a hand or a foot in the coldest winter any of them would ever live through. The days never seemed to end, but then, all at once, a whole season would be gone. Summer, fall, winter, another spring. Harry can remember the cold, the second-hand foxholes that still smelled like someone else's death, the killing. Other than the clinging hands of Sergeant Eldridge Stevens, though, it has all blended into a merciful haze, a melange of mud and ice, fatigue and fear.

And he remembers when it all ended, deep in Germany. They stayed drunk for two days, and when he woke up one morning, staring at a rainy sky, he saw that it was almost summer again.

Ruth's letters kept her alive in his mind, made her grow, even. Without them, she might have receded into his memory, an imagined creature who once seemed perfect only because the world was so new. And already, he was finding that there were things he needed to express that were best revealed to someone other than Gloria, whom he loved, God knows, but sometimes it was better just to tell Ruth instead.

Where was the harm in that?

EIGHT

"THERE WERE DAYS," Ruth wrote Harry after he went home to Richmond, "when I envied you, out there saving the world while I changed diapers and kept books."

Ruth had moved into a one-bedroom apartment over McCrory's dime store in Newport in January of 1944, as soon as she felt she and the baby were strong enough. Jobs would be plentiful for the next couple of years.

No act of blatant cruelty drove her to seek her own way with a four-month-old in tow. It was the looks, even in her own home. She was tired of the women crying in their rooms and of T.D. going into another part of the house when she came in carrying Naomi. She had stopped going to church, her old friends didn't seem to know what to say to her, and they had already filled her job at the lumber mill. It was time to move.

"Naomi has never been a problem," Ruth wrote Harry after he sent $50 for his daughter's second birthday. "I love her more by the day. She's already talking up a blue streak, and when I look at that curly jet-black hair of hers, I see Harry Stein, straight up and down."

The letters weren't always so cheerful. Sometimes they just started out, "Harry," and these would barely be legible, written by a young woman, half asleep, trying to do one more thing at the end of an 18-hour day.

In Newport, though, she thrived. She got a job as a bookkeeper in the shipyards and then was promoted to office manager. She was amazed then, as she would be all through her life, at how disorganized most people were. Even before the baby, even as a girl, she knew what she was doing and when she was doing it. She found it easy to direct others, because she came to understand that others needed directing.

She made friends with other young women, some also rearing children by themselves. In truth, they raised each other's children. She went to an occasional movie. She ate out once a week, three weeks out of four, at the Coastal Queen Hotel. The other week, she kept her friends' babies in addition to Naomi and they brought dinner back to her. After T.D. gave her a second-hand Plymouth for Christmas of 1944, as a peace offering, life got a degree or two easier.

By the end of the war, she was receiving $15 a month from Harry and saving at least half of it. She would, after that first year, go home to Saraw for Sunday dinner. They would cook ham, chicken, five vegetables and three desserts, and send half of it back to Newport with her on Sunday night.

T.D. Crowder dropped dead in late June of 1945, halfway between VE Day and VJ Day. He was sitting in his office at the mill, and for a couple of hours, they thought he was just sleeping. They could see him through the glass, his chin down on his chest. But he had been known to nod off after lunch. He was entitled, being 75 years old and still showing up every day for work. He and Matty would walk over, T.D. going to his office, Matty to his own special woodworking shop in a little add-on building next to the railroad spur line.

After T.D. died, Sudie started having memory lapses, and she turned over most of the cooking and housekeeping to Jane, who served a dutiful daughter's lifetime labor of love and was taken for granted as a reward.

There was no one left with the interest or know-how to look after the mill, and the Crowders soon sold it to Pembroke Lumber, which would keep it open for 10 more years of diminishing returns from forests whose oldest, best trees had long been replaced by scrubby pines.

Without T.D., his lifelong protector and friend, Matty got worse.

During the war, one of Ruth's older cousins built a triangular diner to fit the three-sided lot where Turpentine Creek Road joined the Beach Road at a 45-degree angle from the northeast. Matty began spending time there, wandering over when no one was looking and sometimes making a nuisance of himself. Inevitably, he would launch into a tirade about "that damn Randall Phelps," about how he was going to find him and kill him, even if he had to go all the way to Germany. To the end, Matty had it in his mind that Randall Phelps was hiding out in Germany.

When the war ended, so did Ruth's tenure in Newport. "The problem is," she wrote, "I did my job too well. When they promoted me to office manager, I replaced Will McLaurin, who went to the Navy. Will McLaurin, whom I have never even met, got back to Newport last week. Mr. Harper called me in two days ago and said he'd love to keep me, and there probably would be something else for me soon, back in bookkeeping."

Bookkeeping, though, would have meant a step backwards and a cut in pay. And Ruth had something else she needed to do.

"When Momma and Daddy died, the rest of my family was all that stood between me and the orphanage," she wrote Harry. "They did their duty, and now it's my turn."

Don't do it, Harry wrote back. You could be so much, you could do such great things. Don't plant yourself in Saraw.

But Ruth had made up her mind.

She had spent a week imagining life in Saraw, reading magazines for culture and taking care of her older relatives, raising Naomi in the same house in which she herself had been raised, reconnecting with the people who were her girlhood playmates.

And she thought she could do it. Ruth could, she was coming to believe, do anything if she had a little time to steel herself. She knew that those around her had always thought of her as flighty and a little spoiled, "used to getting her way," but she knew more than they did. She had developed an orphan's self-sufficiency, able to do whatever was needed, able to imagine great disappointment or hardship and then imagine living through it. It carried her through the loss of Harry, carried her through unwed pregnancy and single parenting, carried her back to Saraw and duty.

"I know what you've written me before," she told Harry, "that I should get out of here and move to a real city somewhere. I know I could take care of Naomi whether I was in New York City or Saraw, and it sounds conceited, but I know I could make a living anywhere. I've seen enough dimwits making good government salaries around the shipyard to know that."

She knew Harry was right when he told her no one would think any worse of her if she stayed in Newport or moved to a bigger city. Charlotte had told her as much.

Ruth was not returning to Saraw because she had to. She was returning because she ought to, and she knew the difference.

When she moved back, Ruth Crowder was 20 years old. Despite being as attractive as any girl in Newport, she had not dated since Harry left. When she lived in her small apartment with Naomi, she was constantly turning down offers to go out with the best of what men the war had not taken. She knew eventually she'd say yes, but not yet.

She had learned to sew well enough to make most of Naomi's clothes. She filled her letters to Harry with the various firsts that would never excite her as much with her other children. She worried about pushing Naomi too hard, but she couldn't stop herself. She wanted her to be the first to walk, the first to talk, the first to be toilet trained. She never had to scold her much, because Naomi seemed to be born sensing how much was expected. Harry expressed the opinion that first children were practice, and Ruth wrote back that she didn't think that was one damn bit funny.

"Next thing up for Naomi," she wrote Harry in early 1946, "is swimming lessons. I know you're going to think I'm crazy, but I am determined that my daughter is not going to live right next to the Atlantic Ocean and be afraid of it like I was. And the younger the better."

She forswore many possibilities when she packed her belongings into the back of a pickup truck, with the help of a couple of male cousins, and moved back to Saraw.

Martin was born the day before Christmas, 1946. The Stein and Tannebaum families joked about the fecundity of the Stein seed. Harry had been home less than 11 months.

As a married couple, he and Gloria had so far known only war and pregnancy. They missed the newlywed phase where the attractive, charming, lovestruck young couple drinks champagne from shoes and dances until dawn, the way they did before the war. Gloria had a difficult pregnancy, and Harry went to a few parties by himself.

His father kept trying to interest him in law school again, but Harry had given up on that in 1942, and four years in uniform had only made him more determined to go his own way. He'd made one grand concession for the general good, he thought but couldn't say, and he was damned if he'd make another.

By May of 1946, with fatherhood approaching, Harry had to accept that the world was not going to forever buy him drinks and throw him parties because he'd once lived in a foxhole.

Harry had majored in English, but he had neither the talent for writing nor the patience for academia. Renaissance man that he was, he minored in mathematics; he'd always liked numbers. But what could he do with that? The idea of never going back to school, law or otherwise, appealed to him greatly. The family business was always a fallback position, but neither Harry nor his father really wanted him to spend the rest of his life in men's furnishings.

"This I did so you could be something bigger," Old Harry told him. Actually, it seemed to Harry that his father's life had been a rather pleasant endeavor, hardly the orgy of abnegation recounted with damp eyes for the benefit of Freda and himself.

In June, opportunity came calling in the form of the return of Bobby Weinberg. He spent a weekend with Harry and Gloria, the three of them talking about the now-distant good times at Princeton and in New York before the war. Bobby had gone back to Wall Street after he was mustered out and claimed he was on the verge of making "a killing, an absolute killing." Harry thought he saw something he might want to do, might be able to do. Bobby Weinberg wasn't that smart, and even he was getting rich.

The day his friend left, Harry talked it over with Gloria and then made an appointment with Martin & Rives, one of Richmond's oldest investment firms. He chose Martin & Rives because it was one of two firms in the city that possibly would employ a Jew to invest gentiles' money. This Harry knew, without even asking, without having any idea where he'd first heard it.

Bobby and Harry actually had little in common except that they were approximately one-eighth of the Jewish population of their class at Princeton.

Jews roomed with Jews. If this was not so at the outset, it soon was corrected. There were no fights, no direct confrontations, nothing unpleasant, unless you objected to catching the punch line of a Yid joke as you came around the corner.

"We are the elite of the elite," he once wrote Gloria at Mt. Holyoke in an uncustomary fit of bitterness. "Private clubs might be OK for the great majority, but we Sons of Israel, we'll have none of it. I'm sure they hesitate to invite us only because they know we would turn them down. We are the utility infielders on the World Series champs, the cheap bungalows on Country Club Lane, the world's tallest midgets."

In June of 1946, Harry Stein was 27 years old, and other than working in his father's stores and drawing a paycheck in World War II, his experience was almost nil. But Martin & Rives' only Jewish broker, Mo Green, had been killed in the war, so there was an opening. Harry had a handsome face, a face Richmond's old money could be comfortable with. He had a winning personality and Ivy League credentials. By the end of the week, he had begun his chosen profession: making other people's money grow.

Harry was the fastest learner anyone in the firm had ever seen. And he could charm the clients, and his bosses.

His years of being immersed in the clothing business, of listening to his father talk at the dinner table and on those long trips across the state, had given him a sense of style that had everyone else at Martin & Rives aping his choices in suits and shirts and shoes.

He could explain and understand the beauty of numbers, and he could recite Shakespeare and Milton. He could tell a joke, and he always knew which joke to tell to which client. They enjoyed talking to him even when they were losing money, which wasn't often, because Harry was good. If the market dropped dangerously, Harry could keep the anxious from stampeding; he could convince them that it would come back stronger than ever. If there was a new trend in human life that promised a profit, Harry was soon an expert on it. He would see computers coming before anyone else; he would see Detroit going.

Even Old Harry had to concede, the day in 1957 when they made his son a partner, that Harry Stein was born to make people money.

"If it weren't for your name," Peyton Rives told him that day as they shared some very old Scotch, "I wouldn't know you were Jewish."

Harry knew he meant it as a compliment.

Harry and Gloria decided that Martin would remain Martin until he got big and rowdy, and then he would be Marty. He was a colicky baby, then an easy, large-eyed child who wanted to please, who cringed at raised voices. Harry thought at times that he was too malleable, that he ought to do something really bad once in a while — break a window, say "fuck," something. But how do you encourage your child to misbehave?

When they get together now, Martin is still Martin. To Harry's knowledge, he has never been Marty to anyone.

Harry thought Gloria was a good mother, and as good a wife as he deserved. She worried too much about everything with Martin, a little less with Nancy, who came two years later. At 4, Martin would cry when Gloria tried to discipline his sister, who was more of a handful than he had ever dared to be.

Gloria never knew about Ruth, until there was no option except to tell. Harry believed (would keep believing) that what he and his wife had was love, despite everything. Even now, he is almost certain, almost all the time, that it was a kind of love that they shared, and that he eventually ruined.

Harry had known Gloria Tannebaum since junior high. She was valedictorian at a rival high school, and she finished second in the school beauty pageant. She was graduated from Mount Holyoke (a member of her own excluded, exclusive group) in 1944, already married a year, robbed of her youth not so much by Harry as by everything.

They first dated when he was home between his sophomore and junior years at Princeton, but he had first noticed her when she was 13. Later, he would see her in her cheerleader's outfit when his high school played hers, was aroused by her tan, perfect legs. They knew each other; they went to the same parties. But she always seemed to be going steady with one boy or another.

That summer, though, they found themselves both available and attracted. Everyone, in both families, was so pleased. Even if they had despised each other, it would have been hard to escape the path that led to that hurried wedding in February of 1943. Once they began dating steadily, neither Harry nor Gloria ever saw a point where not getting married was a feasible option, until he met Ruth.

If Harry's life were a movie, he wrote to Ruth one day many years later, it would be entitled, "It Would Have Been a Wonderful Life If It Hadn't Been For That Schmuck Harry Stein." You'd have all the flashbacks, he told her, showing what everyone's lives would have been like if Harry hadn't been there to screw them up:

Here's Gloria Tannebaum Wolff, married more than 50 years to the same devoted husband, the incredibly rich and loving capitalist Howard Wolff. She and her husband are surrounded by their four children and 11 adoring grandchildren, in front of their Georgian brick mansion overlooking the James River. Gloria has thrived as an interior designer, and she has never been to a therapist.

Here's Ruth Crowder Johnston, still lovely and celebrating this year her 50th year of wedded bliss with Malcolm Barnwell Johnston, former governor of North Carolina, whom she met when she was a student at Flora MacDonald College and he was in law school at Duke. She's beloved by an entire state, the Queen Mum, but most especially she's loved by her husband, three children and nine grandchildren. None of her children holds a grudge against her; she has never been struck in anger.

"Don't take me back, Clarence," he concluded the letter. "Give everybody a break."

By the summer of 1947, Harry and Gloria were more settled than he could have imagined. Their son was taking his first steps in the new brick Cape Cod with its treeless yard, theirs thanks to a downpayment by their parents, a mile from his old neighborhood. Harry was on the verge, already, of pulling down more money than good brokers 10 years his senior.

He had managed to compartmentalize Ruth. Every Thursday, he would stay 45 minutes after work, when he knew he should have been drinking with present and future clients, to write her. It wasn't as if he planned to someday abandon Gloria and Martin, but still he couldn't let go. He thought he would, in time; he was just hanging on to his options. During the week, reading the newspaper or sitting on a park bench, he would see something and think of how it would amuse or touch Ruth in his next letter.

At home, he was able to more or less shut her out of his life. Although the Crowders got a telephone after the war, neither he nor Ruth ever called. That would have broken the spell, Harry believed, and Ruth told him, decades later, that this was how she had felt, too.

She sent him a photograph, in 1945, and he sent her one from Germany.

In his, he was kneeling in front of a German sign, a friend on either side. His cap was off, and his black hair was long and bushy. He was squinting into the sun, the eyes Ruth loved squinched almost shut.

In hers, she was leaning against someone's car in what appeared to be a churchyard, her hands primly together in front of her, smiling at someone to the photographer's left. She was just as beautiful as he remembered, the baby fat in her face melted away but the beauty not diminished a whit.

She would put his photo, Harry at war, with the letters, under lock and key. Sometimes, over the years, she would take it out and look at it, when she was alone.

He would keep her picture, tucked away in the back of one wallet after another.

Most of the pictures she sent, though, were of Naomi. Those he kept in the locked trunk in his office.

Through the sober, back-to-work year of 1946, the letters got more daring, more full of the heat neither Harry nor Ruth had experienced since he left. He started it by writing about all the things he wanted to do with and to her, including some they'd never tried in their brief season together, some he'd never tried with Gloria. To his amazement, she responded in kind, sometimes going farther than he had. He would read them at his desk, often more than once, and they always made him hard.

Occasionally, he will take one from the chest and read it now, and they still stir him. Did he ever engender such heat?

"I am in bed now," she wrote him late that year, in response to a fantasy he had shared with her involving an act that was illegal in either of their states at that time. "I am naked beneath the covers, and I am wet. The sheet below sticks to me. It is so dark I can't see my hand in front of my face, except of course it isn't in front of my face. I hear the doorknob turn and then the sound of your clothes as you take them off and drop them roughly, hurriedly on the floor beside my bed; the rustle of a shirt, the heavy clump of your pants.

"Then you're beside me. I open to you. I reach to feel you with my free hand and you're as big as I remember. You kiss me all over — my mouth, my ears, my breasts — while your fingers explore me. My nipples ache from your nibbling. Then you go lower and lower, to my bellybutton and lower still, and now I can't stop. I know others can hear me. I don't care.

"You give me no mercy, spending the rest of the night penetrating me in every way possible with your tongue and your fingers and especially the part of you I particularly like. You make me do things I will blush to think of in the morning. Now, though, I only want more. . . ."

In 1947, though, her letters got more demure. Harry sensed a pulling back, and then he read what he'd already deduced.

"Harry," she wrote him that spring, "I've met this man. . . ."

Like half of any couple attuned to each other's rhythms, he pulled back, too. He didn't want to lose her entirely.

By late summer, Gloria was pregnant again. They had never had the kind of sexual rapport he would have preferred; despite her outward worldliness, she was reserved in private. She didn't like what she called "the dirty talk," she tried to accommodate his tastes, but he could tell her heart just wasn't in it. He wished he could show her one of Ruth's letters and say, "Here. This is what I want you to do. Be like this."

Still, they seldom argued. They had a million friends in common. They loved their children and, they were sure, each other. Gloria was thrilled with Harry's ascending stardom at Martin & Rives, enough so that she was willing to have dinner alone a couple of nights a week, content to share a nightcap with a man who didn't need one.

NINE

ON SUNDAY AFTERNOON, Harry, Freda and Artie sit on the back deck, where the October sun warms them. Harry nods off and wakes up again at irregular intervals, and no one seems to mind. The three of them talk about the things they have in common — the old neighborhood, the synagogue, their parents, their friends, living and dead. Freda starts every other sentence with, "Remember, Harry?" Usually, he does.

Lately, the temperature is almost always too hot or too cold for Harry Stein, or the wind's blowing, or there's ragweed in the air, or his stomach is upset, or he's depressed for no discernible reason other than the major one.

Today, though, on the sun-kissed back deck of Freda and Artie Marks, he has reached an equilibrium. The chaise longue fits his contour like a mold. The small table alongside is at the perfect spot for his slowly-sipped beer.

"Remember, Harry?" Freda says. "Remember how I used to send those letters, those checks down to North Carolina during the war? And nobody knew?"

And Harry nods and chuckles. It was so serious at the time, but it seems like the stuff of childhood pranks now, no more or less momentous than terrorizing the neighbors with bottle rockets.

"Nancy and Alan and the kids came by last month," Artie says. "Nancy doesn't look a day over 40."

Harry will nod and say something kind about the Marks boys, both living outside Washington now, a lawyer and an accountant. Artie has mentioned a visit by Harry and Gloria's daughter twice now, but Harry finds comfort in the way their conversations loop back on themselves, the words less important than the way they're said.

It is all so sweet to him, a balm. Sometimes, he hears them out of a half-dream asking him something, one of them, and the other will mutter, "I think he's sleeping," and they let it go at that.

Just after 3 o'clock, though, the sun dips below the top of the oaks and the wind comes up immediately, and they have to go inside. Harry tries to stick it out, tries to make rare perfection last a little longer, but soon he is shivering.

"Come on," Artie says. "Let's see how the damn Redskins are doing."

At halftime of the 1 o'clock game, Hank, Paul and Stephen go outside to throw a football around.

Paul stands to one side, beer bottle hanging loosely from his right hand, and watches Hank hit Stephen perfectly in stride with a 40-yard spiral as the boy sprints down the hard, wet sand beyond the dunes. Hank Flood was as good a natural athlete as Paul ever saw. The family line on Hank: He could have done anything.

Paul still sees Hank the way he did when they were kids, still thinks in some irrational corner of his own brain that his brother really could do anything, still could.

Paul knows he will always be a source of amused pride for Hank, who can't quite believe his little brother is rich enough to afford a large home outside Atlanta and a beach cottage, too.

He also knows Hank would readily give the good right arm he's exercising now to be the way he once was.

Shortly after the second-half kickoff, they go back inside. Paul and his son settle in to watch the rest of the game; Hank goes in the other room to check on the race, then joins them for the fourth quarter. Earnhardt, he informs them, has won again.

Paul has the remote control and switches back and forth between the Tampa and Miami games, checking other scores when they appear across the bottom of the screen. He has a $50 bet riding on Atlanta, and every time anything happens to change the score, he either curses or cheers. He needs the excitement, needs for something to happen.

The 4 o'clock game has just started when the shoppers return. Naomi, Tran, Leigh and Ruth come walking in with only a few inconsequential purchases in their arms. Ruth looks happy, even though she's only carrying one bag that could hold, at most, a blouse or a shirt, some early Christmas gift.

Ruth tells them that she is tired, that she needs to take a short nap. Tran and Naomi are busy in the kitchen, putting out sandwiches and paper plates, along with cold steamed shrimp and cocktail sauce.

They eat an early supper, and Ruth says she would like to walk along the beach. Hank offers to join her; Naomi says maybe later.

The wind has picked up as they walk along the flat, seemingly endless coast. They get their bearings from a flash of red in the far distance, the roof of the Sugar Beach Inn.

"They said on the radio that the hurricane is stalled out there," Ruth says, looking toward the horizon as if she can see it.

"Looks pretty clear to me."

"Well, they can come up quick. We ought to tune in the Weather Channel when we get back to the house. That is, if all the football games are off."

He tells her there is a one-hour window of opportunity between the end of the 4 o'clock game and the start of the 8 o'clock game.

The sun is within an hour of the horizon, and the sky is already starting to show orange and yellow. This is the perfect time of day to be at the beach, Ruth believes. Even she can find beauty in it now.

"Did you find anything worth buying?" Hank asks his mother.

"No, but I bought something anyhow."

"Well, as long as you're happy."

They walk along the Gulf beach with its miniature waves and sand dunes. Even the shells, Hank notices, are smaller than life.

About half an hour out, Ruth says she's tired, that she wants to turn around.

Where they are, the island juts out into the water in a dogleg, and they turn away from the setting sun into a rising moon, almost full. By the time they get back to the cottage, it's dark enough that the moon and sky are bright orange and deep purple.

They stop at the steps leading up from the beach to admire the colors for a moment before the chill drives them indoors.

Ruth stares out at the approaching night.

She's quiet for a while, then she says, "Does Naomi seem a little distant to you?"

"No," Hank lies, "she just needs time to get settled. We don't see her that often. It takes a while to get so you can just talk normal."

Ruth sighs.

"It's been a long, long time since we could do that. I know parents and children grow apart, that you can't keep them with you forever, but I never thought it would be that way with me and Naomi."

"We are two women against the world," Ruth wrote once to Harry, when Naomi was 4. She was so proud of her: how early she walked and talked, how quickly she took to swimming, how pretty she was.

Even after Ruth's marriage, she wrote more about her daughter than she did her two sons combined, as much as she loved them. She had always thought, without even having to actively imagine it, that they would be the mother and daughter who lived in the same town, went out to lunch together, grew old and very old together, best friends for life. She had believed what they'd built in that cheap Newport apartment and then on Henry Flood's farm would outlive the years, the men, everything else.

As Naomi was becoming a teen-ager, Ruth started hinting in her letters to Harry that all was not right, wondering if it was just a phase.

Ruth was just starting out with the diner, and between that and the usual uproar of life with Henry Flood, she knew that she had sometimes taken capable Naomi for granted.

Then came the Olympics, and then college out West, and Naomi was gone permanently. And then Hank's problems caught Ruth like a thunderstorm out of a clear blue sky.

"Harry," Ruth wrote in early 1963, "there are times I think there will never be a moment when I can just sit back in my easy chair, take a deep breath, and say 'Everything's safe. Everybody's all right. Nothing is wrong. There is nothing to worry about.' Nothing is safe. Hardly anybody seems all right, and everything is wrong. There is everything in the world to worry about."

It was about as close as she came to visible despair, and she closed the letter with an apology and a promise that she would be in better spirits the next time she wrote. And she was, ready again to fight nature and bad luck.

Harry and his sister sit up late, by his standards. Artie has gone to bed. Harry is leaving in the morning, and he supposes his brother-in-law — old golfing buddy, winking co-conspirator against "the girls," excellent dirty-joke teller Artie — knows he and Freda would like to be alone for a while.

They chit-chat for a few minutes, the TV turned down low. Harry is back in the seat of honor, the one in which he slept so well in the pre-dawn. Freda, who walks three miles a day, sits up straight in a wing chair 10 feet away, facing him.

"So," Freda says, at last, "have you seen Gloria?"

He tells her of his last visit.

"She was a good girl," Freda says. "But you were a good boy, too, Harry."

"Thank God for little sisters," is all he can think to say, and suddenly they're both crying.

They talk some more, about their children, about Ruth, about the place in Safe Harbor. Freda asks him, in a low, conspiratorial voice, how he's doing, really.

"I'm hanging in there," he tells her, unwilling to either lead her on with false promises or fall on the floor, hug his knees with his arms and moan, "I'm dying, Freda. I'm dying!" Better for all concerned, he feels, to be "hanging in there."

Too soon, it is after midnight.

"Well," Harry says, trying to rise, "I guess I'd better get to bed."

"You've got a big day tomorrow," Freda says, helping him up. There is something in her voice like doubt, perhaps about Harry Stein's ability to weather a big day.

He shuffles off to bed, then lies there in sleepless pain, wondering why they didn't just stay up all night, talking about the good times.

TEN

"I GUESS," HE wrote, "that I'm going to have to come down there and marry you myself, just to save you. Give me a week to take care of the divorce."

"Harry," Ruth wrote back, "don't even joke about something like that. I am not going to be a homewrecker. And besides, I've already got a fella, haven't I?"

That was in April of 1947. Three months later, after a letter in which Harry presumed to advise her against marrying the young war veteran to whom she had become engaged, she put her foot down.

"You seem to believe only what you want to believe," she wrote. "Well, believe this, Harry Stein. I am going to marry Henry Bullock Flood on the eighth of September, in the living room of my grandmother's house, in Saraw, North Carolina. He is a fine man. He is the most courageous man I have ever known. He will be a good husband and a good father. I'm sorry, Harry, but it is time for strong words."

Ruth had become somewhat exasperated with Harry Stein. She had put from her mind any thoughts of his ever returning, no matter how much he hinted of it. She knew she loved him, but she was a sensible woman. It was time to get on with her life, and she knew Henry Flood was the man with whom she was supposed to do that.

She is sometimes amazed these days, when she thinks back to those clear-eyed, certain times, at how much she "knew."

"You dismiss my plans as if they were the dreams of a child," she wrote. "I know he's 10 years older than I am. I know he's a farmer and I'll be a farmer's wife. I can do that, Harry. I can be a farmer's wife."

Ruth was content, had made herself content, with the fact of living her life in Saraw, North Carolina. She was settling down with a man who did not care that she had a young daughter of somewhat-mysterious provenance, who was brave and hard-working and kind, a man who needed her.

"You have your life, Harry," she concluded that letter. "Let me have mine. . ."

Harry's next letter begged forgiveness.

"If you truly love this man," he wrote, "I am as happy for you as you are for yourself." They both knew he was lying, but the thread between them had never seemed so fragile, and above all he didn't want to sever it.

She forgave him, and the letters continued.

When Ruth came back to Saraw, she went to work again at the mill, keeping the books for the company her grandfather had owned. She met Henry Flood in December of 1946, at a party given by some of her old high school classmates. She rarely went to parties, she said, but this night Jane and Charlotte insisted, told her they would take care of Naomi.

Her friends and her aunts had conspired to bring her and Henry together. He was not an unattractive man. He was six-foot-three, with curly hair that had been blond in 1942 and turned mostly gray somewhere in the Solomon Islands. He had a strong chin, the hint of a dimple, a long, patrician nose and piercing eyes.

If a soldier had managed to stay alive long enough in Europe or the Pacific, he probably had brought home some medals, the way Harry saw it. He had a few himself, earned just by being there. You kept your head down. You tried to look out for your men. You definitely looked out for yourself.

Henry Flood, though, was different.

He was a North Carolina country boy who joined the Marines two weeks after Pearl Harbor. He was already 26 years old, already running the family farm. He might not have been drafted for a long while, might have avoided combat.

He spent most of the war in the South Pacific. Ruth learned his stories mostly from newspaper clippings, his family, a war buddy who came through Saraw to visit, and then through relentless questioning of a man who was an uncooperative witness to more than he wanted to remember. She fell in love with the sweet, shy killer Henry Flood had become in his late 20s.

Twice, he had gone into caves to flush out Japanese soldiers who were somewhere within. He went in voluntarily when no one else was willing. He killed three enemy soldiers with a knife. Henry Flood was not afraid to get blood on his hands, wasn't afraid to feel flesh yield to steel.

He told Ruth that the big guns were so loud and were fired so close that his ears often bled. The headaches that would get worse were already bothering him when he came home in 1946. Ruth had to be careful not to make any loud noises around him. Once, at a cousin's birthday party after they had started seeing each other, a child popped a balloon and Henry dove and landed flat on the floor, face down, his large hands covering his ears and much of his head. In the quiet that settled on them, broken only by a child's question and a mother's whispered "hush," Ruth helped Henry up and led him away.

He was injured three times, and he came home with so much shrapnel in his legs that the doctors in Newport called him "Scrap." He would start a lifetime of pain medication at the VA hospital where they shipped him when they decided he'd done his share.

Harry knew he and Henry Flood had much in common, the way many men of a certain age did after the war. In 1947, they both walked and talked, lived and breathed in a world each thought, more than once, he would never see again. They were into their second and third lives. They came back to parades and adulation that was gone before they had a chance to grow tired of it. They had lived to see a world where all things were possible. They were part of the greatest fraternity in the greatest country on Earth.

And yet, Harry wondered sometimes if anything had changed, really. He went back to his life and Henry Flood went back to his. There were plenty of farm boys like Henry in Harry's unit, sergeants and corporals and privates who helped keep an Ivy League lieutenant alive. They had shared chores and food, fear and misery, enough so that it would seem they were bound together for life, blood and bloodied brothers.

But that wasn't how it was. If one of those bus drivers or cotton-mill workers who shared a bottle with him on VE Day had looked him up in Richmond, he knows he probably would have taken him out for a drink, but not to the same bars the other stockbrokers frequented. A sick child or an early appointment the next day would have made an overnight invitation improbable.

Harry sees, from this distance, that much of what men brought home from the war was just a worse version of what they carried over. He has no interest in watching the old movies: good-hearted guys working out their problems in a foxhole. Nine-tenths of the men Harry knew before the war and after were less admirable human beings in 1945 than they were in 1941.

Henry Flood was 10 years older, but Ruth was a very old 21 when they met. She was taken by his reserve and his good looks, but she also was touched by what she could only describe as need. She knew, in 1947, that she could cure the hunger inside this man she so admired and was learning to love.

They went to church picnics. Ruth had started going back to the church of her youth, where no one ever said anything to her any more about Naomi's murky nativity, although she was certain that some of them doubted the story her grandfather had planted four years earlier. They went to the beach; they took long boat trips back into Kinlaw's Hell, which Henry Flood knew like no one else, having grown up on the edge of it just half a mile north of Ruth's family. From the very first, she marveled over his knowledge of every turn in the vast, unmarked wilderness that had been his boyhood backyard.

He didn't ask her about Naomi's father for some time.

It occurred to Harry that Ruth might well be better off with her hometown hero, the boy from just up the road. When he urged her not to rush into anything, he was just trying to keep the door open.

One night, a month before the wedding, Harry went out for drinks after work and didn't get home until 9 o'clock. He had flirted some with a secretary, an agreeable brunette. He knew, for the price of some guilt and a little risk, he could arrange to have drinks and all that followed at her townhouse the next night, but he hadn't cheated on Gloria yet, not really. He arranged nothing; he went home.

That night, Gloria and he had the biggest fight they'd had yet. Gloria smelled the brunette's perfume, from where they'd brushed faces when she leaned over to whisper the punch line of a dirty joke in the booth they shared with four other people.

Her jealousy made Harry furious. He thought of how wicked he could be, he thought about the choice he'd made, alone and unappreciated. He thought about Ruth and Henry Flood.

He stomped up the stairs, and he thought of just packing his bags and leaving. He'd stop and call Ruth from the phone at the bar on Belmont and then head south. He'd breeze into Saraw, North Carolina, and Ruth would forget that Henry Flood ever existed.

Even as he thought it, though, his confidence collapsed. He did not doubt that Ruth loved Henry, although never, he was sure, the way they had loved each other. And, Ruth had her code. She kept promises.

At the top of the stairs, he looked across the hall. A sliver of light spotlighted Martin's cradle. He had his thumb in his mouth, and his eyes were wide open. He hadn't started to cry yet, and Harry picked him up before he did. It was as if he knew what his father was considering.

Harry held Martin, humming softly and rocking him back and forth in his arms. Gloria had followed, still full of argument, but when she saw her husband and son there, she walked over, without a word, and embraced Harry. It was as if the two adults were shielding their child from the outside world.

That was the night, they both were certain later, when Nancy was conceived.

By this time, Harry was sending Ruth $20 a month, faithfully slipping the money out of his account and mailing it to Mercy with a letter. Ruth told him more than once not to send it, but he wrote that it was not for her; it was for Naomi.

On Ruth's wedding day, Harry had white roses shipped to her home. Matty, by now on his last legs, so weakened by a bad heart that he was barely able to wander down to the diner, leaned over to sniff the flowers, which were a puzzle to everyone except Ruth, and muttered, "That damn Randall Phelps."

Ruth had her own bank account and stocks, something that Henry accepted at first without complaint. The same Ruth who didn't give up her baby refused to surrender that little piece of independence, even for love. Henry Flood would learn the magnitude of her strength a little at a time. It would take him a lifetime to learn all of it.

For years after she moved back to Saraw, Ruth never touched a cent of the money Harry sent her, and she added much of her own, after she was able. Occasionally, Henry would try to get control of Ruth's account or her stock portfolio, or at least find out how much money she had in them, but Roy McGinnis, an old friend who had known her since high school, made sure he never knew, no matter how much he threatened.

The wedding was large. Ruth had many friends, Henry was a war hero, and it was something of an oddity in Saraw to attend a ceremony in which the bride's daughter was the flower girl. Ruth thought the main sadness she would feel would be over moving out of the only true home she had ever known. Her grandmother had passed away just two weeks before the wedding, and the knowledge that Ruth would be only half a mile away did not seem to ease Charlotte's and Jane's anguish.

"I wish we had never set you up with that Henry Flood," Charlotte told Ruth at the wedding, her face red and raw from crying. "Now he's stolen you away from us."

The morning of the wedding, Ruth did something she really couldn't explain. She picked two petals from one of Harry's roses and kept them in her left hand. She carried them to the church, set them aside while she dressed, then picked them up again. She had them as she walked down the aisle, her left hand in a light fist. When she held that hand up to receive Henry Flood's ring, the wilted petals fell lightly and unseen to the carpeted church floor. The ache that hit her made her hesitate, a slight bump in an otherwise seamless event. She found her place again and didn't think about Harry Stein again for most of the day.

The farm to which Ruth and Naomi moved had more history than promise.

"As soon as the loan comes through from the bank," she wrote Harry in early 1948, "I am sure we will be more secure financially. Henry has such great plans for the future." Most of the letters Ruth sent in those days dealt more with the future, the if and when of it, than with the present.

They raised tobacco, along with corn and soybeans. Henry had inherited 120 acres from his father. His mother, after his father's death, had moved in with one of Henry's sisters in Laurinburg. A tenant family, living in a wooden shotgun shack out back beside the railroad line, did much of the hard work.

Henry and Ruth had hogs and chickens and a pair of mules that wouldn't be replaced with a tractor for many years.

Ruth had grown up in approximately the same world as Henry Flood, but she knew little about farming. She had not correctly gauged the difficulty in switching from town life to the cooking-canning-cleaning existence that awaited her at Henry Flood's. It was harder, she soon knew, than her years as a single working mother.

At first, Ruth kept her job at the sawmill office. She made relatively good money there, and she could still get most of her work done at home, although Henry already was complaining about the quality of her cooking and housekeeping.

But when she became pregnant with Hank in 1948, and the morning sickness hit her harder than it had with Naomi, she had to quit and devote what energy she had left to helping Henry keep the farm afloat.

It wasn't all work. They would go on picnics, to places only Henry knew. On long winter days when there wasn't so much to do around the farm, just repairs and preparation, sometimes they would talk for hours on end. Henry was a book, although not easily opened, when it came to the natural life of Kinlaw's Hell, and Ruth loved to hear him when he got carried away describing the swamp's beauty and mysteries. Sometimes, he would have a bad day, when the headaches would squeeze him so hard that he couldn't get out of bed. And there were a few nights when his screaming would scare Naomi in the next room, and Ruth would have to soothe them both. Mostly, though, she was optimistic.

"Harry," she wrote when she had quit her job and was seven months pregnant with Hank, "this is all I ask of life: a good man, a wonderful little girl, another child on the way, a clean, comfortable home with enough space that you can hardly see the next house beyond the line of pine trees that bounds our property. I work harder than I have ever worked in my life, but Naomi is with me until school starts for her next fall, and there is always time for talking and reading and listening to the radio in the evening. I hope your life brings you such peace."

In truth, though, her peace ebbed and flowed. Sometimes, a month would pass between letters, and the letter that arrived would have a note of worry to it: "Henry grows increasingly exasperated with the VA hospital, which can't seem to get him the proper treatment and medicine." "I have made it clear to Henry that Naomi is not to work in the tobacco fields. He says that he was working in them when he was 5, and I tell him that I don't care if he worked in them when he was 2."

Even now, Ruth remembers that there were good times, too. She really did love the land and the life, and Henry Flood, and she thought everything would end well, that she could grab it and shake it and make it end well.

Hank was born in March of 1949. Henry Crowder Flood. Naomi ran away when he was five weeks old. They found her walking along the Beach Road, already across the river bridge in Saraw. The move to the Flood farm was traumatic for her anyhow; she was adored by her aunts. And while Naomi liked Henry, Ruth wrote that she sometimes rebelled against him, even telling him once, "You're not my daddy." Henry just smiled, according to Ruth, and said, "Well, then, little girl, who is?"

"Randall Phelps," Naomi told him. "He didn't come back from the war." Ruth had told her that.

"Someday," he said, "we're going to go to Germany, so we can find out where your daddy is buried. It's a shame to leave him like that, all alone in the cold, cold ground where he doesn't know anybody."

Naomi bit her lip and left the room.

He was still smiling, but Ruth knew at that moment that she might someday be expected to explain more about Randall Phelps than she wanted to.

ELEVEN

IN A LETTER dated Aug. 5, 1950, Ruth told Harry that the family who lived on Henry Flood's land and did most of the farm's manual labor had departed one hot summer night, with no warning, in the middle of tobacco cropping, before they had even been paid for that season. The stress of losing the Farrises seemed to have made Henry's headaches worse. He could hardly get out of bed some days.

Ruth ached for him, for the pain in his damaged legs, for the headaches and nightmares. She tried to make sure that she and Naomi gave Henry Flood every reason to be of good cheer. Hank was 17 months old, and often it fell to Naomi, only 7 herself, to take care of her step-brother.

"Speaking of Naomi," Ruth wrote, "can you imagine the daughter of Ruth Crowder Flood and the granddaughter of Theron and Belle Crowder winning medals for swimming? Is this not more amazing than pigs flying?"

That year, the YMCA in Newport had held swimming competitions by age group for the first time. Those 8 and under competed together.

Ruth had known that her daughter could swim well, seemingly against all genetic odds. The instructor the previous summer had pulled Ruth aside one day and told her that Naomi was better than any of the little boys her age and many of the older ones. After that, Ruth would observe Naomi swimming when she could, amazed at the perfect way she glided across the water, with almost no wasted motion.

"She's like a little fish," Ruth told Henry, who did not seem as impressed as she had hoped he would be.

Naomi, who kept her own counsel, had casually mentioned at supper one night that there was going to be a swim meet, and she supposed she ought to be in it, because her teacher wanted her to.

Ruth called the instructor, who said that by all means

they wanted Naomi to compete, that they thought she was pretty special.

Ruth told the man that she thought Naomi was pretty special, too, although she had no idea where she got her swimming ability. The coach said maybe from her father.

In the swim meet that made Naomi's talent impossible to ignore, Naomi won every race she entered, against girls one and two years older. She beat the best boys' times in three events.

"Were you a fast swimmer, Harry?" Ruth asked in her next letter.

Yes, Harry wrote back, as it turns out there were some swimming genes in the Stein family pool. The 1935 Virginia state age-group breaststroke champion was none other than Harold Martin Stein. And Freda had a trophy case full of medals before she quit.

"We've always been good swimmers," he wrote, and he told her the story of Hyman Stein, who swam his way to America.

Harry's fraternal grandfather emigrated from Germany in 1882, when he was 23. He had grown up in a village along the Rhine, between Bonn and Koblenz. A Jewish man from his village had gone to America many years before and had gotten relatively rich. The man sent back word that he needed a bright, hard-working young Jew to work in his garment factory, that he would sponsor a man from the village and help him become an American citizen, because he only really trusted the families from the place where he grew up.

A cousin still living in the village, a wealthy merchant who saw no reason to leave Germany, was empowered with the choice. Money was sent for passage by ship (and more, Hyman Stein would always claim, that the merchant kept for himself). The cousin who was to decide which young man would get a ticket to the promised land was of a sporting nature. He announced that all who were interested should be at his shop at a certain time, on a certain day.

Six men, all in their teens or early 20s, came to the cousin's shop, and he led them down the street, to the water's edge. There, where Hyman Stein always would claim the river was at least a mile wide, the cousin told them how he would choose. Half the town had followed them, for the entertainment.

He pointed toward the water and said, Swim. On the other side, there would be a tree with six ribbons (and here he gave to each of the young men a different color). The one who swims across the river and returns first with his ribbon, he told them, will go to America. Hyman Stein's color was red.

He was the youngest of eight children, and there was little for him to do in Germany other than stay and take care of his parents and work for his brothers. So he swam. It was early in the morning, in May, before the fog had even lifted, and the water was very cold.

One man went home, but the other five took off their clothes and dove in. They all swam in their long underwear, to the amusement of the crowd that gathered. Harry's grandfather couldn't see the other shore until he was almost there, already exhausted but ahead of all the others. He came up through the mud and found the tree, a good 50 yards from the water's edge, and he took his ribbon, the red. A witness was there to be sure no one cheated.

He said, years later, that his underwear felt as if it weighed 50 pounds. On the way back to the river, the man just behind him, a fast runner, passed him and jumped back into the water first. Hyman Stein, perhaps more desperate to reach America than the others, took off his remaining clothing and started back across, naked, as slick as a seal.

He passed his main rival somewhere in the middle of the river and was never caught. One of those behind him was pulled down by the current and drowned. Hyman Stein got his ticket, leaving behind all the family he knew and a legend that would outlive them, of the boy who swam to America.

He did not get rich in his new world; most of his energy and intellect was required merely to set the stage for his seven children, to place success within their grasp. He never admitted any regrets, though, and he seldom talked about Germany and the family he left there. He had been dead three years, having expired quietly in his own bed in his son's home in Richmond, when the Nazis came to his old village in 1942 and took every Jew there to a pit outside of town and murdered them all.

So, Harry wrote, tell Naomi to swim on. Travel light and don't look back, as my grandfather always advised.

Naomi, in the picture Ruth sent, is grinning from ear to ear. Her teeth are too large, and Harry could see that someday his surreptitious money would help pay for braces.

When Naomi was young, she smiled all the time. Around the house, she and Ruth would sing together. She wasn't really shy, Ruth believed; she just didn't say anything unless there was something to say. But everyone could see that she was happy.

Ruth would send clippings from the Newport paper as Naomi won one swimming competition after another. By the time she was 10, she owned four state age-group records. She was no larger than the other children, although she would grow to be 5-foot-9. But she was always in the middle of the picture, always the star.

By the time Gloria was back in swimsuit shape after Martin, she was pregnant with Nancy. After Nancy, she seemed to accept the fact that she wasn't a girl any more, and she displayed a maturity that Harry wasn't able or willing to match. It irritated him.

He was 29 when Nancy was born. She was pretty in the way of the Steins; Nancy and Naomi, were they to appear in the same room today, might easily pass as cousins, even sisters.

Harry saved all his maturity for his job, where he was thriving. He still wanted Gloria to do the spontaneous, hedonistic things they once did (and he still did). Too often, she couldn't find a babysitter, or she was too tired, or she just found the things that used to make her giggle now made her shake her head.

They still had good times, but Gloria was forcing it, trying to be a good sport, Harry could see. More and more, she was wrapped up in Martin and Nancy. Harry was jealous. He can see that now. He was the much-admired center of attention all day at work, then at happy hour, and then he came home to a world of diapers, home repair and need.

Harry sees his marriage, the whole of what he thinks of as his first life — the first one that he himself crafted — in terms of the race his grandfather swam. Hyman Stein gave it everything he had; he held nothing back. He never hesitated that day, never thought of the embarrassment he'd face as he came running out of the water with his red ribbon tied around his wrist, stark naked. He never thought about how foolish he would look if he took off all his clothes and still lost the race. He never hesitated or second-guessed himself. He never considered quitting, never wondered if another plan for getting to America might work better and require less risk.

Harry loved his grandfather dearly. People used to say they were much alike. The old man would lecture him about duty and responsibility and tenacity, and Harry took it to heart. He is sure that someone in Richmond in the 1930s would have observed young Harry Stein and said to his neighbor or his wife, "There's a young man with some backbone, some stick-to-itiveness. There's a young man who won't let you down." Harry kept the same paper route for six years. He never missed a basketball practice in four years of high school, despite not starting until halfway through his senior year. He went eight years once without missing a day of school.

Was he more susceptible than most, Harry wonders now, because of that single-mindedness? When he did look back, and see that there were alternatives, that there was some other way, probably a happier way, for his life to proceed, was he more vulnerable for never questioning his path before? Until he met Ruth Crowder, Harry's path had seemed relatively straight, with few side trails beckoning.

He thought, for a long time, that the path he took, away from Ruth, would eventually come to seem the straight and right one, that with a fine and loveable (though not loved enough) woman, he eventually would learn not to look back.

TWELVE

"THE THING THAT makes me so sad," Ruth wrote, early in 1953, "is that Henry is a sweet man. He knows he's doing wrong, even when he's doing it, but it's as if he can't stop himself. Later, he sometimes cries like a small child, when we're alone together.

"He scares the boys sometimes. He even scares Naomi. Now that she gets her picture in the paper now and then, she sometimes acts as though she thinks the sun and moon revolve around her. But even she gets scared when Henry has one of his spells. Thank God they don't last long."

He struck Ruth for the first time in March of that year, when she was two months pregnant with Susanna.

"Last night, Henry did something he's never done before," she wrote. "We were alone, at the end of a hard day. (With this farm, hard days seem to be in the majority.) I mentioned a bill that was overdue at the store, not intending to nag, but not sure that he was aware that the payment was late.

"I didn't even see it coming, Harry. We were sitting beside each other, on the end of the bed, and he must have backhanded me. It knocked me over. I remember putting my hands over my face and closing my eyes; when I opened them, he had gone into the bathroom and locked the door. I looked in the mirror, and there was no blood, just the mark of his hand, a red splotch that went away within a few minutes. . ."

He apologized, begging her forgiveness and promising never to do it again.

At the end of the letter, she wrote, "I wonder, Harry, if things ever get better. I would like to hope so."

The first time Gloria left, it was late June of 1954. Martin had just finished second grade; Nancy would start first grade in the fall.

The specific, obvious reason was Marianne Nobles. She was 23, not long out of Westhampton College and working for a law firm just down Main Street from Martin & Rives.

She was blonde, she had a heartbreakingly perfect body, and she could handle the sometimes rough give-and-take of the after-work drinkers at the bar most favored by the lawyers and brokers in its vicinity.

She attracted Harry in some way he couldn't define, some combination of how she moved her hands when she pushed her hair out of her face, the way she smelled, the color of her eyes. He never really gave it much thought at the time, just knew, somewhere below the surface, that she had his number. One night in March, she asked him for a ride to her apartment because her car was in the shop.

He could have stayed in the car, could have declined her invitation to have "one for the road," could have turned away from those lips instead of meeting them halfway. He made love to her at least two afternoons a week that spring and early summer. She would sometimes not even bother making her bed in the morning, and they would fall into sheets already smelling of her. He saw this carelessness as a kind of intimacy, of letting go, and it aroused him further.

Harry didn't truly understand, until some time in May, what the attraction was. He was at his desk, writing to Ruth, when he picked up her most recent letter and the scent of her perfume, unchanged since 1943, reached his nose. It triggered memories of how she smelled, the deeper aroma that was Ruth herself. And that triggered memories of Ruth's voice, the musical quality of it. Marianne Nobles didn't really resemble Ruth Crowder Flood. In a dark room, though, with the blinds drawn and other senses taking over, he knew now to whom he had been making love.

He voluntarily told only one person about his fall from grace, and his discovery, and she wrote back that he ought to get on with the life he had before the past did him in entirely. But Harry didn't stop seeing Marianne Nobles. He always told himself, one more time, that's it, but around 3 in the afternoon, the mere thought of what they had done the last time gave him such an erection that he had to sit and read the *Wall Street Journal* for a full minute before he could get up and go to the water cooler without drawing unwanted attention.

The one person he definitely had no plans to tell was Gloria. Instead, she had to find out from her best friend, whose cousin's daughter lived in an apartment in the same complex as Marianne Nobles.

Harry had committed his share of heedless acts as his star rose closer to partnership. Famously, he and another broker had started drinking one afternoon, began talking about a jazz club Harry favored in Greenwich Village, and before it was over, they were on a train headed for New York City. For that one, he had to buy Gloria a diamond necklace.

He told himself that Gloria wasn't hurting for money, that Martin and Nancy were going to the best private schools little Jewish children in Richmond could attend, that they did enjoy nice vacations together, that they still did have their good times. And Gloria was not always so great, sometimes more interested in her birth family than him, always talking about when — not if, when — her mother would move in with them. He was entitled, he told himself, although the ultimate entitlement he had not allowed himself until Marianne Nobles invited him inside.

The day Gloria left, Harry called home at 4:30 to tell her he would be late for dinner, and no one answered. He didn't think anything about it. She could have been at the community pool with the kids, or visiting her mother. His main response, he realized later, was relief.

He was caught unawares by the empty house when he came home at quarter past seven, twilight bringing a welcoming glow to all the windows on Dabney Lane except his. Gloria always had dinner ready, even if it had to be reheated for him. He turned on the lights, checked the children's bedrooms as if everyone might be hiding in there, ready to surprise him, and then came to his and Gloria's room. And saw the note lying on their properly-made bed.

"Harry," she wrote, "I have left you. I have taken the kids. You will hear from my lawyer tomorrow. Enough is enough. Gloria."

He called his mother-in-law. Eileen Tannebaum informed him that his wife and children would be out of town for the next few days. He could not bring himself to ask what was wrong; he knew and was certain she knew as well.

Gloria's leaving shook him badly. Once he confirmed the reason for her leaving, he swore off Marianne Nobles forever in his mind, and he would keep that promise. He spent four days haggard at work, almost sleepless at home, calling his mother-in-law twice just in case Gloria had checked in with her. He had to concede that Eileen probably was kinder to him than he deserved.

On the following Tuesday evening, Harry was at home when the doorbell rang. He closed his eyes, praying for another chance. When he saw his wife and children, he fell to the parquet floor and tried to encompass them all at once, finally wrapping his arms around Gloria's knees, almost causing her to fall. He cried the way he hadn't cried since he was a child. She said nothing, just patted him on the head.

He told her almost everything; she had already decided to come back.

Nothing, though, seemed the same to Harry afterward, once the relief and false honeymoon passed, except the love they both felt for their son and daughter. He remembered an older broker who once told him about a sexual fall from grace. His wife found out eventually, they went through "some rough times," and finally things settled down. The word the man used was "stabilized," and it stuck with Harry in the months and years after he stopped seeing Marianne Nobles.

All through this first real crisis of his marriage, Harry kept writing Ruth, telling his troubles, sympathizing with hers. Her letters in return were never judgmental, and he loved her for that.

"Maybe I should just drop everything, drive down to Saraw and carry you away," he wrote her that August. He was only half-kidding.

"Harry," she wrote back, "I have enough problems as it is."

THIRTEEN

THERE HAD BEEN a long silence from Ruth late that fall, while Harry and Gloria were applying damage control to their marriage.

Harry thought it might be her way of ending their old friendship at last, although he could not see the end coming in her most recent letter, and he had read it over many times, taking it from his locked trunk at work to study it for clues and portents. There was nothing there except a straightforward account of a woman trying to raise a family on a withering farm while her husband slowly lost his mind.

The next letter he received from Saraw was postmarked Dec. 3, and it was not from Ruth, but rather from the only other resident of that town who knew his address.

Ruth had wondered once if things do get better. After reading Mercy's letter, Harry could understand her doubt.

"Dear Mr. Stein," it started, "I am writing for my cousin, Ruth Crowder Flood . . ."

At the end of the letter, Mercy allowed herself a rare uncharitable gesture:

"Mr. Stein, it is a terrible thing to say, but why couldn't it have been Henry Flood instead?"

The house where Ruth Crowder Flood spent her married life looks solid enough now, as if a century of storms and hard times had bounced off it forever without leaving a scratch.

It is an illusion.

What is still known as the old Flood place, out of the family now in all except name, looks much as it did at sunset on Nov. 5, 1954. The exterior was barely damaged.

It was typical of farmhouses in the area. It had a screened-in porch facing east. Downstairs, there was a long hallway with kitchen, dining room, living room, bedroom, parlor and bathroom doors leading off it. Upstairs were two bedrooms and a plunder room.

Naomi was 11. She had her own room upstairs. Hank and Paul, who were 5 and 3, had the other one. The baby, Susanna Lee, was 14 months old, barely walking.

Susanna had been sleeping in the same room with Ruth and Henry, but Ruth decided it was time for her to move upstairs, too. They could have kept her in their room for another year, but Ruth had read that it was best to separate yourself from the child at night, to give it a sense of independence.

"Naomi and I slept in the same room, same bed, until she was 3," Ruth would say later, "and it never seemed to be a problem. Why I put my faith in that book, I'll never know."

They had waited until Hank and Paul were 2 to move them upstairs.

Ruth had to accept, finally, that they moved Susanna out of their room at least in part because they wanted to.

The baby hardly ever cried, but she kept Henry awake at night, making little noises. He was a light sleeper who suffered terribly from insomnia, and when he was awake, Ruth felt she should be awake, too. If there was to be any peace, she thought, they would have to put Susanna in another room.

They could have left her downstairs, next door in the parlor, but Ruth thought the child needed to have someone in the same room with her, and besides, Naomi was a sound sleeper.

Naomi was not pleased when they put the crib in her room. She and her brothers adored Susanna, a chubby blonde dumpling who grinned and drooled and was never colicky, but she thought she was too old to share her bedroom with a 1-year-old.

After Naomi sulked for two days, though, she got used to Susanna's presence, even let the child share her bed whenever a thunderstorm frightened her.

The plunder room was a catch-all, full of old clothes, old newspapers and magazines deemed to be worth keeping by someone at some time, decades of empty jars saved out of thrift and habit, and kerosene lamps.

When Hurricane Hazel had come through in October, saving its worst damage for areas west of Saraw, it knocked down power lines, disrupting electrical service for a week at the Floods' and elsewhere. A tree fell against the side of the roof. Did all this trauma somehow change something inside the walls of the Crowder home? Did some thin piece of wiring somewhere disconnect, or almost disconnect, waiting until the middle of that dark November night to do its worst? Ruth still thinks about it, still wonders.

The fire started in the plunder room, sometime after 2 a.m.

Nothing was more frightening to the farm families in rural Pembroke County. Most of them remembered the pre-war days when kerosene lanterns placed them always one false move from a fire that could only be fought, hopelessly, with water hand-pumped from a well. Even in 1954, the nearest fire department was in Newport. Afterward, the town of Saraw would buy its own water truck and start a volunteer company.

By the time Ruth and Henry were awakened, by smoke and heat and the distant crying and screaming of their children, it was almost too late. Twice Henry tried to climb the stairs in tar-black smoke, before it overcame him. Meanwhile, Ruth had run outside.

On the front of the house, there was a tin roof over the porch, with a window above it. Naomi, awakened by the choking smoke, grabbed the baby and carried her through the suffocating blackness, holding her breath and putting her hand over Susanna's mouth, to that window, closed since summer and stuck shut. It usually took Henry's strong arms to open it again in the spring, but Naomi somehow got the window up. The smoke blew past her as if it were going up a chimney.

Hank and Paul were at her heels, hanging on to her gown. Naomi stood there, with the heat already singeing her, knowing what she had to do, working up her nerve. She heard her mother, below, screaming for them to jump. She couldn't see Henry lying on the ground, left where Ruth had dragged him out through the porch and down the brick front steps. It was a cloudy, moonless night, lit only by flames.

From the lip of the tin roof to the ground was an 8-foot fall, and with the speed built up from sliding down the 30-degree pitch, it would not be an easy landing. Ruth and Naomi both knew that.

Still, there was no choice. Naomi could hear her mother's voice below, instructing her.

She grabbed Hank first, forcing him through the opening, into the cold night air. She said later that she figured that if Hank went, Paul would follow. The force of a 5-year-old sliding off the roof almost knocked Ruth's breath away when she tried to catch him. She had never in her life held on to anything so hard. She rolled Hank away from her, still crying and moaning, and waited for Paul.

Ruth could see nothing above her by this time. She had to depend on Naomi to tell her what she was doing.

"Here comes Paul, Momma," Naomi screamed, and Ruth had to position herself by sound. Paul was making so much noise that it wasn't hard to do. She caught him more easily than she had Hank, laid him gently to one side, with his brother.

By this time, Henry was on his hands and knees, trying to vomit and cough the smoke away.

Now just Naomi and Susanna were left. It had been easier to send the boys down; Susanna was whimpering quietly. Naomi would always remember that, and how the child clung to her legs. She picked her little sister up and pried her hands loose, then pushed her through the opening. Ruth could hear Naomi, through the smoke and noise, telling her to get ready for Susanna.

From the time Ruth awoke until it was all over was less than 5 minutes. All four of her children came down the roof in less than 60 seconds.

At the very moment when Naomi slid her baby sister down the tin roof, Henry righted himself and charged back into the house. Ruth was distracted for no more than a second, but when she strained to hear cloth against tin (for Susanna was now silent), she couldn't.

There were hydrangea bushes all along the front of the porch, and a more kindly universe might have deposited Susanna in one of those, the miracle baby in next day's paper, saved from death by soft green foliage, cooing for curious strangers.

From where Naomi slid her forward, the baby actually would have stood a good chance of landing either in shrubbery or Ruth's arms. Perhaps Susanna made some panicky sideways movement as she slid.

She landed on the brick steps, with a solid thunk like an ax as it first strikes a stump. Sometimes, even now, Ruth will hear an approximation of that sound and have to stop, grab hard onto something or someone nearby, and close her eyes for an instant.

Susanna's skull bore an indentation of the left side, a sharp right angle where it collided with the bricks.

Naomi, half sliding and half jumping, her nightgown smoking, suffered a dislocated shoulder and first-degree burns. There was no one to catch her. Ruth was already holding the body of her youngest, caressing her desperately, trying to wake her up.

Hank broke his arm. Henry, overcome by smoke inhalation, spent two days in the hospital, getting out just in time for Susanna's funeral.

Over the years, Ruth has played it back in her mind thousands of times. She has never, will never be able to forget that almost inaudible sound that screams to her now, the one she didn't hear in time — the sound of her baby sliding away from her.

Against all odds, the fire department from Newport, called by a neighbor, arrived in time to save the exterior of the house. Half the town's adult male population showed up, and several of those were employed to keep Henry Flood from running back intc the structure again, assuring him over and over that everyone was out.

When he learned about Susanna, he had to be restrained and then sedated. He cursed Ruth loudly and bitterly before they took him away to the hospital.

Ruth and her three living children stayed at her grandparents' old house, where now only Charlotte and Jane lived, Matty having died in his sleep the previous year without ever getting to lay his hands on the rascal Randall Phelps. That first night, the four of them slept together on the bed of her childhood.

It would be six months before they could move back into part of their damaged home, and Ruth didn't want to go back at all. Always afterward, she was aware of an acrid underscent no amount of cleaning could erase. Henry, though, insisted. It was the only home he had ever had, he said. And there was no way that he could get along with Ruth's aunts. For most of the six months, he slept in a tent in the old farmhouse's front yard. He turned down many offers of shelter, saying he preferred the outdoors.

From Mercy's letter, Harry knew only the bare essentials: Ruth had lost her youngest daughter in a fire. Ruth needed him.

He could have called her aunts' home, but he hesitated, even then, to break what he had come to regard as a spell.

Instead, he called Mercy.

She didn't seem surprised to hear from him.

"She has given up, Mr. Stein," she said, and he told her to call him Harry. "Ruth Crowder Flood has more life in her than anyone I know, but she's just quit. She acts like the boys and Naomi aren't even there."

And so, almost 12 years after he had watched Ruth Crowder shrink from his vision on the Newport depot platform, Harry Stein made hurried, furtive plans to return, if briefly.

He told Gloria he had to go down to North Carolina the next day, to Newport for God's sake, to check out the viability of an up-and-coming company that was making cheap furniture out of the local pine. He told her he would be back late that evening.

The trip down was a blur of self-doubt, plans of action routed by restlessness and nerves. There had been an unwritten but understood contract between Harry and Ruth: They would live the rest of their mutual life secretly, on paper. What if the Ruth who waited at the Saraw station couldn't match the one he remembered? What if he didn't match her memories? He almost left the train at Rocky Mount, prepared to catch the next one back north.

As the Saraw platform grew larger, Harry could make out individual people. He studied every woman there, trying to find her.

He got off the train with no Ruth in sight. Then, he felt a tap on his shoulder and spun around. For a second, he thought it was her, more drab and washed-out than he remembered.

It was Mercy.

"Come with me," was all she said, taking his arm and hustling him into the station itself, then through a side door into a poorly-lighted, dingy train-station cafeteria.

At first, he didn't see her. He looked to Mercy for guidance, then followed her eyes to the back corner, where a lone woman sat stiffly in one of the uncomfortable wooden chairs and stared straight ahead, out one of the windows opening on to the platform. Harry knew that, if she was actually looking, she had already seen the 1954 version of Harry Stein. This knowledge might have been all that kept him from running out the door.

Ruth had not aged much, outwardly. Even in her despair, she was as beautiful to Harry as she had been the day he left her there. He didn't see any way a woman could look that good and want to die.

Mercy nudged him forward, and then he was standing directly in front of her, blocking her unblinking view.

Ruth looked up. He could see the dark circles under her eyes.

"Hello, Harry," she said. She tried to smile, but her eyes, already red, teared up, and then they were crying together. Harry hoped Mercy was right about no one from Saraw being there; they were far from inconspicuous.

"You haven't lost much, Harry," she said, motioning for him to sit. "It's a wonder you don't have to carry a stick around Richmond to beat them off you."

He told her she hadn't lost much either, then colored as he realized how it sounded.

"It's OK," she said, patting his hand. "The way everyone tiptoes around me, whispering outside doors like I can't hear . . . Sometimes, I wish they'd just say, 'Look, you lost your child. Now get ahold of yourself.'"

To make matters worse, Ruth told him before their brief visit was over, her husband didn't seem to have the will or desire to say anything at all, except to blame everyone, himself included, for Susanna's death. After thc funeral, he came to Charlotte and Jane's, where she and the children were. He said not a word that day, and by nightfall he had gathered what belongings he could salvage and moved into his tent.

Two hours was all the time Harry Stein had before another Atlantic Coast Line train would take him back to Richmond. He could have stayed overnight, cooking up some excuse, enlisting an ally to deceive Gloria, but he knew it was better this way. They had talked, had reconnected with each other instantly. They had promised to try to look out for each other, to be each other's friend, for as long as they lived, speaking the words as solemnly as a wedding vow. What was left to say?

She had already told him that she was not going to divorce Henry Flood. And he knew that, despite the bruises, he was not going to leave Gloria and his children. Henry loved her, in his way, Ruth said, and he needed her desperately. He was her husband.

She showed Harry some recent photographs of Naomi and told him how proud he should be of her.

Harry said he had no right to be proud, and she let him off the hook, the way she always had, telling him he was doing what he could.

"Someday, I'd like to meet her."

Ruth thought about it for a few seconds.

"Yes," she said at last, "I'd like that, too, someday. Right now, though, Naomi thinks her father is some man named Randall Phelps, who died in Germany. I'd like her to be a little older before she finds out about Harry Stein."

Harry imparted no timeless wisdom to Ruth to get her up off her spiritual sickbed and walking among the living again. All he did was talk with her a little, like the old friends they had already become, like the lovers they had been and, in some world parallel to their everyday lives, still were. They held hands while they talked, and when he embraced her, that scent came back, that same sweet smell that was her rather than her perfume, something he had always associated with autumn and the ocean.

He wanted so much for her to ask him to stay. He wanted so much to say that he would.

But that wasn't even on the table. She couldn't. He couldn't.

They talked about old times, about new times. Ruth had managed to be as well-read as anyone Harry knew, despite not yet having taken one college course. In a farmhouse full of the needs of children and a half-crazed husband, on the edge of a desolate swamp, she found time to educate herself.

Harry had known friends who went away for six months and came back as different people, but he and Ruth never missed a beat.

He told her that he loved her, although he had sworn to himself that he wouldn't do that. What if she didn't respond in kind? But she did. He made her promise that she would somehow get over Susanna, and she promised that she would, somehow.

"If you don't get better," he said, leaning down to kiss her forehead, "I'll just have to keep coming down here."

Tell me to keep coming down here, he willed her to say. Tell me to keep coming. But she said nothing, just held tightly to him, and the moment passed.

Ruth did, though, allow him to see Naomi.

Her elementary school let out at 3. If Harry would take a later train back to Richmond, he could be there, parked across the street, when she exited. So he rented a car at the station and drove inland, to Saraw.

He waited alone. Ruth had to return, and it would have been unwise for her to be sitting in Saraw, in a strange man's car. Their leaving was hurried, and neither of them could find a fitting punctuation for their visit.

Harry had a photograph of Naomi that was less than a year old. She reminded him of his sister Freda at that age.

When she did finally emerge from the old wooden school building, he had to restrain himself. What he wanted was to rush out of his car, run up to her and tell her he was her daddy. But he had promised Ruth he would not do that.

What he saw, even from a distance, disturbed him a little, though. He had assumed that Naomi would be surrounded by friends, as would befit the girl who wins all the swimming championships, the girl who saved her brothers from the fire. He had figured that she would be smiling.

But she wasn't smiling, and she left to walk home by herself. She didn't look sure to Harry, not the way he would have wanted a kid of his to look at 11.

She was a pretty girl, tall and thin with dark hair and the great tan that bespoke the Southern sun and the Stein genes. But she didn't seem confident. He wondered if she would have been more confident if her father hadn't caught a train long ago.

Before he returned to Newport and then to Richmond, he couldn't resist taking a slow drive down the street, past the church and then right by the old house where they had been so happy for a while, Ruth's past and present home.

As he eased along the dead-end lane, amazed that he could still find what he needed in Saraw, North Carolina, he saw a woman standing at the open front door. It was Ruth, waiting for Naomi, leaning against the doorframe, her arms folded. The afternoon sun reflected off her hair and made it shine back, golden. She and Harry made eye contact across the long front yard, and he almost stopped. But then he saw her shake her head, fiercely, and he kept going.

At the end of the lane he turned around. When he came back by the Crowder house, Ruth was still there, and Harry could see Naomi approaching, a block away.

So much of my life, he thought. Right here.

He looked left once more, and Ruth Crowder Flood, standing a little back, out of sight of anyone but him, seemed to blow a kiss.

When he passed Naomi, she lifted her eyes briefly to his, and then lowered them again as she walked on to her waiting mother.

FOURTEEN

MONDAY NIGHT, COMING from an early dinner at Gumbo Jim's Oyster Shack, they drive into a cloud of moths. Paul has his brights on, and to Ruth it looks as if they're in the middle of a blizzard. Instead of snowflakes, though, thousands and thousands of bugs splatter against the windshield of Paul's minivan. The wipers only succeed in smearing the protein in semicircular streaks across the glass.

Ruth is sometimes undone by Florida's fauna. There is a cockroach in her room so large that she can see under its body as it scurries along the floor. Every time she goes into the bathroom, she instinctively looks to the ceiling, to find out what kind of large insect is perched there, ready to pounce.

The air is heavy outside, and Ruth is wishing they were headed for the cottage instead of away from its superior air conditioning when she realizes Paul is slowing down.

They ease onto the sand shoulder, less than a mile from the causeway bridge, and Ruth first thinks they must have a flat tire, or engine trouble.

Then she sees that it's Hank.

He's out the door before the minivan has completely stopped, walking off in a straight line toward an abandoned gas station turned into a roadside bar 100 yards ahead.

Everyone is quiet at first.

"Too many people, too crowded," Ruth says at last, breaking the silence and shaking her head.

Naomi gets out and goes to walk with him, but he doesn't seem to want her company. She has to move fast to keep up with him. Her shoes are not made for walking in powdery sand.

Hank stops beside a live oak tree. He's leaning against it, breathing as hard as if he had just run five miles. Naomi stays with him for another minute, then comes back and returns to her seat.

"Poor Hank," she says as she lights a cigarette. Naomi's hand, in the neon light of the bar, is shaking. The air-conditioning is going and the windows are rolled up, but they can all feel the beat of the roadhouse's country band working its way up through the dirt. Leigh and Stephen, who have never seen their uncle like this, are as quiet as the rest.

Harry finally drifts off to sleep half an hour before his plane touches down, after he has given up all hope of catching a nap on this long, airborne day.

First he had to get up and get dressed and packed and, with help from Freda and Artie, on the 2 p.m. flight out of Richmond. Sitting there in front of his gate, flanked by his sister and her husband, he felt like a kid going off to camp. He saw Freda have a furtive word with the woman behind the counter, who looked his way and nodded.

They let him get on first, with the halt and lame and mothers with young children. Freda hugged him so hard when he stood up to go that he almost fell over.

"Hey," he said. "Hey, sweetie. I'll be back. I will."

"Damn right you will," Artie chipped in, but even Artie, salesman deluxe, wasn't doing such a good job of selling, it seemed to Harry, who hugged the big oaf anyhow.

"Take care," was what they said to each other at last, in unison, and then he was walking down the ramp to his plane.

He's seen men, younger than he is now, who didn't handle it so well when they found out they weren't going to live forever. He's seen them just stop doing anything, pull down the blinds and close the store. Harry feels their pain. It makes him sad to go out to a favorite restaurant and order a favorite dish for maybe the last time, to see the state of his health reflected for half a second in the maitre d's face. But Harry isn't ready to go home, sit in the dark and watch television.

When he was 7, his parents threw him a birthday party. All his friends were there; his relatives all gave wonderful gifts. There were pony rides and a clown. No kid on the North Side of Richmond had ever had such a birthday party.

Harry felt loved by everyone. But late in the afternoon, it hit him that it would soon be over, and the next day couldn't possibly be as good as the one he was living right then. They found him in his room, crying. No one knew what to do, and the party broke up soon afterward. His parents were upset; Old Harry kept bringing up the cost, and neither Harry nor Freda ever had such a party again. But he couldn't find the words, at 7, to tell them he just couldn't bear to see the party end.

That's what Harry thinks he understands about the old guys he doesn't want to be like: They don't want the party to end, and they're too big to cry in public.

He saw his father turn old friends away toward the end, and he promised himself, right then, that he would take every scrap life offered rather than sit home and watch the second hand steal from him.

I've given up on living forever, he told Freda, but I haven't given up on living.

When the plane landed, Harry was escorted to his connecting flight in one of the airport golf carts that used to annoy the hell out of him, coming up behind him and beeping him out of the way so some codger could keep from walking a few steps. Now, he was the beeper instead of the beepee. He was embarrassed, and grateful. It was at least half a mile from his inbound terminal to his outbound one.

After a 90-minute wait, in which Harry was afraid to drift away from his uncomfortable seat into the hard-charging traffic that would lead him to a hot dog or a newspaper, he was ushered on to another plane, again at the head of the line.

Then there was an hour wait for takeoff. It was 6:30 by the time they cleared the ground. Wedged against the window by the overweight businessman next to him, Harry wondered why he wasn't asleep. An attendant had brought him some water to take with his pills, and the pain had subsided, but yet he was awake.

And then, he wasn't.

The dream is on him, has him right back in that same bloody stream. He is thrashing to get away from Sergeant Stevens.

"Sir! Hey, sir!"

The attendant is looming over him, and the people in front are sneaking furtive glances at him.

"Bad dream," Harry mumbles.

"Are you OK, sir?" The attendant, a middle-aged woman with reddish hair, looks concerned that he might die before they land.

"Fine," is all Harry can say, and then they finally leave him alone, with one last admonition: Fasten your seatbelt.

Harry takes his baseball cap off and rubs his head, where the hair is only coming back as stubble, not long enough to comb, too coarse to be pleasant to the touch. Who, he wonders, would want to see such a person?

When they first met, Ruth loved to say his name. Later, she sometimes would write it out three times — "Harry Stein, Harry Stein, Harry Stein" — usually as prelude to commiseration over some confessed misdeed on Harry's part. Reading such letters, he could imagine a slight shake of the head, a small smile, a certain tolerant exasperation.

In his letters to Ruth, Harry unburdened himself, admissions and complaints that might better have been directed to Gloria.

Ruth responded in kind, although Harry came to know finally that she soft-pedaled the bad times more than he had.

When her world with Henry Flood began to tilt dangerously on its axis, she hinted more than told.

"What's the use in whining?" she asked Harry years later, when he knew what she hadn't written.

"If you've got a good whine in you," he told her, "you have to let it out. Otherwise, it just turns to venom and kills you. Self-pity should not be hoarded."

She told enough, though. Maybe her store of self-pity was not as massive as Harry's, but such unburdening as she did, she did in her letters. He likes to think he was there, if only in the form of clandestine mail.

Hank seems calm now, at least calm enough to continue their trip.

Ruth knows that Naomi remembers Hank as he was before he couldn't bear to be in tight spaces with other people. She never really lived at home after everything changed for Hank, and in some ways, she has never accepted it.

Ruth's strategy toward Hank's "spells," at this late date, is to just let them slide. She knows he'll be better soon, and she knows how much it hurts him to be pitied.

They ride the rest of the way in silence, Ruth staring out the window and wondering why she couldn't have just had a nice quiet birthday back in Saraw.

The plane lands, and Harry Stein waits, obedient as a child, until they have come to a complete stop before unbuckling his seat belt.

He reaches into his pocket to make sure he hasn't left his key ring, with his car and house keys on it, back at Freda's. These days, he's forever double- and triple-checking. He's almost worn out his plane ticket by now, pulling it in and out of his coat.

He fishes out his keys, and the piece of bright plastic attached to the ring catches his eye, an old friend. The letters on the garish, orange-and-yellow rectangle are almost worn off. The establishment itself has been out of business for years.

Everything he touches lately, even this cheap trinket barely bearing the name of the Fairweather Grill, reminds him of Ruth.

He feels, from somewhere, a surge of energy.

He is glad to be here.

FIFTEEN

IN 1956, RUTH became, out of sheer necessity, a business-woman.

Between then and 1990, when the interstate was completed and immediately siphoned most of the traffic off the Beach Road, the Fairweather Grill would be an essential stop for almost anyone going to White Oak Beach or the other resorts along the coast below Newport. It offered simple fare: grilled hot dogs and hamburgers and what many considered to be the cheapest, best ice cream in the state — only five flavors — plus produce from Henry's farm. It became famous for the Fairburger, a cheeseburger with a fried egg on top that Ruth had been making for her family for years.

Ruth's cousin told everyone how he had skinned her on the deal. But she had done her homework. Her old friend Roy McGinnis assured her that the Beach Road would only get more crowded, that all the hurricanes in the world wouldn't keep people from wanting a place by the ocean. Even Ruth didn't believe Turpentine Creek Road, which joined the main highway there and was barely paved, would be a state road one day.

Ruth did not completely and clearly foresee a day when people would laugh at Ben Crowder for selling the Saraw Diner for only $15,000, but she did think it had promise.

"And we do need the money, Harry," she wrote that summer, "whether Henry admits it or not. This land is played out. If it wasn't for the tobacco allotment, we'd be better off selling the farm right now, but it would kill Henry, I believe. He still thinks he can support three children, and ourselves, with a farm that's about one generation past going."

They opened on the Fourth of July, 1956. Ruth changed the name to the Fairweather Grill, gave it a paint job, hired good help and spent most of her waking hours there.

Henry, who had never fully gotten over Susanna's death, seemed to take Ruth's new venture as a betrayal, an insult to his manhood. He accused her of "carrying on" with Roy McGinnis, because he couldn't see why else Roy's bank would loan a woman of Ruth's limited means $15,000 with almost no collateral, and she couldn't tell him about the $5,000 she had saved and the rest that was loaned to her by an unnamed party in another state.

More and more, Henry would go off into the swamp by himself. Ruth knew he had built a cabin of some sort in a part of Kinlaw's Hell she had never seen, and sometimes he would spend the night out there.

"But he hasn't hit me since we lost Susanna," Ruth wrote that summer, "and we have some good times. There are days when he seems as bright as a new penny. He and I will sit and laugh and talk, and afterward, when the children are in bed, we'll make love, and it seems, at times like that, as if I can get the old Henry back, that I can fix whatever's broken.

"Some days, he'll play with Naomi and the boys, but they know it won't last, and it makes me cringe to see them cringe, because I know he sees it, too. All five of us try to pretend that Henry Flood won't have any more bad days."

The Fairweather Grill was just far enough from the beach to justify stopping on the way there or on the way home, and a family of beach-goers or -comers could not miss the orange and yellow cinder block triangle (Ruth let Naomi and the boys pick the colors).

It was in need of repair the first time Harry Stein saw it. By 1956, it was temporarily closed and had become an eyesore even to a town with forgiving standards. But Ruth knew it had potential. Harry's letters were full of news about the ways in which the world was booming.

"Anything anybody starts now," he wrote her, "is only going to get bigger and bigger, assuming it is not run by idiots."

Ruth did not think she was an idiot, and she could see from the vantage point of almost a decade where Henry Flood's farm was headed. She visited her cousin, who hemmed and hawed in the careful, phlegmatic way that always defined Saraw's nickel-and-dime business transactions, then sold her a property for $15,000 that he had despaired of unloading for 12.

Under Ruth's careful yet imaginative management, it thrived. Not even the chain fast-food restaurant that opened a mile away 15 years later could make a dent in the Fairweather Grill.

Ruth had never imagined herself an entrepreneur. Such dreams as she had in those hard early years on the farm mostly starred her children, and after Susanna's death, she hardly dreamed at all. And Harry never meant to push her into the business world, but he started her thinking about ways to save her family from a life that she could see was becoming more and more second-rate.

Ruth didn't mind the long hours; Hank was in school, and Paul would be the next year. Some days, she was able to get by with a few hours and a couple of scowling walk-throughs to make sure the help wasn't cleaning out the cash registers, but there were many others when she had to depend on Naomi and Henry to look after the boys and the house, days when she left before sunrise and fell into bed exhausted after 10.

"I would rather be with my children all day, waiting with milk and cookies when they get home from school," she wrote Harry, "but I do not have the luxury of doing that, if we are to thrive."

She resisted all entreaties to build another Fairweather Grill or two in Newport or at the beach itself. By the time she had gotten the grill up and running, McDonald's and its emulators were starting to devour the market, but Ruth knew she would dilute what she had if she branched out.

She told all who offered to make her a franchise queen that she didn't think the world could support more than one Fairweather Grill. Ruth knew she could make more money, in the short term, by doing this, but she knew she would never sleep well knowing that someone somewhere, some ambitious but inexperienced young couple yearning to get rich in a hurry or some business-school graduate willing to cut corners, was playing fast and loose with the name of the Fairweather Grill.

"You're right," she wrote Harry. "I am too particular. I know that. I can't help it."

She worried, when she had time to worry, about Naomi, who never seemed to be satisfied, who was always trying to swim a little faster, work a little harder. Where, Harry asked her once in a letter, do you think she could have gotten that from?

The grill didn't make them rich, but it did allow Henry Flood to keep his farm, and it did keep the Floods from sinking to the next level down, where they would be receiving rather than giving hand-me-down clothing. Henry, the boys and such help as he could hire took care of the tobacco, their only real cash crop. They would make a few dollars more selling watermelons, cantaloupes and tomatoes at the grill's produce stand. Ruth had spared Henry's pride, although she got little credit for it. In the first year, he twice came to the grill, half-drunk and listening to the demons who were whispering louder and more frequently into his tortured ears, and accused Ruth of cheating on him.

Finally, she told him what the rules were. He could rant and rave all he wanted in the privacy of their home, but if he persisted in embarrassing her in public, to say nothing of endangering the prime source of their livelihood, she would leave him. For a time, this seemed to work.

Harry gently suggested that she leave her husband anyhow. In her return letter, Ruth asked who would take care of Henry Flood if she didn't.

"I am here," she wrote, "for the long haul. Sickness and health, Harry."

In 1956, Naomi swam the fastest time of any 12-year-old girl in the country in the butterfly, her specialty. "In four years," a sportswriter reported in the Newport paper, "Pembroke County will not just be pulling for the red, white and blue in the Olympic Games. We'll be pulling for one of our own, Naomi Jane Crowder."

Naomi's success, though, seemed to irritate Henry.

He badgered Ruth to have Naomi's last name changed to Flood, but Ruth said that was up to Naomi, who would prefer to remain Naomi Jane Crowder.

"Doesn't she want me to make her an honest woman, too?" he asked Ruth one morning after the children had gone to school, on a rare day when she didn't have to open the grill herself.

"There aren't anything except honest women in this house," Ruth told him.

"Then tell me about Randall Phelps," he'd thrown back at her.

He seemed to enjoy quizzing her in front of the children, especially Naomi, who still occasionally asked about her father.

Ruth was adept at preserving the integrity of the sacred family lie, although she knew the best policy was to say nothing at all. She worried more about Charlotte or Jane giving it away.

But one evening, when Naomi was hounding her for information, at the end of a long day when Ruth's nerves were a little more frayed than usual, she slipped. Worse, she slipped within earshot of Henry. Ruth told Naomi that her father had dark hair, like hers. She was exhausted, she wrote to Harry later, and she just wanted to get Naomi off this tiresome subject. She thought that she had told the lie long enough that it came automatically, that the truth would never slip past her by accident.

Henry looked at Ruth for a couple of long seconds and then walked off, smiling a little. Randall Phelps, he knew, had yellow hair.

That night in bed, Ruth expected to be interrogated. Instead, Henry Flood just lay there. Ruth was afraid to go to sleep until she could hear her husband snoring.

The next morning, he waited until Naomi and the boys had left for school. Then he went down to the Fairweather Grill, where Ruth had been since 6 a.m. and where the breakfast crowd was thinning out enough so that the one waitress Ruth could afford would be able to handle things for a while.

As soon she saw Henry jerk open the door and walk inside, not even bothering to close it, Ruth was slipping out of her apron. She guided him out into the parking lot without a word. Her hands were shaking when she closed the door behind them.

Once outside, he was leading her, to his pickup truck parked on the side of the building that had no windows. He even opened the door for her. Then he got in and started to turn the ignition key, but she put her hand over his and told him that whatever he had to say, he ought to say it there.

"All right," he told her, and he took the key out. "Here's what I have to say. I think you're a goddamn liar and a whore. I think you slept with half of Camp Warren and don't have any idea who your little bastard's father is, unless it's that pansy-ass McGinnis. Can queers have children?"

He said it all in a calm voice, almost no inflection at all. Ruth could barely hear him. In the background, the Sam and Willie's lone engine was creaking back and forth along the lumber yard's spur rail, occasionally clanging hard like an anvil into a flatcar.

Ruth knew this moment would come some day, but she still was not prepared for it. She pointed out that she had a perfectly good marriage certificate, to say nothing of divorce papers.

"Bullshit," Henry told her. "I don't know how the Crowders pulled it off, but I don't believe a word of it. It's time to tell the truth. Lyin' time is over." He moved closer and reached across the seat as if to put his arm around her. Instead, he grabbed Ruth's right arm and, before she could move, he twisted it around behind her, pushing her forward so that her head hit the metal dashboard.

"Time to tell the truth," he whispered.

She almost gave it away then. She had seen little boys do that to each other in the schoolyard, but she never knew how much it hurt. Henry eased up enough so that she could sit back up and get her breath, and talk. He was close enough to her that she could smell the liquor that the VA doctors had told him to stop drinking.

When the pain subsided, she realized that she had been through worse, and she was damned if she was going to give in. She had fought for too many years. She had created a world in which even those who knew perfectly well at one time that there was no such person as Randall Phelps had conveniently "forgotten," the way people can, Ruth understood, if they like you. It was worth a lot, she concluded sitting there next to Henry Flood, to keep that world intact.

He still held her arm behind her back, but his grip was light now. Without even thinking, she yanked her right arm free and simultaneously reached over with her left hand and grabbed him by the testicles. His face grew beet-red as he tried to pry her hand loose. Then she reached into her dress pocket and pulled out the little paring knife she kept there when she worked, just in case. She stuck it into his thigh, not far from where her left hand was squeezing. She let him know she could push the knife a little deeper, squeeze a little harder.

Henry Flood finally did what Ruth told him to do: He sat still and listened, blood forming a dark spot on the fabric of his work pants. Later, she would start shaking so hard from the memory of it that the cook thought she was coming down with the flu.

She told Henry that there weren't going to be any more questions about Naomi's father.

Henry Flood had never really had it all spelled out to him before then. Ruth had long ago made sure that the lawyers put everything related to the Fairweather Grill in her name. She had made sure that her business with the brokers in Newport and later with Harry Stein himself was hers and nobody else's, and especially not Henry Flood's.

"You want the truth?" she asked him. "Here's the truth, and you had better heed it."

She explained to Henry, as to a child, chapter and verse, just how quickly the farm would be taken away from him without the money the Fairweather Grill brought in. It was explained to him that Ruth had "other money" that was none of his business and not in his name, money that could sustain her and the children, if need be. It was explained, although Ruth never wanted to bring it down to that level, how little he would have in the world, how quickly he might find himself alone and broke if he continued to press the issue.

"I don't ever," she told him, "want to hear about Naomi's father again. Naomi's father was before your time. You are not to concern yourself with him any more."

Henry, his hand over the flesh wound Ruth had inflicted, told her that she was bluffing. She said to try her, then, and he was silent for a very long time, just the two of them sitting in the truck looking straight ahead while the sun worked its way up in the sky. And then he said, "Get out," which she did. And Henry drove away.

"Harry," she wrote when she told him about it, "it bought me some time, at least."

They had been married nine years almost when she bought the Grill. They would stay married for 19 more. It wasn't all bruises and silence. Henry was "good" for some time after Ruth explained how things were.

Ruth's letters to Harry emphasized the sunny days, days when Henry was a gracious, smiling presence at the grill as he pretended to be the part-owner he never was, evenings when he would play baseball or basketball with his sons until dark, nights when he would beg her forgiveness for the other times.

For a very long time, she always forgave him.

By the time Ruth opened the grill, she was receiving $15 a week from Harry Stein, who had it to spend. Even with Gloria, Martin and Nancy to consider, his ability to make money for others, and himself, had allowed him the luxury of painless generosity. The Steins only became more affluent when Gloria's mother and father died within eight months of each other and their only child inherited three-quarters of a million dollars.

Harry and Gloria got along. They made their own peace in the aftermath of Marianne Nobles and found enough substance in their lives to keep their marriage anchored. They never doubted that they loved their children, and they supposed that they loved each other as well.

They took solace in the comforts of family and a lifetime of friends in Richmond. Gloria became more fond of her upward mobility than Harry ever would have imagined, and there was an unspoken covenant between them, he felt: As long as Harry could provide all this — a life that opened almost all of Jewish and Christian Richmond society to them — she was able to forget the past and sometimes turn a blind eye to the present. Harry knew he was to blame, that he was the one who forced the woman he had loved and married to either lower her expectations or leave, but still he couldn't forgive her, not really, for selling her acquiescence and forgiveness.

At Martin & Rives, they called Harry "The King of the Jews," and he laughed right along with them. There was still only one other Jewish broker working in the city of Richmond.

Harry made money for many people whose clubs he could enter only as a guest. This bothered Gloria more than it did him, but she was thrown enough crumbs — a charity chairmanship, an invitation to join a lesser women's club, what she felt were genuine friendships with some of the old-line Anglophiles in the boxwood-and-azalea neighborhoods — to pacify her.

Ruth never forgot what Harry told her about the way money grows. She had been almost 19, with a one-year-old daughter in tow, when she walked into the oldest brokerage house in Newport, wearing her best dress, and told them she wanted to buy some stock, something not too safe, not too risky.

"Why don't you just put it in the bank?" an amused broker asked her.

"The same reason you don't," she told him. He shrugged, but he let her start with just the $100 she brought. She added to it every month, keeping just enough in the bank to pay her bills. For a long time, it didn't amount to much, but finally it did what Harry had told her money would do: It took on a life of its own. Then she finally let Harry manage her investments. Even for men who told Yid jokes to his face, Harry Stein made good money. For Ruth, he took advantage of every whispered, just-for-you-and-nobody-else inside tip.

Now, Harry considers the evil entity devouring him, two bad cells becoming four, then eight, 16, 32, 64. If his cancer were a stock, he thinks, he would certainly advise everyone to buy.

SIXTEEN

Harry knows that a wiser man might have chosen another road, the much-recommended straight-and-narrow.

A wiser man might have written Ruth Crowder off in 1943 as a casualty of the times.

But Harry stayed his brambly course. He wonders now if all his will could have pulled him off it.

And eventually (to his wonderment), he emerged stumbling and bleeding from the undergrowth to find that long-abandoned, long-yearned-for path, cool and smelling of honeysuckle and the ocean.

Paul lets everyone out at the terminal building, then drives away to park the minivan.

"Are you sure you want to walk all the way to the gate?" Hank asks his mother. "We can get him."

She doesn't even answer, just walks straight ahead. The others follow.

It takes Naomi three tries before she gets through the metal detector without setting it off. She wishes out loud that she had smoked another cigarette before they entered the terminal.

Finally, they're at Gate 24, staring out into the darkness. Paul, who never leaves anything to chance, called ahead to make sure the flight from Atlanta would be on time.

Fifteen minutes later, the passengers start coming through the door in ones and twos. Ruth can't believe a plane can hold so many people. It seems to her as if a thousand have departed before one tired-looking old man in a baseball cap and a tan suit emerges, an attendant by his side as if she expects him to fall presently.

Ruth half-runs to his side, almost knocking him over.

"Be careful, old lady," Harry Stein says. "A good gust of wind would do me in right now."

Some of the crowd at the terminal have never seen people their age kiss with such passion.

"Hey," Hank says to the teen-age boys gawking next to him, "what're you lookin' at? That's my momma."

Even Naomi laughs.

It would have been easier, everyone agreed, if Harry had just paid someone to close the Safe Harbor cottage for the winter. He could have called Freda and told her he'd spend some other weekend with them in Richmond.

But by the time Paul came up with his idea for Ruth's no-surprise surprise 70th birthday party, Harry had already bought the super-saver ticket. He always went back up for a few days by himself in late September, long after he and Ruth had returned to Saraw, long after Martin and Nancy and their kids had paid their last visits. It was a good time to be alone out there.

And he thought he might not have the luxury of rescheduling visits.

"I don't think I can bear to ride in a car all the way from Saraw to Florida," is the way he explained it to Ruth.

Now, she sees that the 10 days they've been apart have not been restorative for Harry. Maybe, she thinks, he looked this sickly when he left and I just wasn't noticing. Maybe he's just tired.

She leads him through the long hallway and down the escalator to the front door and the car. He eschews a wheelchair, and she doesn't insist. They all take short, controlled steps, trying to pretend that he is not slowing them up.

"I think this is just what I needed," Harry says as they step outside into the still-warm night air.

"Me, too," Ruth says, squeezing his hand.

The second time around, she was 51 and he was 57. Harry had not been with a woman anywhere near his age for several years. He was becoming a little intimidated by the 30-somethings and 20-somethings who turned up at his beach place. He wondered when wit and charm and money and what was left of his looks would be overbalanced by the gray in his hair, the failure to pick up on everything currently, ever-changingly young, the general sag of age.

But the thought of being together again with Ruth after all that time was disorienting. He wondered if they would have some convenient friendship of the mind. He wondered if that was what Ruth wanted. He would have settled for that, until he saw her again. They had shared almost everything in their letters.

Still, they had not seen each other undressed since Hitler ruled Europe. Harry thought it might be like the marriages of his mother's and father's generation, when the bride and groom had yet to see each other naked.

The first night, Harry was not sure where he was supposed to sleep. Ruth had taken him in like an abandoned puppy, as he had hoped she would, but that evening, he wasn't sure at all about where he stood.

When Ruth yawned and said it was time for bed, he followed her up the stairs, uncertain as a teen-ager and just as aroused.

Then, Ruth Crowder Flood reached out to him, gently and unexpectedly. He jumped back, startled, then let her caress his penis through his pants.

"You seem glad to see me," she said, and he could only nod, speechless for once.

She began stroking him and led into her bedroom, the same one where they had made illicit, delicious love so many years before. She pulled Harry to her and kissed him for a very long time, and then she stepped back.

She was wearing a red-and-black kimono. With one motion of her right hand, she undid it and threw it off. She was wearing nothing underneath. Harry looked at her breasts, sagging a little, at her pubic hair going slightly to gray, at her stomach, not so much the worse for the wear after four children. And he thought she was beautiful.

"If I looked as good as you after all this time, I'd do that, too," he told her, his voice as unsteady as the rest of him.

"Let's see," she said, and she started undressing him.

"Mmm," she said when she was finished and had stepped back, her right hand on her hip. "Not too bad, Harry Stein. Worth waiting for."

Harry had taken care of himself, after a fashion. He had a good tan, he worked out five days a week at the club. He was capable of being at least tolerated by women half his age.

Ruth turned him on more than any of them, though. He was so relaxed that they might have been sexual partners forever, and he marveled at the mind's ability to preserve what it wanted to preserve.

Ruth was amenable to just about anything Harry wanted, and he was more than willing to return the favor. She led the way when she thought he might be too timid, amazed at how their roles had switched over the years.

"I'm trying to make up for lost time," she murmured, and later she would tell him how often she had imagined that he was with her, inside her.

"I've made love to you ten thousand times," he said.

His second week there, they succeeded in breaking the double bed she had taken for her own when she moved back to her old home. A pine plank firming up the old mattress and box springs snapped like a twig, and even Harry blushed when they had to move the splintered wood and ancient bed down the stairs and later carry a new, queen-sized one up, aided by a poker-faced Hank.

It didn't continue like that forever. The tide receded, but slowly enough that neither of them ever felt out of step. They ebbed together.

The cancer brought a large dropoff. In remission, though, Harry's lust came back, along with his hair, for a while.

Even now, Harry marvels at the way physical attraction works. When he was 15, most girls and women between 13 and perhaps 30 were desirable to him, assuming they weighed less than 200 pounds. At 40, he was affected by a range of women that stretched from teens to approximately 50.

Now, at the unkind, unseemly age of 76, he is capable — or he was, until the last little setback — of being stirred by just about any marginally attractive woman born between 1920 and the late '70s.

He figures that, taking into account population growth, there are at least 10 times as many women capable of arousing him as there were when he was a teenager.

Life, he says only to himself, because nobody likes a whiner, is a bitch.

When they get back to the cottage, Harry feels strangely rejuvenated, as if at the end of his long, tiring day he has been granted an Indian summer.

He eats a sandwich of cold cuts and has some potato salad, even has room for a small slice of the cheesecake Tran bought. By then, it's 10:30, and Ruth tells the rest that she and Harry are going to bed.

In their room, she tells him that she has a small present for him. It is in a department-store bag, and she apologizes for not wrapping it.

"It's your birthday," he tells her. "I should be wrapping presents for you."

He takes out the dark blue shirt, exactly his size, the size to which he has of late shrunk. It is the perfect color, the shirt Harry would have bought for himself.

Harry used to make fun of shopping. Gloria would endure his jibes after an afternoon in a shopping center or a mall. It wasn't the money. He just couldn't understand the purpose. It never occurred to him that it might be fun, and if not spiritually uplifting, as least as intellectually stimulating and worthwhile as watching professional football, and that it might be driven by something so simple as generosity.

Now, this late, he has come to recognize shopping as a meaningful, even therapeutic activity, a leisuretime pursuit, almost a sport. He sees no reason why it shouldn't be one of the demonstration events in the Atlanta Olympics; surely it is the equal of bowling.

Women, Harry concedes, spend all their lives tolerating men. They endure massive doses of sports spectatorship passed off as male bonding. They forgive deep-sea fishing trips that yield no fish. They don't begrudge the happy hour.

While men are ogling sports cars or younger females, women are making mental notes of what kind of shirt would look best on a dried-up old coot like him.

Harry is grateful to have learned this, but he wishes he had been a quicker study.

"Thank you," he says, moved by her kindness, moved by all he never will be able to repay, his eternal debt. "It's beautiful."

Her smile makes him believe anything is possible.

SEVENTEEN

HARRY WONDERED, IN a letter he wrote in the spring of 1959, how different things might have been if they had never met or, having met, never parted. She told him not to dwell on such things, as she admonished herself not to.

"Don't torture either of us," she wrote. And then she told him a story about her earliest days as an orphan.

She had brooded over her lost mother and father, and she became an angry, resentful child. She would tell T.D. and Sudie, when she was in a particularly hurtful mood, that they weren't her real parents.

One day, after she had said this, reducing her grandmother to tears, T.D. pulled his chair up next to hers, facing her. She was 7 at the time. Her grandfather leaned over and down so they were eye to eye.

"Ruthie," he told her, "you know the Bible stories you hear about in Sunday School? You know about Jonah and the whale, and Moses parting the Red Sea, and Jesus raising that dead man up after three days?"

Ruth was silent.

"Well, those are just stories, ain't nothin' but stories. They might have been true once upon a time, but they ain't true now. And even when they were true, the dead that rose back up hadn't been dead long."

He put both her hands in one of his.

"Your momma and daddy are gone. They are not ever coming back. All you have is today, and tomorrow if you're lucky."

Tears were rolling down T.D.'s cheeks by then. Even at 7, Ruth sensed that he didn't believe in anything much any more. Even if it was directly in front of him, so that he could touch it, he was afraid it would disappear the next minute.

"And I guess some of that has rubbed off on me," she wrote to Harry in 1959. "I know for a certainty that I didn't mention my mother or father again to him or my grandmother, even when we would go out to the cemetery to put flowers on the graves. We remembered mostly in silence. And I haven't done very much looking back. It hurts too much, Harry.

"Besides, things are better around here now. We seem to have reached some kind of truce. Either that, or the VA has finally gotten Henry's medication right."

Harry had come to believe, by that spring, that he and Gloria had settled on the rules by which they would live the rest of their lives. They hardly ever argued anymore, and never in front of the kids (although Harry came to understand later, from a grown Martin and Nancy, that his children had missed less than he had hoped they had).

Harry would go on weekend deep-sea fishing trips off Hatteras; Gloria would take the kids to the beach for the week while Harry worked and played bachelor back in the city. Gloria and her friends would go to Charleston or New York and leave their husbands to play poker, drink, burn burgers on the grill and keep the children.

Sex was comfortable, predictable. Sometimes Harry would wake with an erection and want Gloria. When the children were younger, waking at dawn, sex in the sunlight was impossible. Now, it seemed exciting, something different. Gloria preferred the night, though, when Harry was sometimes too tired. Three times a week became twice, well on the way to once. But, Harry thought, they had it at least as good as most of their friends. Wouldn't it be selfish to demand more?

Then, one week that spring, Gloria went to New York for four days to meet some old classmates from college for shopping and the theater, as they did once or twice a year. On the second night, Martin, who had been bothered for a week with a cough that resisted treatment, woke up and couldn't breathe. When he coughed up some phlegm, there was blood in it.

Harry took him to the emergency room at 2 on a Saturday morning and sat there trying to talk the pain away from his son as the drunken fight-losers and car-wreckers filled the room with their blood-ruined shirts and thoughtless cursing.Finally, a doctor saw them. Martin had pleurisy. "Probably pneumonia as well," he added. "We probably ought to hospitalize him."

Harry went home and slept a few hours after Martin was admitted. When he awoke, he thought at first he would be noble and let Gloria enjoy her carefree weekend with the girls, but by visiting hours he had convinced himself that she would want to know her son was languishing in a Richmond hospital, would want to rush home.

But he didn't even know what hotel she was staying at, hadn't bothered to ask. He did know the names of the other women. He got the address book and called Teresa Linder in Rochester, N.Y., figuring Teresa's husband could tell him where their wives were staying.

Teresa Linder herself answered the phone. Harry had not spoken with her in 10 years, and she seemed surprised to hear from him.

No, she said, she wasn't supposed to be in New York. But, she added too quickly, she did recall Gloria inviting her, wished that she could have gone, darnit. Harry thanked her and hung up.

He called the other two women and found that they were spending quiet weekends in the Boston suburbs and a small Pennsylvania town.

He took Nancy to the hospital with him and spent two hours with Martin, who was resting comfortably, on penicillin, still coughing up blood, already getting bored. Harry had time to think while his son dozed and his daughter went down the hall to watch television in the lounge.

He spent the weekend going between home and the hospital. He told her family and his that he didn't want to disturb Gloria in New York; she had a long weekend coming to her.

Monday afternoon, he met her at the train station. She gave him a quick kiss on the lips, and then he drew away, holding on to her hands.

"Martin's in the hospital," he told her. "He has pneumonia. I tried to call you, but nobody knew where you were."

He could see it in her eyes.

The room, had Harry been able to remember the hotel, would have been in another name anyhow: Thomas Gray Daniels. Gloria was so stricken with guilt and embarrassment and almost physical pain that she never even bothered to ask Harry who it was he tried to call. She would find out later, when three old college friends all phoned her, each during the day, when Harry wasn't home.

They had to pick up Nancy from school and then go to the hospital, where Martin was in better shape and would be released in two more days. They didn't have a real moment to themselves until late that evening.

Harry knew she would tell him, and she did.

Thomas Gray Daniels was descended from two United States presidents. His grandfather had been a senator. Harry knew Tommy Daniels, had made him a lot of money over the years, had been Tommy's guest at the Commonwealth Club, one of the many of which Harry could never be a member. He was a lawyer in an old Richmond firm; they had played golf together.

Gloria had gone away with Tommy Daniels twice before, she told Harry. He would discover that many of his friends knew about it long before he did, and he had to finally admit to himself, and Ruth, that the humiliation of having the brokers and golfers and drinkers with whom he spent much of his time know his wife was being screwed by Tommy Daniels hurt him worse than the betrayal itself.

Harry wondered, not for the first time, if it was worth it. Nothing had been the same since the days of Marianne Nobles, although he had slipped only once since then.

He asked Gloria if she wanted a divorce, and she shook her head violently, no. She never again, to Harry's knowledge, slept with Tommy Daniels.

"Why Tommy Daniels?" he asked her. "He's got a face like a horse and he can't hold his liquor. What was it? His money? His dick?" but Harry knew. He knew the lure of those serpentine gentile walls, those soft old bourbon-soaked accents that they both should have hated. He knew how much Gloria loved all the trappings, especially the ones they couldn't have. He also knew Tommy Daniels would never leave his cool blonde wife, at least not for a Jew.

He thought seriously about trying to arrange a tryst with Beth Daniels, a revenge fuck. But she wasn't his type at all, and he wondered if he could even get aroused for her.

Throughout the summer of 1959, Harry and Gloria danced around each other. They never really talked everything out, because they knew what was down there at the bottom of the bottle if they threw the cap away, started drinking and really opened up. So, they pretended everything was all right, and soon, it seemed to be.

That summer, something took hold of Harry's life, and by extension Gloria's, and for a while they thought it would be their salvation.

Harry had always had a peripheral interest in politics, but after they made him a partner in the firm in 1958, doors were opened. And the times were with him.

Peyton Rives had been a mover and shaker in Virginia state Democratic politics — one of the old boys who decided who ran the state — for 20 years. With the world changing, though, with Eisenhower leaving office and the whole world coming out of its self-satisfied '50s slumber, it didn't seem appropriate for Rives, head of the commonwealth's largest investment firm, to be backing John Kennedy. Besides, Rives was uncomfortable with Kennedy, could see already that he himself wasn't really going to be a true believer in this new Democratic party.

Harry Stein, though, might do. He would never, Peyton Rives knew, be on the real inside of Virginia politics. It might, however, be good for Martin & Rives to have someone on the Kennedy inside, "just in case the sonofabitch wins," he explained to his wife.

It was arranged, then, for Harry Stein, already a minor functionary, to direct the presidential fortunes of Jack Kennedy in Virginia.

"A Jew and a Catholic," Rives said one night, having bourbon after dinner, with two old friends, one of them a U.S. senator, in their deep leather chairs within the bowels of the Commonwealth Club. "That's about right."

Nineteen-fifty-nine was a good year for Ruth. Henry applied himself to farming and appeared, most of the time, to be relatively sane and stable. Hank and Paul were growing up bright and strong.

The whole Flood family looked as if it was recovering from the bad years after Susanna's death. Their repaired house was more substantial than the original. There was more hope in Ruth's letters than Harry had seen in years.

Ruth's only real worry was Naomi, her pride and joy. There was a distance there that hurt and puzzled her. Naomi was withdrawn, then irritable when her mother tried to draw her out. Ruth figured it was something she would outgrow; Naomi would be 16 in September.

"In some ways," Ruth wrote, "it seems I have never been without her, and in others, it seems only yesterday I brought her home from the hospital.

"But now, she doesn't talk to me. We used to talk about everything. If Henry was in one of his moods, she and I would just exchange a look and know what the other was thinking: Better tread lightly today. We laughed at the same things. And she just threw herself into helping with the grill, always trying to make it easier on me.

"Now, she avoids my eyes. And she gets irritated with me when I try too hard to cheer her up. I am sure it is a stage, Harry, and that it will pass, but I miss my old Naomi."

Still, there was relative peace. And, with the Fairweather Grill a success almost from the start, Ruth didn't have to be there every minute of every day.

She didn't squander the extra time.

There was nowhere in Saraw for children to swim, except the muddy river. There was nowhere to play basketball indoors in the winter. The only baseball field was a flat, grassy spot by the lumber yard where thousands of hurrying feet had carved out basepaths, with feedbag bases and a chicken-wire backstop. It had bothered Ruth for years that Naomi had to go all the way to Newport to swim, and now her boys had nowhere decent to play.

She petitioned the town council, but there was no money for such frivolity, so she took matters in her own hands, as much out of pique as public-spiritedness.

She had been an active member of Crowders Presbyterian Church since she returned to Saraw, gradually settling into acceptance among her old friends and her extended family. She knew the congregations at the Baptist and Methodist churches in town, where almost everyone else in the white community worshiped.

"I am no public speaker, Harry," she wrote, "but this was important."

So she went around to each of the churches, soliciting money.

Eventually, the churches raised enough to build a gym and then a pool. And then Ruth petitioned the county to put a branch of the public library in Saraw after a child was hit by a car as she crossed the road to reach the bookmobile on its weekly run.

Ruth never planned to be a mover and shaker, in Saraw or anywhere else, although she admits now, to herself and to Harry, that she does relish being recognized in a restaurant, being able to call powerful people and have them put other calls on hold. She pleads guilty to misdemeanor vanity.

Mainly, though, she came to understand that she had more courage than many of those who lived around her. If she thought she could do some good, she wasn't afraid to take on much of anything. In Saraw, a person could become important just by having the nerve and energy to take on the fraternity of farmers and small-businessmen who made the decisions.

In 1960, Ruth (who was spending a good deal of her own time working toward a better Saraw) was persuaded to run unopposed for a vacant seat on the town council.

Most of those serving on the council didn't take their jobs as seriously as Ruth would, and some came to rue the day she joined them.

"Harry," she wrote not long after she was sworn in, "I know that this can be a better town than it is. And I mean to make it so. What you are doing in Washington, I can help to do down here."

Harry Stein had shown a great talent for raising money and votes on behalf of John Kennedy. It was a labor of — at least — respect. He believed in what Kennedy promised, and he felt empathy for a man who might be denied the presidency because of his religion.

Harry was not able to carry Virginia for John Kennedy. but he gave the Byrd machine and the old Episcopal money a scare. And when it was over, Harry Stein, seen as a hardened capitalist with a social conscience and an Ivy League education, was offered a chance to go Washington as part of a pre-inauguration task force.

His firm sent him with its best wishes, basking in the reflected glow of Harry Stein's sudden stardom. Peyton Rives exchanged winks with bourbon friends.

For more than six months, Harry commuted up U.S. 1, eyeing with impatience the piles of Virginia dirt and the caravan of heavy equipment that marked the achingly slow progress of the new Interstate 95.

He rented an apartment near a bus line, close to George Washington University, and that was his home, most weeks, from Sunday night until Friday afternoon.

Harry missed his family, and especially his children. In June of 1961, he would move them all to a suburb just inside the nascent Beltway, to a new tri-level brick house in a hilly neighborhood of hardwoods where everyone was from somewhere else. Around them, the red clay was always being gouged to accommodate another housing development, another shopping center. They had traded Richmond, where nothing seemed to change, for a place where six-month-old street maps were obsolete.

He worked in wooden, World War II barracks at first, with some of the finest minds the new administration could gather from throughout the country. When Kennedy was sworn in, Harry was asked to join the Economic Advisory Board, and his office improved.

He knew the powerful people who thought they were creating a new world: Larry O'Brien, Kenneth O'Donnell, Harris Wofford, Ted Sorenson, Robert McNamara. He became a protege of Douglas Dillon. Dillon, 10 years Harry's senior, was head of one of the country's premier investment banking companies when Kennedy made him secretary of the treasury.

The tall, balding Dillon, who had been ambassador to France in the early '50s, took Harry sailing and introduced him to people far above Harry's workday Washington station.

Harry and the other members of the Economic Advisory Board spent much of their time trying to find ways to make Kennedy, who had little interest in either meetings or economics, understand the importance of kick-starting the economy. The recession that Kennedy inherited ended more or less on its own in the spring of 1961, but no one on the EAB thought it was either permanent or the result of anything the new administration had done.

Harry, who could make money or raise it with equal ease, part economist and part entertainer, became known for being able somehow to get Kennedy's ear. Jack Kennedy liked him, remembered him. He teased Harry for his Princeton ties, his Southern accent, his Jewishness.

"I would like to present Harry Stein," he told Jacqueline upon introducing her to the starstruck Harry. "His great-grandfather was the only man in the Confederate Army to get a two-day pass for Yom Kippur."

He would jibe Harry about Harvard and Princeton football games, gloating when Harvard won, making a great show of mock-avoidance when the Crimson lost.

Harry knew his place. He saw himself as a trim, Jewish Falstaff, Puck perhaps, but he also had timing. Once, catching JFK in a rare quiet moment at a banquet, he was able to explain in two short minutes why the EAB felt the minimum wage should be raised. It was accepted wisdom within the EAB that Harry, certainly not the classic economist, could do one very important thing: He could, sometimes, make Jack Kennedy listen.

Back home in Richmond, Harry would tell Gloria and the kids stories about his brushes with people they saw on the evening news. By the end of the school year, Gloria, who had already gotten a taste of high-rolling politics during the campaign, was eager to move north, and Martin and Nancy were grudgingly willing to trade off a lifetime of friends for having a full-time father again.

The woman with whom Harry spent an occasional lonely night, a high-ranking aide for a Democratic senator from the Midwest, understood about his family and its imminent move to Washington. They hardly ever saw each other again after June of 1961. She was 28 that year, and if she had been transported across time and space to a certain railway station in Newport, North Carolina, one late fall day in 1954, Harry Stein might have mistaken her for Ruth Crowder Flood.

"I don't think the federal government ought to be telling us what to do." Ruth wrote in March of 1961, "but something has to be done, by someone. We've always said we could take care of our own mess down here, Harry, but we never have."

The week before, the council had listened to the pastor of Bethany AME Zion Church as he pleaded with them to allocate money for Armstrong School, where 12 grades of black children got such education as they would get. There was no more oil for heat and no money to buy any more. Warren Tabor, who had been on the council for more than 20 years, told the Reverend Waller that he supposed they would have to wait until fall for more oil.

"After all," he had said, "We don't have but three more weeks of winter."

Ruth heard a couple of the other councilmen laugh quietly. The minister said all he could say, and then he thanked them and left. He didn't lose his temper, never showed any emotion at all. But as he reached the front door, Ruth saw him jerk the coat of his suit tightly around him as he stepped out into the cold, his large, grayish hands clenched into fists. She doubted if the rest of the council members even noticed.

She argued the school's case, but she was voted down 4-1.

The next week, Ruth went by Armstrong School. It felt colder to her inside the building than it had outside, with cracks so large that she could feel the wind coming through if she stood near a wall. All the children and teachers were wearing their jackets. The rooms were half-empty, and one teacher told her many of the parents wouldn't send their children again until it got warmer.

From the town's only hardware store, Ruth bought a thermometer. She went home and got her camera, and she went back to the school. She took photographs of the children bundled in their winter clothes inside, and of the cracks admitting daylight and wind. The temperature in the classroom where she left the thermometer was 54 degrees.

Then she went back to the Fairweather Grill and put a jar by the cash register with the pictures beside it and a sign taped to the jar: Emergency Relief for Armstrong School.

Pembroke County, and Newport in particular, had been the site of several lynchings in the first half of the 20th century. Harry wrote Ruth and warned her to be careful. The violence that would soon immortalize the names of previously anonymous Southern hamlets was just starting to bubble to the top.

But people knew Ruth, and they knew what they saw in those pictures, and the school had heat two days later, paid for by the patrons of the Fairweather Grill. None of the four men on the town council spoke to Ruth unless necessary for the next two meetings.

It was too early to think seriously about school integration in Saraw, but Ruth could see that coming, too. Part of her rebelled at the idea of others imposing their will on her town and her state, but she knew it was inevitable if justice was to be done, and she saw a way to get her neighbors used to the idea.

"These are not bad people," she wrote. "But they are set in their ways, and sometimes you have to give them a little nudge."

The "nudge" was the athletic complex for which the white churches had paid. What if, Ruth wondered, the AME Zion church was to contribute time and money? ("They have more time than they have money, I'm sure," she wrote.) If the white congregations could be persuaded to share time at the gym and the baseball fields and swimming pool, it would be a step.

"I imagine," she wrote, "that the black children would just as soon have their own gym and their own swimming pool, but I can't see the white churches building them one of their own, or the black churches being able to afford one. And I surely can't see our town council building them one, so we ought to share ours."

Ruth had to cajole and badger the white churches, whose charity did not extend as far as she had hoped it would. It wasn't so difficult to sell them on the idea of letting the AME Zion church baseball and softball teams use the fields occasionally, as long as the black deacons helped with the upkeep and maintenance, and they finally relented and allowed the black church teams to use the gym on occasion.

The pool, though, was the sticking point. Even the city pools, such as the one in Newport, were segregated, and there was great force brought to bear by the white community to keep them that way. The whites were sure the blacks would urinate in the water, transmit unspeakable diseases and lust after their bathing-suited daughters.

It took Ruth four years to integrate the Saraw pool, and she lost some friends along the way. She was even afforded the Southern white liberal's ultimate Croix de Guerre, which was burned in her front yard one night in the fall of 1962.

*   *   *

Harry looks over at the bedside table, where the travel alarm clock glows the same soft green as the one back in Saraw, the color of insomnia. He can feel it burning through his eyelids when he awakens at 3 a.m. and tries to will himself back to sleep. The pain diminishes when he sits up, something he is always loath to concede, because it involves admitting that the night is shot to hell, that he will spend the rest of it in an easy chair in the den or, in this case, the chaise longue on the deck.

He staggers down the hall like a man on a small, unsteady boat, stopping at the guest bathroom to get some water to help him swallow his pills.

Standing over the toilet as he urinates, he is hit with a sudden and frightening nausea that would have served him better if it had come all the way up rather than leaving him with the taste of bile.

As he leans forward toward the mirror with both hands on the counter, the vision facing him is almost too much to bear.

One night two months ago, on his and Ruth's yearly late-summer return to Safe Harbor, at the end of what he considered to be a good day, they risked a party, given by friends in Sagaponack with enough money to possess an ocean view. Harry slipped out on their deck around 11 to smell the salt air and to relish and mourn one more sweet evening. There weren't any lights, and Harry was very quiet. After about five minutes, he heard the sliding glass door at the other end of the deck open. Two younger men whose voices he recognized, friends of friends, walked outside.

Harry could only pick up parts of their conversation, but he heard clearly as one, an intense, tough-talking Wall Streeter out for the weekend, said he'd been told "the best way is to just drive up to Vermont on a January day, hike up a mountain, take your coat off, and leave the trail. They find you in the spring."

Then he heard the other man say something about "quality of life . . . Never let it get that far, I swear to God."

Harry tried to disappear into the weathered wood, but then the younger man's voice stopped in mid-sentence, and a few seconds later the door at the far end softly opened and closed, and Harry was alone again.

Quality, my ass, Harry thought to himself. Quality is in the mind of the beholder.

He figures that if he can keep a couple of meals a day down, if he can keep his eyes on the sunrises and sunsets and off the mirror, he has quality enough.

If you get close enough to smell the brimstone, Harry Stein wishes he had told both of them, you'll trade 10 pounds of quality for a gram of quantity.

It's chilly on Paul and Tran's deck, but Harry has a blanket, and there is something soothing about being here, with the darkness and silence in front of him broken only by the put-putting progress of one small, sad shrimp boat, trying to find its way home.

EIGHTEEN

IT IS ALMOST DAWN. Harry figures he might as well give in to consciousness. It hurts, but he's loath to miss another sunrise at the beach.

He goes down to water's edge in his robe and slippers. Far to the left, he can see light creeping up from the place where the sun will soon appear. He hobbles back up to the deck and fetches one of the short chairs that Paul and his family like to plant in the sand so the incoming tide can wash over them.

Harry Stein digs in and waits for another day.

Many years ago, Harry heard a man at a party in Richmond talk about the green light, a brief flash of pigment sometimes visible to the human eye at the exact split second when the first centimeter of the sun breaches the horizon. Harry read the scientific explanation, and for each of the next three summers at the beach, he would get up at dawn at least once, searching in vain for the green light. Friends and family would tease him when he came back, bleary-eyed and frustrated, from the pier.

But now, expecting nothing, he sees it. The green flash is there and gone before he can blink, a hidden emerald not even a tenth of a second long, the length between night and day.

Once, as Harry sat alone on the back porch of their new home in the Northern Virginia suburbs, a deer materialized in front of him, not 20 feet away. It was a beautiful buck, at least an eight-pointer. It made eye contact, showing neither fear nor surprise, then turned and crashed back into the woods, never to be seen again, witnessed only by Harry, who always afterward watched in vain for its return. Now, as then, he looks around for corroboration. Only the gulls are there to share his green light.

He watches the sun rise. This near the horizon, he can actually see it move, if he looks long enough. Harry does look. He is not concerned about cataracts.

When the sun is half-exposed, some bit of color makes him look out to sea again. This time, the flash is red.

Harry's eyes are still good, and he can see soon enough that it's Naomi, out for a swim, alone in the Gulf of Mexico. She is doing the butterfly, which Harry thinks is one of the strangest athletic endeavors ever invented for humans. According to Ruth, Naomi chose it because it seemed an event that she could master by sheer hard work.

Naomi's one-piece red bathing suit lurches in and out of the water, resembling the dolphins he and Ruth see off the Carolina beaches. When he first spots her, she is far away, but in almost no time she is near the shore, swimming easily in the weak Gulf current.

She doesn't see Harry until she stands up in waist-deep water and starts walking toward the shore. Harry knows this because she jumps slightly. Even a mile swim after a night's sleep, he thinks to himself, isn't enough to rid his daughter of her tension.

Naomi walks a few yards over and picks up her terry cloth robe where she left it in a protected pocket between two dunes. Then she comes over to where he's sitting.

"Jesus, Harry," she says. "You ought to let somebody know you're out here."

"I didn't know you were such as early riser."

He wonders if she is reacting to his appearance, which he's sure hasn't improved since he looked into that 3 a.m. mirror. She is already fishing in her robe pocket for cigarettes and matches. She finds them, lights one, then sits, yoga-style, watching the sunrise with Harry.

"Did you see the green light?"

"The what?" She looks back at him as if he has reported a mermaid sighting. Then she remembers Harry explaining it to her, years before.

"Oh, the green light. You finally saw the green light? That's nice."

She smiles as if she might be humoring him.

They are both quiet for a while as the sun slips into a cloud bank. To make conversation, he asks about Grace and

Gary, not expecting much except the usual boilerplate. But Naomi surprises him.

"Well," she says, putting out a spent cigarette in the sugar-white sand and reaching for another one, "it isn't a picnic, Harry. It definitely is not a picnic."

Harry observes that it usually isn't. At best, he adds, you've got ants. Feeling a rare moment of kinship with his oldest child, he tries not to frighten the moment away with overeagerness.

He talks about Martin and Nancy, more than he has before — about how, after things fell apart, Martin seemed to choose him while Nancy chose Gloria, like kids picking players for a softball team.

"And then there's me," she says, turning and smiling with a little mischief, Harry thinks, a little life. "Should I want you on my side?"

Harry puts his hand on her shoulder. At least she doesn't jump.

"You're entitled not to," he says. "You've got a grudge coming to you."

She turns toward him and rubs his foot, which looks bruised and swollen although he doesn't remember running into anything recently.

"Does that hurt?"

"Only when I laugh," he starts to tell her, but his throat catches, and it takes all his strength to keep from crying. Where the hell, he wonders, did that come from?

"It's OK, Harry. It's OK." She strokes his ankles and feet, and he's grateful that she looks away, as if she has seen him naked, until he can pull himself together.

"So," he says finally, trying to pick up the thread, "what's not a picnic?"

She scoops up a handful of white sand and lets it sift through her fingers.

"Well, Grace is OK, I suppose, although she's a little too much like me for my liking, if you know what I mean."

"She should be so lucky."

"I mean, she's breezing through law school, not a problem in the world, but she doesn't have, I don't know, a lot of sympathy, a lot of compassion. I really wanted her to come east with me for Mom's birthday, but she said she didn't really know anybody back here anymore.

"Do you think I'm hard-hearted, Harry?" she asks, looking right up into his face now. "Do you think I've passed that on to Grace?"

Harry tells her he thinks she's passed a damn good work ethic on to Grace and, no, he doesn't think she's hard-hearted; he just wishes she and Ruth were better friends.

"We used to be," she mutters.

"What she said about, you know, gays . . ." Harry had been there, too, that day, was left to deal with Ruth's self-recrimination afterward.

Naomi bats away his sentence with her right hand before it is even completed. It is so much like the gesture Harry's father used to deflect compliments or apologies.

"She didn't know. Hell, I was in denial at the time, myself. Thomas is still in denial. He claims he believes the boy Gary is living with is just a friend, a buddy, a roommate. We can't even talk about it, Harry. I'm afraid it's going to tear us apart. You think I'm hard-hearted? No, don't deny it; let me finish. Well, I can't shut my child out of my life because of something he's got no more damn control over than he does red hair.

"But Thomas, he'll never accept it. He's got to know, though. He's gotten into all this macho stuff — mountain-climbing, dirt-biking. He's talking about taking up parachuting. It's like he's trying to prove that, by God, it wasn't anything he did, not something wrong with his family's chromosomes. Thomas likes to control, and he can't control this."

It occurs to Harry that Gary has a tough row to hoe, if Naomi is the flexible, sympathetic parent.

He decides to make a small leap.

"Are you afraid," he asks her, "that you and your kids will wind up with the kind of relationship you've got with Ruth? Are you afraid of history repeating itself? Things can change, you know."

He feels so helpless. He should be able to say it better. If he could say all he knew, it might come out right.

She looks up at him and frowns. She doesn't speak for so long that Harry wonders if it's still his turn.

"Harry," she says finally, "you and I both love my mother, but even you don't know everything. You weren't there, and I don't mean that in a nasty way. I just mean, you weren't there. You didn't live through the reign of Henry Flood. You didn't pray for deliverance and have that prayer answered with lectures on how 'you've got to try and get along with him.'"

She's never before opened up this much. Maybe, Harry thinks, it's because soon-to-be-dead men tell no tales. And maybe he should tell one of his own, one he swore he never would. Whatever the reason, he's glad for the moment. First the green light and now this. He is struck, not for the first time, with how any given day, no matter now large the odds against it, can be worth the effort.

Naomi says the winter before the Olympics was the worst. It should have been the time of her life, but it wasn't. She was working harder than she'd ever worked or ever would again. She felt her whole life would be a failure if she didn't make the U.S. team and go to Rome. She had skipped a grade in school and would graduate that summer, before she was 17. And Ruth was determined that Naomi would be the valedictorian Ruth always thought she should have been.

"Nobody around Saraw knew how hard it was," she says, "just to get on the U.S. team. You look around and there are — what? — several hundred big-league baseball players, over a thousand pro football players. But we were competing for just two spots, two lousy spots out of the whole country, for each event. And afterwards, you might get a college scholarship, maybe a parade back home if you won the gold. It probably wasn't worth it, Harry. But it was something I had to do. Who needs a childhood, anyway?"

Naomi looks as if she is either trying to remember something or forget something, and before Harry can find a way to make this, the most real conversation he's had in years with his oldest child, last a little longer, Hank and Paul come walking toward them, surfcasting rods in hand.

"What are you all doing, looking for the hurricane?" Paul asks.

"No," Naomi says, standing. "I've just been telling him what a couple of little assholes you two were as children."

"Oooh," Paul flinches. "Do you kiss your mother with that mouth?" She throws a shell at him.

He tells Harry that they intend, sometime today, to get him out in the surf with a rod and reel in his hands.

"Maybe later," he says. Naomi is brushing sand off her legs and bottom. Harry finds that the only way he can get out of Paul's sawed-off chair is by half-falling forward on his knees and then rising.

"I've already had enough excitement for one morning," he tells them. "First I see the green light, and then I get to talk to a mermaid in a red bathing suit. Who deserves to be so lucky?"

Naomi shakes her head, walking back ahead of him. Ruth is standing on the deck, looking out to sea.

NINETEEN

NAOMI, WHO WAS still specializing in the butterfly, finished second in the 1960 national championships and then in the Olympic trials in Detroit, where she also made the 400-meter relay team. She almost qualified in the breaststroke, as well. Harry, reading this, wondered if his grandfather was smiling somewhere.

Naomi was upset that she didn't finish first and had to be convinced that making the United States Olympic team did not qualify as failure.

Ruth's portfolio had continued to grow, aided by smart investments and the Fairweather Grill; she was independent. She didn't have to ask Henry's permission to fly to Rome that September.

Harry, unable to tell anyone what he wanted to scream out, that his daughter was an Olympic swimmer, grew distracted at Martin's baseball games, Nancy's recitals. He felt himself splitting a little, like the pear tree in their backyard that was coming apart at the crotch where the two dominant branches pulled north and south. Only his work on the Kennedy campaign kept him focused.

He almost told Gloria everything, but he didn't.

The Games began late that year and ran well into September. Ruth, who had never flown before, was with a small group from Newport, all richer than she and treating her like royalty, to her amusement. In Rome, they stayed in a small hotel near the Spanish Steps and had tickets to several venues other than swimming. She met Rafer Johnson, and Naomi introduced her to the great Australian swimmer, Dawn Fraser.

Ruth was not yet 35 years old. She was mistaken for Naomi's older sister on two occasions. She had studied Italian for six months beforehand, and she took great pride in bailing language-challenged compatriots out of tight spots. The others from Newport started calling her "the great Floodini."

She didn't get to spend as much time with Naomi as she would have liked, though. Naomi preferred to be with friends and competitors her own age. The two of them went shopping twice and had dinner together three times. Ruth had hoped for more.

But she was thrilled when Naomi's relay team won the gold medal, especially after her disappointment in the 100 butterfly.

Naomi wasn't expected to win the butterfly. She wasn't even the fastest American. And then she got sick before her semifinal heat, Ruth suspected from nerves, and didn't qualify for the final. Hearing about it and then reading about it in thc paper the next morning, Harry felt sick for her.

So the relay was Naomi's last chance. The night before the final, Ruth was able to have dinner with her, at an outdoor cafe near Ruth's hotel. Naomi was so nervous she could hardly eat.

Ruth tried to calm her, with little success. Finally, Ruth paid the bill, and they walked to the Spanish Steps. They climbed halfway up and found a quiet spot in the sea of young people there.

Ruth told her that she loved her, that she couldn't be more proud of her, that nothing was going to change whether she won or lost.

"Well," Naomi asked, "what was all this about then? What have I been working my tail off for?"

Ruth looked across at the crowds filling the Via Condotti. She had always taken it as an article of faith that you worked hard for what you wanted, if you were to have any chance of getting it. Talent, she had told Naomi after the girl won her first state championship, can't get you all the way there.

"Nothing you ever do with a full effort and a good heart comes to nothing," she told her that night in Rome. It was a speech she had been giving since Naomi was old enough to listen. Naomi just rolled her eyes, but Ruth thought it was a good sign that she didn't reject the weatherbeaten wisdom outright.

The next day, with Ruth and the rest of the cheering section from Pembroke County screaming encouragement at the natatorium on the banks of the Tiber, Naomi turned a short American lead into a long one and got her gold medal. She told Ruth that they ought to only give her one-fourth since it was a relay, but Ruth could tell she was proud.

After that, they had four days left in Rome. Naomi, with the weight lifted off her shoulders, partied every night with her teammates. Ruth didn't see much more of her until the trip back.

Naomi was to return with the Pembroke County contingent. On the last morning, Ruth took a taxi to the Olympic village, and she could tell, as soon as she saw Naomi sitting on her bags outside the compound, that something was wrong. She never found out what. Maybe, she thought, it was just the letdown after all that work.

There was an incident checking the luggage. The security guards wanted to open one of Naomi's bags, and Naomi made such a fuss about it that she almost got them arrested.

She was in tears by the time things were smoothed over by Ruth and others. They made the flight with 10 minutes to spare.

On board, a doctor from Newport got Naomi to take two sleeping pills, and she slept most of the way to New York.

There, Ruth and two of the men had to virtually carry Naomi through customs and then to the terminal where they were to catch the connecting flight. She cursed Ruth, and then she sank into a crying jag. Ruth was able to strong-arm her into the women's bathroom, where she made her wash her face. Then she waited while Naomi vomited what little she had eaten in the last 12 hours into one of the toilets. On the flight to Newport, Naomi cried softly on Ruth's shoulder.

Ruth, looking out at the water as they banked toward Newport, knew that she might never again feel so much like Naomi's mother, so needed. She stroked her daughter's hair and wondered at the perversity of a mother who could enjoy, even a little, such misery.

When they landed, and Ruth reminded her that there might be a crowd waiting for her, Naomi snapped back as if nothing had happened. She looked, to Ruth's amazement, like anyone else who had been on a long flight from Europe.

There were a couple of hundred people at the terminal. Naomi, very patiently and with great composure, signed autographs and shook hands, smiling all the time. Some of those in the party from Rome wondered if they had dreamed Naomi Crowder's bad behavior.

Henry Flood seemed glad to have his wife and stepdaughter back with him. The aunts had kept Hank and Paul, but Henry had persuaded them to let the boys come home and stay with him the last week, and they appeared to have enjoyed this time with their father.

But the next day, at the Naomi Crowder Day parade in Newport, Henry turned up drunk, cursing spectators from his seat in the convertible behind the one in which Naomi and Ruth rode. Ruth wondered if anything ever really changed for good.

"It often seems to me," she wrote Harry that September, "that the best times for Henry are the times when nothing at all is happening. He hasn't been this bad since I bought the Fairweather Grill, four years ago. It doesn't matter whether it's good news or bad news. Henry Flood simply is not equipped to handle the extraordinary."

Naomi slept for the better part of the next two days, and then she packed and took another trip, by plane again, to Los Angeles, where her freshman classes had already begun.

"I don't expect to see her that often from here on out," Ruth wrote to Harry. "This was our last big thing together, like a graduation before she entered the big, wide world. It does seem as if she tried to get a scholarship at the school farthest away from me in the whole country, doesn't it?

"But she is bright and talented, and I am sure that she will succeed. Whether she will be happy, though: Well, that's another question, I suppose."

Naomi would graduate from UCLA in four years. She was a member of one of the nation's best swim teams, full of kids — many of them much younger than she — who were lured to Southern California from all over the country so that they might compete against the best.

But Naomi lost interest in swimming her junior year and didn't even go to the Olympic trials in 1964. She put all her effort into her studies and, that year, was admitted to law school.

She finished near the top of her law class, meeting and falling in love with Thomas Ferrell III, a classmate and fellow North Carolinian, along the way. They were married in 1969, and by 1972, when Grace was born, Naomi had almost completely retired from the law. Ruth confined her disappointment, for the most part, to letters.

"She is so good at everything," she wrote Harry. "Why can't she stay with it?"

If I can stay with Henry Flood, Ruth wondered only to herself, why can't Naomi stay with swimming or law? How hard can that be?

TWENTY

SEVERAL TIMES IN early 1961, Gloria and their children came up to see the trilevel on Balsa Drive as it slowly rose from the red clay to become their home for the next six years. The chain stores and strip malls and gridlock would overtake them soon, but in the beginning, Harry thought of himself and his family as pioneers, starting over.

He worried that Gloria wouldn't bond. Since college, she had never lived anywhere except Richmond. But she enjoyed the country, while it lasted, and she came to love the Washington scene that beckoned at the other end of Shirley Highway.

During his extended leave of absence from Martin & Rives, Harry more and more came to think of himself as a Washingtonian.

He felt he was making a difference. The Economic Advisory Board was committed to stimulating the economy, and to educating a president who never quite saw where they were headed but sometimes, with the aid of his advisors, did what they wanted anyhow.

And, Harry had to admit to himself, he did love the power, the clout that came from others knowing you had JFK's ear.

Gloria was always running into old Seven Sisters acquaintances. She amazed Harry with how well she blended into the social scene, how much she loved being invited to Hickory Hill by Bobby and Ethel, how she shone at Perle Mesta's parties. She was still, Harry had come to realize during those months when he went without seeing her for five days at a time, a very attractive woman. He was less inclined to take her for granted.

"Harry," Jack Kennedy said when he was introduced to Gloria, "are all the men in Richmond ugly? They must be, for you to land a woman this beautiful. The competition there must be minimal."

Harry would retell the story at parties, perfectly mimicking Kennedy. "The competition theah must be, ah, minimal," Harry would say, and everyone would crack up, delighted to be one degree from the president.

Gloria was as happy as Harry had seen her in years, and it made things better, he felt, not just for him but for Martin and Nancy, too. She laid it on a little thicker than he might have liked at times, reveling too much in what he felt deep down they couldn't sustain. He knew they were in a town where all the jobs changed in the time it took your kids to get through high school. But what was the harm?

Martin and Nancy were adapting well to their new schools, which were full of the sons and daughters of congressmen and cabinet staffers. In their neighborhood, every kid was a new kid on the block. The outsiders were the ones who had been there all along, now outnumbered and badly outspent.

"Harry," Gloria said to him often that heady first year, "I'm so proud of you."

He pointed out that he had taken a rather large cut in pay to go to Washington and couldn't be sure he'd be there forever.

"Money," she said, shaking her head at his inability to grasp the big picture. "We've got enough money, Harry. What money did for us is give us a chance to get into all this. You can be somebody, Harry."

Harry, under the impression he already was somebody, knew Gloria meant somebody in Washington, not somebody in Richmond. He wondered if he had created a monster, but he was pleased that at least they were both enjoying their lives at present, that their children seemed to be enjoying theirs.

By November of 1963, he was assistant director of the EAB. He played a key role in getting Kennedy to lower taxes and enlarge the budget, and it occurred to him often in years to come that the national debt actually started with him and a few other idealists whose original plan mutated into something they had never envisioned, helped along by a war and then by greed and short-sightedness. He imagined his obituary reading, "Harold Martin Stein, who helped his country take the first small steps toward fiscal irresponsibility. . . .” How, he would wonder over the years, did such a high-minded, simple-ass desire to make America the land of opportunity for everyone get so screwed up?

Harry and Gloria seemed to know all of Washington socially and, in his case, professionally. He came to be seen as a man who could cut across boundaries, an economist with an English degree, an Ivy Leaguer who could talk Southern, a facile fund-raiser who really believed in making a better world. Gloria complemented him well and was happy enough to be known to most as the wife of Handsome Harry Stein. In a city where youth and glamour were suddenly in, the Steins’ timing was perfect.

They were accustomed to seeing their names mentioned in Washington’s daily newspapers, Harry’s in the A section, both of theirs in the society pages. Gloria would clip out each mention and put it in a scrapbook that she kept hidden from everyone except Harry, ashamed to let any of their new friends know how proud she was.

In the summer of 1963, a group of Kennedy insiders was sent on a fact-finding tour of Vietnam. Harry was included; the word was, he was recommended by the president himself.

The war looked, from that vantage point, not like a war at all. Maybe it would, in time, become another Korea; maybe it would be some small exercise like the one in the Dominican Republic. Harry, like all his friends in the World War II alumni club, had a rather straightforward approach to Vietnam: The Commies are trying to take over the world; we’ve got to get them out, save the planet for democracy. The idea of a war not being “right” was a concept none of them had really considered.

It was unbearable when they landed. They had not listened sufficiently to the warnings about the heat and humidity. After all, they were only going to be there four days.

“Hell,” Harry had said to Gloria at the airport, “how can anything be worse than Richmond in July?”

They got the royal tour of Saigon, which Harry conceded might be a pleasant place on days when the temperature was under 100 degrees. They all shook hands with Ngo Dinh Diem, who would be shot to death three weeks before Jack Kennedy. They saw what they were meant to see of the army. They heard what they were meant to hear. Even Harry could understand that there was no way he or any of the other Americans on this miserable junket was going to peel back even the first layer of jungle that hid whatever Vietnam really was.

"Can you believe," asked a state department aide with whom he shared a hotel room, "that anybody is willing to die for this shithole?"

The last day there, Harry and the aide went out walking by themselves in Saigon, against orders. They turned on to one of the broad avenues the French had built. Harry thought, not for the first time, how it really was a beautiful city, if he could only breathe. Up ahead, a crowd was gathered, and Vietnamese soldiers were wading through the civilians.

The two Americans walked up, knowing they shouldn't be there but unable to resist.

Harry didn't see much, just what appeared to be a charred leg as three of the teen-age soldiers threw the monk's body in the back of a truck. The smell, burned skin and gasoline, was nauseating in the heat. The charred remains of the dead man's clothes were burned into the surface of the street.

"Shit," the aide said, and turned to one side. Harry couldn't look away, though. In the shade of the truck, he got a quick glimpse of the monk's blackened face, the gritted teeth. He saw a soldier stick a bayonet into the monk's body and realized that he was still alive.

A Vietnamese officer advanced on them, shouting and pointing, but the aide flashed his identification, and the officer, a short, round man, became instantly obsequious, ushering them away from the scene as gently as if they had been the next of kin. Behind them, the young soldiers dispersed the crowd with threats and rifle butts.

Harry thought he might pass out in the still heat. He wondered how much hotter the fire could have felt to the monk than the actual air did. He and the aide walked two blocks and retreated beneath an awning, where they ordered beers beneath a slow-moving fan.

The aide had to explain to Harry that no one set the monk on fire; he did it himself. Harry would see photographs, later, but they didn't have the impact of that one hot July day in Saigon — the smell, and the little dark place where the monk patiently melted into the pavement.

For some reason, the state department man explained, the Communists had gotten to the monks.

Harry thought about that monk, and when he got back home, he did some reading about the French occupation of Indochina. When he was asked for his assessment of Vietnam, he was not as optimistic about America's chances of success as were the others in the mission.

Kennedy sent for Harry one day two weeks later. With Dean Rusk and two other state department officials in the office, he read an undersecretary of state's report, full of optimism, promising that a six-month campaign would fix everything, and then Harry's more pessimistic note.

Kennedy put down the reports and looked at Harry.

"Harry," he said, "may I ask you something? Were you two gentlemen in the same country?"

Everyone laughed, and it was generally understood that this was the kind of misinformed jeremiad you might get when you sent amateurs on a fact-finding mission.

Martin was 16 that summer, with two years of high school left. Not long after Harry sent his report on Vietnam to the president, he paid a visit to a National Guard major, an old friend of his, to make sure Martin Stein would never set foot in a country where the enemy would set themselves on fire and peacefully burn to death rather than submit. He was abusing what little power he had, and he didn't care.

When they got word that Kennedy had been shot, Harry and one of his assistants, a young woman from Oberlin, had just returned from lunch. As soon as they knew he was dead, everyone went home.

Harry would always remember the traffic jam on the Shirley Highway that afternoon, and the sight of two grown men, in suits and white shirts, fighting in the median strip, apparently as the result of a minor accident. Both men were flailing away, doing almost no harm. Both were weeping openly.

Nothing much changed for Harry after Kennedy's death, at least not professionally.

He wondered that he could get along with two men as different as Kennedy and Lyndon Johnson, and perhaps if he had been closer to the fire, he might not have. He saw more than one high-level official cowed and humiliated by Johnson's tantrums and bullying. Harry never took what Johnson did or said personally, though. In fact, his greatest fear was that he might break out laughing while in some small group that was the momentary target of LBJ's wrath. He knew Johnson could send him back to Richmond in two seconds, but he always had the strange feeling that the president was on the verge of stopping in mid-diatribe and winking at them. And this lack of fear seemed to carry back to Johnson, who saw in Harry Stein a man who respected him with an unaverted eye. They got along well enough.

Then, in the summer of 1966, the ambassador to The Netherlands stepped down unexpectedly. A week later, Harry answered a summons from Walter Padgett in the state department. Padgett had been a year behind Harry at Princeton and had created over the years the myth of a college-days friendship.

"Harry," Padgett said when they were both seated, "how would you like to move to the Hague?"

Harry would be amazed, throughout his life, at the odd directions from which opportunity came at him. Padgett, who probably called him a Hebe behind his back in college, was pushing him for a European ambassadorship, supported by a Virginia senator whose politics were anathema to Harry and by a member of Johnson's cabinet to whom Harry had never, to his knowledge, spoken.

He went home in a daze. When he told Gloria about it, she had a brief moment of anxiety, and then she became, in her mind, the wife of the ambassador to The Netherlands, and she realized this would make her life complete. Martin was a junior at the University of Virginia; Nancy was getting ready to start her freshman year at Mary Baldwin. The timing seemed perfect. Harry, whose first thought upon being approached was that Gloria never would give up Washington, the same as he thought she never would give up Richmond, knew that she would be the perfect ambassador's wife, that she was born to play this role, the one she had been honing in Washington society the past five years.

There were no major objections to Harry Stein as ambassador to Holland. No wealthy industrialist or retiring senator coveted the post. Harry had been sent on the occasional junket to foreign lands and had become known, in his circle, as a loyal Democrat and a charming generalist.

By September, when Nancy left for college, there was almost nothing standing between Harry Stein and what he and Gloria had come to see as their destiny.

TWENTY-ONE

"DEAR HARRY," RUTH wrote on a wet, cold February day in 1964, "Isn't it amazing the way, no matter how much you try to anticipate disaster, it always sneaks up on you anyhow?

"It never occurred to me to worry about Hank, any more than I would worry about the sun not coming up in the east."

The previous Tuesday, she and the rest were just starting to clean up after lunch when she heard the door open. Thinking that they had one more hungry truck driver to feed, she looked up and saw Hank. He was moving toward her very slowly, tentatively, like the stray dogs out back who weighed fear against the chance for a free meal from a stranger's hand. Hank usually wore his confidence like a neon sign.

Ruth came from behind the counter, ready to ask him what was wrong.

"Momma," he told her, "I can't go back to school."

She assured him that he most certainly could go back to school, not knowing what else to say.

"You haven't been expelled, have you?"

The idea of Hank Flood being expelled was beyond Ruth's belief. He had never even gotten a spanking.

"No," he said, "I haven't been expelled. But I can't go back. I really can't, Momma."

He had been in fourth-period algebra class. He had not felt well all day, and there had been a ringing in his ears since he got to school.

Hank had never liked tight spaces. Once, when he was 5, Naomi shut him up in one of the closets, thinking they were just playing, and he almost tore the door off trying to get out.

But that day in algebra, it occurred to him, suddenly, just how small the classroom was, how there wasn't enough space and how he didn't think he could bear to be in a room like that any longer. He told Ruth that if anyone had tried to stop him from leaving, right then, he was afraid of what he might have done.

She left the grill with him. They walked down to the river and back, in the freezing cold, and they talked. Hank told her he could not stand even to sit inside a car, that he did not know if he could bear staying in his room at home. He wasn't crying, but he was shaking so hard his teeth rattled.

"I have set up an appointment with Dr. Sherman, a psychiatrist that Roy McGinnis recommended in Newport," Ruth wrote. "We are to go see him day after tomorrow, and I pray he will be able to find some way to fix what's wrong with my boy. I am so scared, Harry. . . .

Eventually, Ruth would take Hank to two psychiatrists in Newport, then to the university hospital in Chapel Hill, then to Johns Hopkins.

To have done otherwise, Ruth felt, would have been like quitting.

Nobody in Saraw had ever heard of agoraphobia. Neither of the first two doctors even mentioned the word.

Hank was the golden boy, as promising as Naomi in his own way. He had never made anything except A's until the grading period before he came home from school that last time. On that one, he was given a B-minus in algebra, mainly because he was up the night before the midterm exam helping Ruth keep Henry from beating Paul with a belt.

In Saraw, where everyone knows everyone else's business, much was made of the hard-hearted teacher whose B-minus was generally given as the cause for Hank Flood's "breakdown." Ruth was not among those affixing blame. If all it took was one B-minus, she wrote to Harry, then he must have been very close to the edge, anyhow, and she blamed herself for not noticing. She had been relieved, in a way, when he made something less than an A; she thought it would help him live with the reality that no one is perfect, that even the perfect are done in by an imperfect world.

Hank was a starter on the junior varsity football and basketball teams, and he was even better in baseball. The day he told Ruth he couldn't return to school, all that ended, too.

By New Year's Day of 1976, when Harry Stein first met the gentle, intelligent man he had only seen in one of Ruth's photographs, the damage had been contained. Accommodations had been made. He earned his high school degree via correspondence school. He would eventually graduate from the University of North Carolina's branch at Newport in 1978, taking some courses by mail, venturing like a skittish animal into college classrooms for others.

People wondered why a 29-year-old carpenter needed a college degree, but Ruth knew it was as important to Hank as it would have been to an aspiring doctor or lawyer. It had been a cornerstone of her life and his that you were rewarded for good, honest, well-intentioned effort, no matter how useless it might seem at the time.

For a very long time, Harry Stein was unconverted to this philosophy. It seemed too simple. Say you spend your entire life trying to find a cure for a form of cancer, he once wrote Ruth, and one day you realize that you've been on the wrong path of research for 40 years, that you turned left when you should have turned right somewhere in the distant past.

Ruth wrote back that the diligent researcher probably would have made several meaningful discoveries he never even meant to make, along the way. He probably would have developed a much greater understanding of mortality than most people ever have. His stubbornness and will might have inspired a younger scientist who would someday find that cure.

Harry's father would have called that meshuggah. But over the years, without even noticing its insidious creep into his brain, Harry has come to believe in the Ruth Crowder Flood Theory of Human Behavior.

Late Tuesday morning, after he's napped for a couple of hours, Harry finally is coaxed into some surf fishing by Hank and Paul.

The sky is almost white, the watery-yellow sun warming them through the thin cloud cover. The storm is reported to be on course for a landfall somewhere in Louisiana, but it might as well be in China for all its apparent effect.

"Doesn't a ring around the sun mean it's going to rain?" Hank asks as he reels in an empty line.

Paul looks up at the circular rainbow prism.

"It always rains down here," he says. "You don't need any signs." He's drinking a beer, his left hand on his hip. He's screwed his fishing rod deep into the wet sand. Harry is the only one catching anything, a couple of red snappers that Paul judges to be large enough to eat. It is not a good time of day for surf fishing, but when they asked, he didn't want to hurt their feelings.

Hank cuts off another half a shrimp, then asks if Harry doesn't want to see if anything's taken his bait. Harry shakes his head. Hank shrugs, loads the hook and tries again. It is beyond Harry's ability this day to cast past the waves, so he wants to make very sure there's a reason to reel his line in. He can barely even hold the rod up, and he considers planting his in the ground, too. Ruth's sons really seemed to want him to come with them, though, and Harry appreciates the gesture.

"Don't worry," Paul says, looking seaward. "If the storm changes course, we can get off this island in five minutes flat, I guaran-damn-tee. And there isn't much chance of it sneaking up on us as long as Momma's here and The Weather Channel stays on the air."

Hank smiles.

"I guess I'd hate 'em, too, if I'd been her. You know, I caught her yesterday standing on the back upstairs deck looking over at the sound, like she was trying to figure out exactly how long it would take to get across that bridge."

Paul goes over to get another beer.

"Well, there are maybe 200 cottages out here. I'll bet you not more than 50 of them are occupied right now, with the storm out there and all. That's the best part about being out here during a hurricane panic; it keeps the riff-raff out. I'm not expecting any major traffic jams.

"Besides, tomorrow's her birthday. We've got to stay long enough to light the cake and blow out the candles."

Hank reels in his line.

They stay for perhaps an hour, maybe, Harry thinks, the best hour of the day. Hank and Paul are both experienced anglers, having lived all their lives near the coast. Paul claims he even managed to get some gear and go fishing when he was in Vietnam. They make a big deal, when they all return, over the fact that the ancient mariner Harry Stein has led the way, with three fish to their one each.

Tran, the only one in the cottage who actually studies the Bible as a source of wisdom and guidance, picks up one of the smaller fish, looking dubiously at it. "All we need now, Harry, are two loaves of bread," she says.

"That I can't manage," he tells her. "You need a New Testament guy for the fish trick."

Later, after lunch, Ruth and Harry are alone on the deck. He went outside because sometimes if he can get away by himself and be very still and quiet, he can lull the pain to sleep like a fussy baby. Ruth went outside because she knows it helps if she just sits beside him and holds his hand, without saying a word, a conduit drawing away the pain.

Harry knows Ruth treasures this time with her children and grandchildren, and he doesn't really want to take her away from them, but there is a growing childishness in him that wants her to kiss it and make it well.

Harry Stein's inner child, he knows, has never been far from the surface.

Harry likes to say that Ruth didn't choose politics; politics chose Ruth.

By 1965, she was the elder stateswoman on the town council. When it was discovered that the mayor had been using municipal funds and the town's two maintenance men to help build his beach cottage, they named Ruth to fill the rest of his term. She was elected to a second term in 1968.

"Harry," she wrote in the fall of 1966, "if I were to walk into one of these meetings with a loaded gun and shoot a couple of councilmen, I don't believe God would look too harshly upon me."

She was a master at getting her way. She always kept her temper, and she never backed down. If she occasionally lost a battle, she didn't do something heedless that would alienate people and keep her from winning the war.

To her, running Saraw was like raising children. She would wait them out, make them abide by the rules and sometimes convince them that her idea was actually theirs.

The year Ruth became mayor of Saraw, Hank was 16 and Paul was 14. Christmas eve that year, Henry got spectacularly drunk, even by his standards. He drank all afternoon and left the house after dinner, not even bothering to answer Ruth's entreaties. She and the boys didn't wait up for him; they knew it was just as well not to be around when Henry Flood had had an evening of hard drinking to stoke his fires. Usually, they could wait him out, lying low until sobriety's welcome return.

Ruth was especially excited that Christmas, because Naomi was coming in the next day with the boyfriend she would later marry. It would be her first Christmas in Saraw in three years. They were even forgoing the Crowder tradition of opening all the presents at or before dawn, because Naomi wouldn't be there until mid-afternoon.

Sometime before 1 a.m., Henry Flood came stumbling into his house and saw the Christmas tree with its lights still on. Hank and Paul, the last to bed, had left them burning, thinking it would be a nice effect when they came downstairs the next morning.

"Who left this goddamn Christmas tree on!" Ruth heard

him screaming. "Are you trying to burn the fucking house down? What's wrong with you people?"

Then they heard the crash. They all leapt from their beds to see what was the matter, although they were reasonably certain what was the matter was Henry Flood.

He was waiting for them at the bottom of the stairs. He had knocked over the tree and was stomping on it, breaking ornaments and ripping up presents, tearing open packages and strewing their contents all over the room. He wasn't even saying words any more, just screaming, red-eyed, drool running down his chin.

Hank got down the stairs first and tried to calm him, but Henry swung at him, knocking him to the floor with a glancing blow to the jaw. Paul jumped his father from behind, gripping his neck tightly, hanging on for his life while Hank got up and shook out the cobwebs.

"Hit him!" Paul was screaming. "Hit the son of a bitch. I can't hold him much longer."

Years later, relating the story to Harry, Hank said that he didn't really want to hit his father, but he was afraid if he didn't disable him, Henry might kill Paul when he finally got him off his back.

"So I swung just as hard as I could, right to the gut. And when he doubled over, I got him again under the chin. I was afraid I had murdered him; he dropped like he'd been shot."

He went backwards, Paul breaking his fall. They had to turn him on his stomach because he had started vomiting when Hank hit him the first time, and they didn't want him to choke on it.

The floor was a melange of half-opened presents, regurgitated food and bourbon, Christmas tree and ornaments, and Ruth Crowder Flood's family. The boys were trying to figure, before he came to, how to keep their father from harming them or himself. Ruth wondered if everyone's family was insane and just didn't talk about it in public.

Hank checked his unconscious father's pulse and saw that he had one. Ruth stood frozen, hands on the bannister rail, too horrified to move.

"What'll we do?" Paul asked. "When he wakes up, he's going to kill us." It was not, Ruth feared, a figure of speech.

Finally they determined that he didn't seem to need a doctor. Hank sent Paul out to the barn for some rope, and they tied Henry up in the corner, hands and feet, while they tried to salvage what was left of the tree and the presents.

When they got the tree up again, it was listing badly to the right, because Henry had almost broken it in half. They had to tie it to a hook on the wall with twine to keep it from falling over. The balls and lights, broken and scarred, hung sadly from the mangled branches. Ruth and her sons set about rewrapping presents and trying to save Christmas.

When Henry regained consciousness, still drunk and cursing everyone near to him, they decided they would have to gag him, too. They used a tie that the boys had bought him for Christmas, already ruined by the would-be recipient. Ruth made hot coffee and tried to force her husband to drink some, but every time they took the gag off, he would start ranting again.

The plan they finally devised was to lift Henry and carry him out the front door to the car, bound and gagged. Then, under cover of darkness, they drove him to the diner, where they dragged him inside and put him in the storage room, making very sure he was securely tied.

Then, they went back home to a bleary-eyed Christmas.

At 3 in the afternoon, Naomi arrived with her boyfriend. Ruth and the boys had napped through the morning in the reclaimed living room but were still groggy. Naomi asked them, two hours after she arrived, where Henry was, and Hank told her he was called away on business. Paul grinned and winked. She just nodded; she didn't want her beau to hear whatever the true story was, because she knew how bad the truth could get when it came to Henry Flood.

Hank had gone back to the diner at 2, taking his father some turkey sandwiches and tea. He untied Henry's hands and let him up to go to the bathroom. He had already wet himself once, and the concrete floor smelled of urine. Henry was still out of control, and Hank had to hit him again before his father would let him retie his hands behind his back.

It bothered Hank to do this to his father, and it bothered Ruth to let him, but they decided that the only possible salvation for Christmas at the Flood house was to keep Henry away.

At 8 o'clock Christmas night, Hank went back to the grill, taking Paul this time. Their father had bottomed out by then and was getting the blues, which always followed his outbursts. They took him into the bathroom and got him cleaned up the best they could, made him put on the clean clothes they had brought and told him they still wanted him to be with them for Christmas.

"All the fight was out of him by now," Hank told Harry years later. "Hell, he was probably weak from hunger. It's a wonder we didn't kill him. But he let us clean him and shave him and then lead him home.

"You know what he did? As we're coming up the front steps, he puts an arm around each of us and says, 'Boys, I don't deserve you all.'

"And I know he meant it. Nobody was more mortified than my father when he realized the damage he had done. He tried as hard as he could to make up for the bad times, but he just kept getting deeper and deeper in the hole, so deep that after a while you knew he'd never get out."

"It doesn't scare me or bother me any more," Ruth wrote Harry in the summer of 1967, when his own life was in the sort of free-fall he had never anticipated. "Henry will come home drunk and try to start something, and if I don't set him straight, Hank or Paul will. He knows when he's slipping out of control, and sometimes he'll go missing for two days at a time, and I think he's just trying to stay away from us until the other Henry Flood comes back.

"Why don't I just leave him? You more than hint about it, and I know to you it seems to be your answer and perhaps mine also. He's given me reason enough, more reason I'm sure than you gave Gloria.

"But you have had some control over your fate, Harry. You were not, like Henry, being dragged into hell by some devil not even of your own making. You would have to be here and see what I see, the good and the bad, to understand.

"Why not leave Henry? Well, why bother with Hank? He's broken my heart more than Henry, believe it or not, because I long ago gave up hope of Henry being more than he is, but Hank was going to do great things, and now he is barely able to venture outside this house some days. Every time we go see some new psychiatrist, and he fails to cure this curse, it rips me up all over again. Sometimes I'll see him in the den, watching TV, and I think that I can just go in there and shake him and he'll wake up and go back to being the old, normal, brilliant Hank. But I know it doesn't work like that.

"Neither Henry nor Hank can help it. Hank's illness takes a more passive course and is easier to live with (once you get past the disappointment of promise lost), but Henry's is just as much beyond his control.

"I am here, Harry, for the long run."

TWENTY-TWO

ON THE DAY things started falling apart, Harry was second in command in an agency that he believed was powerful enough, if it used those powers wisely, to almost wipe out poverty. His move from the Economic Advisory Board had been nearly seamless. Lyndon Baines Johnson had come to feel that Harry was one of "his" people.

Now, though, Harry Stein allowed his mind to wander to the appointment that everyone knew was just a rubber stamp away, a poorly-kept secret even by Washington standards. People were stopping by and calling, people whose names and likenesses were in national magazines and on the evening news, to congratulate him and wish him well. He would miss fighting the good fight, he told them, but it was time to move on. He implied that becoming an ambassador was a sacrifice he must, regretfully, make. He wondered if the glow he felt inside was visible to the naked eye.

He thought of his relatives back in Richmond, of all the rich Episcopal boys who had shunned him there and at Princeton. He imagined, for a moment, coming back to America, back to Virginia, in three or four years, still a young man by political standards, with credentials enough to change things that had long needed changing. He could see his life ahead of him, and he liked what he saw.

The phone call came just before noon on a pleasant September day. It was from Malcolm Summers, a man Harry had known since his earliest days in Washington. Summers was a North Carolinian with whom Harry shared a kinship based on region and age, a Duke graduate who had warmed the bench for the basketball team before going to law school after the war, then had risen to prominence in the State Department. They had lunch together perhaps once a year and sought each other out at parties. Their wives were compatible. Mac Summers' inclusion in the informal committee that nominated the new Dutch ambassador had, Harry suspected, been a prime reason for his selection.

“Harry,” he said, “can I come by and see you about something? It won’t take long.”

He wouldn’t be more specific; Harry assumed that it concerned his impending appointment.

“How’s 9 tomorrow?” he asked, and Summers said that would be fine.

The next morning, Harry and Gloria were up at 5:15, making calls to The Netherlands, already into their new life.

They were running on adrenaline, barely able to keep up with their lives. They had gotten Nancy off for her freshman year of college and Martin for his junior year. They had just put the house on the market; the agent estimated they could double their initial investment after five boom years.

Harry, punctual despite the D.C. traffic, walked into the outer office at 8:50. He had forgotten about Mac Summers until he saw him there, a tall, thin, gray-haired man seated on the edge of one of the visitors’ chairs. It flashed through Harry’s mind that he had never known Mac to be early for a meeting.

Harry, though, greeted him with genuine enthusiasm, delighted to have such a pleasant appointment to start his day. Perhaps they could have lunch afterward if Mac was free.

“Maybe later,” Summers said. He seemed nervous; Harry had never seen Mac Summers nervous.

He invited him into his office and closed the door. They were barely seated when Summers opened his briefcase and took out two sheets of mimeographed typing paper. He put them on Harry’s desk.

Mac Summers did not stay long. By 9:30, he was back in the rising early-September heat, without even a token promise of future social get-togethers from either man.

Harry waited another half-hour, and then he left, too. He told his secretary he would not be back, that she should take the rest of the day off. She noticed that the knuckles of his right hand were bleeding.

He walked down a dark corridor, out the front of the building, across a couple of streets and then to the Mall, where he sat on a bench, looking at nothing except the humid air in front of him for the next four hours.

Once, in 1957, Harry had been mildly upbraided by Ruth for absent-mindedly putting the wrong name on his most recent letter. Instead of addressing it to Miss Mercy Crowder, he had put "Ruth Crowder," followed by Mercy's address. It had been delivered to Mercy's anyhow, the postman guessing correctly.

The second time he did it was the February before Mac Summers' visit. This time, the same postman, who had handled Saraw's mail for a quarter of a century and knew everyone in town, delivered the letter not to Mercy Crowder's address but to the farmhouse of Ruth Crowder Flood, noting to himself that the writer had neglected to include her married name.

Ruth was working at the grill that day. Henry came home at 2 and checked the mail. He almost put the letter with no return address, just a Washington postmark, back in the box, replacing Ruth's name with Mercy's, but he didn't. He took it inside, and then he sat down at the kitchen table, opened it and read it.

He could not have felt more betrayed if he had come home and found Ruth naked in bed with another man.

A younger, less-defeated Henry Flood might have reacted to what he deduced by tearing up a couple of rooms, saving some energy for Ruth when she returned.

But the Henry Flood of 1966 had seen better days. He knew, by then, that Ruth held the high cards, knew what his life might be without her. He was also a man whose sons were old enough to humiliate him if they had to. And then there was Naomi. He did not want to upset Naomi, now a grown woman, stronger now than she once was.

He was a man who knew his best damage from then on would be done not by rage but by stealth.

He copied the letter by hand and put it away for the day he was almost sure would come, determined to learn all he could about the man whose name was on the letterhead,

Harry Stein, the man who signed the letter to his wife "Love (as always), Harry." He seemed to be some kind of Washington big shot, and he was almost certainly the long-sought, long-loathed Randall Phelps (who Henry had not imagined, in his wildest paranoia, was still communicating with Ruth). Then he taped up the original envelope, with the letter inside. The next time he went out, he stopped and placed it in Mercy's mailbox.

Henry was amazed to find that Harry Stein was important enough to be listed among the Johnson administration's movers and shakers in the book he found at the public library. For days, he considered his revenge, pondered how he could do the most damage.

Finally, Henry Flood wrote his congressman. U.S. Representative James Nicholson was, Henry knew, an old-school ultra-conservative Southern Democrat who might be able and willing to use the kind of information he was offering. He might be able to bring a certain high-flying Harry Stein down a notch or two. Maybe put Ruth in her place, too.

"Did you know," the letter began, "that a high-ranking member of the Johnson administration had a bastard child in 1943 by a woman in Saraw, North Carolina? That he continues to send support to this child and her mother while he raises another family in Washington, D.C.?" Henry gave Ruth's name, and Naomi's, and Harry Stein's, along with enough educated guesses to give the congressman's office a head start.

Nicholson's staffers checked out what came to them in that envelope with no return address. They were able to track down a World War II veteran named Lawrence Olkewicz in Greensburg, Pa., who remembered a wartime romance almost a quarter-century earlier. They found a birth certificate in Newport, along with a rather suspicious-looking marriage certificate for Ruth Crowder and Randall Phelps, the latter for whom no records existed anywhere else.

They were able, with the help of an accommodating FBI agent, to determine that a certain amount of money had, for many years, found its way south from Richmond and then Washington to Saraw.

James Nicholson, confronted with this wealth of circumstantial information, did not act immediately. He did not necessarily want to scuttle the career of a small-town mayor whom he had met once and actually liked, a woman who was, after all, part of his home state's Democratic machinery.

"But this fella in Washington?" he said at the meeting where all the evidence was presented. "He's maybe not worth it now, but they tell me he's on the rise. Let's wait a little bit. We got all the bullets. We don't have to shoot his liberal ass until he's worth killing."

And so the congressman waited. In late August, he heard about the almost inevitable appointment of Harry Stein as ambassador to The Netherlands, and he considered the man's age and credentials and potential for future damage to a party already torn apart by Communist sympathizers and draft-dodgers. A few days later, he called Malcolm Summers, who had interned for him when he was in law school.

"Mac," he'd told him, "I want you to read this. You're his friend. You can advise him as to what to do. I don't want to make a big to-do about this, don't even want to bring Missus Flood into it if I don't have to, you know what I mean?"

Summers read the report, swallowed hard, thanked Nicholson and left. That afternoon, he made an appointment to see his old friend Harry Stein.

Harry knew about scandals but, despite Ruth, he had never considered himself a target. He had been faithful to Gloria in the recent past; he didn't drink or use drugs, although marijuana was already becoming a regular element at some of the Capitol Hill parties he attended. He did not believe he was associating with Communists.

He didn't expect Ruth to be his downfall, and he found it ironic that what he considered to be this one faithful thing he had persisted in doing month after month, year after year, would undo him.

Harry knew that he could expect to read everything about Ruth and Naomi in the newspapers if he persisted. He knew he could count on his embarrassment staining all those he loved.

He realized, sitting in his office after Summers left, his hand still bleeding from where he had slammed it into the side of his mahogany desk, just exactly how much he loved the life he was leading, the life that was possible for him. Outside, later, he tried to convince himself that he would not be ruining the lives of people he loved, that he owed it to himself and Gloria to not decline the ambassadorship.

By the time he went home, he had convinced himself of exactly what he owed both Ruth and Gloria.

"Time to go," he said to himself as he rose slowly from the bench, scattering pigeons. "Time to be a big boy, Harry."

Before he left the city, he paid a quick visit to the head of the antipoverty program and told him most of the story, how an ongoing affair, involving a child, would make his departure for Europe highly unlikely.

His boss, a cool, tall, stately man whose Harvard credentials had carried more weight under Kennedy than Johnson, and who counted on Harry to do most of the actual day-to-day decision-making, listened patiently, quietly. Harry wondered if he already knew.

"Take a few days off," he said, putting an arm around his shoulder, a gesture so uncharacteristically affectionate that it, along with the day's earlier revelations, almost moved Harry to tears.

Gloria was in the garage. Harry almost lost his nerve when he saw how energized she was, as happy as he'd ever known her to be. She had gone to an ABC store nearby and gotten as many empty liquor boxes as she could cram into her station wagon, in anticipation of packing. She was stacking them neatly in the rear of the garage.

She was surprised to see Harry, always faithful to his work and never home this early. He led her inside, through the house and out to the back porch, which almost touched the unbroken woods where the red of the sumac was already promising cooler weather.

And there, he told her what he thought he never would have to tell her. He knew what was at risk. He knew that he would have been better off telling her years before, when his secret transgression would not have also been the death of their shared dream.

He could have come up with some barely plausible lie, but Harry Stein was tired. He knew the ambassadorship, the bauble he had come to look upon as proof of his worth, was gone.

Watching Gloria's face register the pain for which he was responsible, Harry wondered if he even cared any more about his present position, so glittering a short while ago, now a dingy job in a dingy office far from the glamour he thought soon would be his and Gloria's.

If Gloria had been confronted with the reality of Ruth and Naomi many years before, without the consequences that now leaked from it, she might have forgiven Harry, although not without some terrible price, he was sure.

Even if he had lost the ambassadorship because of some dalliance with a co-worker or secretary, their marriage might have been saved. Affairs can be — had been — forgiven. New leaves had been turned over, also for a price.

But what she could not forgive, when he told her about it, was the secret life he had led, almost completely on paper and in the minds of two people. That betrayal, the knowledge of the clandestine letters and the longing they implied, was what finally made Gloria leave for good.

"You should have told me," she said after Harry had explained why they would not be packing for Europe after all.

"I just did tell you," Harry said, knowing what she meant.

"No. You should have told me a long time ago, right at the start."

Harry had to concede that she probably was right.

"What is her name?" Gloria asked.

"I told you. Ruth."

"Ruth what?"

Harry sat silently, looking through a window at a Dali print he had long detested. He never answered her.

"I think you ought to leave," Gloria said, stubbing out her cigarette and not looking at him. "You are such a bastard, Harry."

Right you are, he thought. Right you are.

Maybe, if their children hadn't been in college, safe from the unfriendly fire of home, grown enough — they each hoped separately — to weather this, Harry and Gloria both would have tried harder. Now, though, neither of them could work up all the energy they knew from experience it took to heal wounds. And there had never been anything this large before. This was a major artery.

Harry never slept another night in the house on Balsa Drive.

He would spent nine more months in Washington. By then, the divorce was almost final. Gloria stayed after he went home, still in the thrall of Potomac Fever, unwilling to return to Richmond. With the career diplomat who eventually became her second husband, she would live in Paris and Brussels for a time. Harry supposed that she was enjoying at least a measure of what he had once cost her.

After the settlement, Harry invested some of his still-impressive nest egg in the house at Safe Harbor. He would, for the next eight years, split his time between Long Island and Richmond, where he resumed making money more or less full time for the still-appreciative firm of Martin & Rives.

By the time he quit his job with the agency he once thought could change the world, he had become almost as disillusioned with Washington as he was with life in general. The two wars, on poverty and the North Vietnamese, were going badly. He feared, in the midst of riots and chaos, that the American people would prove less generous and idealistic than he had hoped and give up on the first, and he had long since come to loathe the second.

Their Capitol Hill friends and some acquaintances were vaguely aware of the circumstances of Harry Stein's demise. After he left Washington, neither he nor they found the time to keep in touch.

When Harry Stein thinks back on his years in Washington, it is with nostalgia and regret, for all the bright, shining days, and all the ones that should have followed.

He wondered, and Ruth wondered, what had happened, how the cover of their long, secret life had been breached. They, and especially Ruth, suspected Henry.

He never let on, though, and Ruth did not then fully realize, would not for most of another decade, all Henry Flood was capable of concealing.

TWENTY-THREE

FOR A VERY long time, Harry Stein thought he and his first daughter would never meet. Too much water over the damn lie, he told himself, too much invested in the face-saving fabrication T.D. Crowder had offered so many years before.

Randall Phelps had developed into an acceptable and accepted story. By 1970, Ruth had not heard anyone except Henry Flood say anything for at least 10 years indicating doubt about the identity of Naomi's father.

By then, Harry wondered what good he possibly could do his oldest child, or anyone else. These were the drifting years, the disappointing years when he weighed what he'd done against all he'd lost, when he fully understood that nothing is as good the second time as the first, and knew he'd already done everything once.

He had Naomi's photographs and Ruth's letters, plus the image of a little girl, walking home from school, who should have had more confidence in herself, and the image of an older girl competing for her gold medal. Other than Martin and Nancy, there was no one from whom Harry needed to hide the letters any more, no one whose approbation he so valued or whose ridicule he so feared that Ruth couldn't send her letters straight to his Richmond townhouse or the cottage in Safe Harbor. Whoever might be sharing his bed at the moment might look curiously at the well-formed cursive script from Saraw, North Carolina, and briefly wonder what that was all about, but nobody really cared enough to ask, and if they had asked, Harry would have told them to mind their own damned business.

So, on the subject of meeting Naomi, Harry had doubts. The idea of being confronted with one more example of and witness to what he had come to accept as his failed life held no charm whatsoever.

Let sleeping parents lie, he and Ruth had long since agreed.

But then Naomi became unexpectedly interested in her family tree.

"Harry," Ruth wrote June of that year, "you know that I have always dissuaded you from seeing Naomi. I have always felt that it would only do harm, that what's done is done and best not undone. You have chided me from time to time for being too 'uptight,' and you could be right. (You see, I am capable of admitting that I am wrong from time to time.)

"Naomi wants to know who her father is. She has doubted what we told her for a long time. If there is a Randall Phelps, she said, she has a right to know who her father is, dead or alive, drunk or sober, rich or poor. And I suppose she is right. And you surely aren't as bad as what she must be imagining."

High praise, indeed, Harry wrote back, but after giving it some thought, he agreed that something could be arranged.

Naomi did not necessarily want to bring her father into her life. But she was determined that, if he existed, she would meet him and know his name. Naomi liked structure, and the idea of her father as some loose thread hanging from her life's fabric was a thought she could not let alone.

So finally Ruth told Naomi the short version of what happened in Saraw, North Carolina, that war winter, and left the rest, the "heavy lifting," to Harry. What was arranged, through Ruth, was a meeting at a neutral site.

Naomi and Thomas already were living in Denver, but she was with a law firm that did occasional work in Manhattan. Harry came to New York on business from time to time and had a membership at the Princeton Club. Naomi was scheduled to fly to New York in mid-July, arriving on a Tuesday and returning on Friday evening.

And so, it was arranged that they should meet at the bar in the Algonquin Hotel at 5:30 on a Wednesday afternoon. Harry told the professional student with whom he was living at the time, a woman one year younger than Naomi herself, a lie about an important meeting in Manhattan, strictly business, apologizing for not taking her with him. She shrugged her shoulders, as Harry noticed women were doing more and more in his presence, and said, "Whatever," the word that seemed to sum up her philosophy of life.

He took the train from Richmond on Wednesday and checked into his room before 3, just in time to wash up and put on something that the heat hadn't wilted. He was as nervous as he'd ever been on any teenage first date.

Here was one woman who had his number, who had always had his number. With others, he could excuse himself for almost anything. Some misdeed on their part, some failing, real or imagined, could be invented to justify almost anything.

But where, he asked himself, is your upper hand when the woman in question is the daughter you never acknowledged? Sometimes he could even justify what he did to Ruth by telling himself she could have had him back on a platter at any time after 1966, if she had only left the combustible piece of garbage to whom she was married. But Harry could not excuse himself for Naomi. He felt she was entitled to spit in his face and walk away forever, to fall on him and try to claw his eyes out. Harry was nervous.

He passed the Algonquin twice before going in. He might have circled another time or two, working on his story, but it was a blistering day on the pavement. It was still only 5:15, but he felt it might be a good idea to get settled, to be perhaps one scotch ahead when she walked in.

Naomi had in her possession a photograph of her father, one Ruth wanted back. Harry knew she probably would recognize him immediately, and he was sure he would know her. So he secured a wing chair out of the light, where he could see her when she walked in but she couldn't see him.

For half an hour he waited. He had ordered his second scotch and soda and was wondering if Naomi had even less nerve than he did. And then, she was there. Her silhouette was all Harry could see at first, but he knew it was her, even before she stepped into the interior light. There was some gesture, something about the way she stood, hesitating, looking. It might have been a memory of Ruth.

Grown, Naomi resembled the Steins more than the Crowders. She was very pretty, but in a dark, quick way.

Ruth had always had — and still does, on the last day of her seventh decade — a languid air about her, an economy and ease that make what she does appear much more simple than it really is. Harry could see, in those first few seconds, that Naomi had the more theatrical genes of the Steins — more movement, a face less able to hide anything.

Naomi was already smoking a cigarette when she came inside, and Harry wondered how an ex-Olympic champion could take up such a habit. Already he wanted to lecture her, before his fatherhood was even acknowledged.

She looked harried, and there was a slight sheen of perspiration on her high brow. She didn't take a seat right away, but asked a waiter something and then disappeared in the direction of the ladies' room, her quick searching glance missing Harry in his dark corner.

Five minutes later she came out, not smoking now, better composed. In those five minutes, the last two tables in the room were taken, and she was standing there, probably debating whether to take a seat at the bar, maybe wondering if her father had stood her up again.

Harry left his half-empty scotch at the table and walked the 20 feet that separated them. Her back was to him, and she jumped when he tapped her lightly, hesitantly, on the shoulder.

"Excuse me," he said in a voice as unsteady as his legs despite all the times he had rehearsed the moment in his mind, "but can Randall Phelps buy you a drink?"

She took the hand he extended and followed him silently back to his table.

That evening, first at the Algonquin and then at dinner, they talked for hours, both amazed that they were so easy with one another, although they were aided by alcohol, and they did keep one subject, The Subject, safely locked away for the most part. The Princeton Club and the Algonquin were right off the diamond district, and Harry had bought her a gift, a necklace she opened and then said she couldn't keep, for fear her husband would think she was having an affair. (In reality, she told Thomas about the real nature of

Randall Phelps as soon as she returned. She kept the necklace and he kept the secret from Hank and Paul, whom Thomas hardly ever saw.)

She smoked half a pack of cigarettes and drank a little. Harry kept the scotches coming.

"Do you always drink so much?" she finally asked him, as blunt as any Stein aunt at a family gathering.

"Do you always smoke so much?" he asked back. They looked at each other and started laughing. They fed off each other's laughter until the people at the nearest tables began giving them sideways glances of irritation. It occurred to Harry that it was the first time he had seen his eldest child either laugh or smile.

"I asked you first," she said when they had composed themselves, so he told her no one in Richmond, Virginia, could drink as much as Harry Stein without getting knee-walking drunk. And she told him no one in Denver, Colorado, could smoke as much as Naomi Crowder Ferrell without dying of lung cancer.

They talked of Ruth more than anything else, she being their common bond. The only time the conversation drifted dangerously close to the Great Unspoken was when Naomi made a disparaging remark about how hard Ruth had driven her as a child.

"If I have children," she said, stubbing out a cigarette hard in the ashtray, "I swear to God I am not going to push them. I am going to let them have a real childhood."

Without thinking, sucker-punched by the scotch, Harry noted that Ruth had been trying to do the work of two parents.

"And whose fault would that be?" Naomi said, registering what seemed to Harry very close to a sneer.

There was nothing he could say.

Naomi shook her head.

"I'm sorry, Mister . . . Harry . . . Mister Dad, whoever the hell you are. You've told me how it happened. Mom's told me how it happened. I don't blame you, not really. It's just that I've been pissed off about this for so long, just mad at the world. I've had this image of some worthless bum who left Mom and me to shift for ourselves. Then, when she told me about you, and about the money and all, it required some rethinking.

"And then I meet you, and you're not a monster or anything. But dammit, you should've been there. You really should've been there. I need to be angry at something."

By then, they had finished dinner and were having a couple of cognacs.

He moved his chair so that he was sitting right beside her. He offered her his right arm.

"Hit me," he said.

"Hit you? Why?"

He took off his jacket.

"Just hit me, right here on the arm, as hard as you can."

"Why?"

"Well, you look like you need to hit something, and maybe I need to be hit."

He wasn't sure she would do it, and when she did, he wasn't prepared for the strength of a woman who had spent the majority of her life engaged in serious physical activity. The chairs in the Park Avenue restaurant were more stylish than sturdy, and Harry had, even by his standards, drunk a prodigious amount. When she punched him, it rocked him backward hard enough that he lost his balance, and then he was on the floor, scrambling to pick up his jacket while Naomi tried to help him up.

They got the bill and paid it almost as quickly as the maitre d' wanted them to and then staggered, weak with laughter, out the door.

They walked for 20 blocks, in places where Harry figured they shouldn't have been walking after dark. They agreed to be friends. They had dinner again the next night and then saw each other twice more the next six years. They would talk occasionally, though, office to office and then at her home after Grace was born. They wrote. They stayed in touch.

They did not become best friends, nor did they become father and daughter in any traditional sense. It is appropriate to Harry that she calls him by his first name. Nowadays, they sometimes talk on the phone. He does get Father's Day cards, and he does remember her birthday, but he always did.

Tuesday afternoon, Harry goes to take his much-coveted afternoon nap. Paul and Tran are planning to drive the rest of them down the coast to Seaside, an instant-Victorian village on the Gulf east of Sugar Beach.

Naomi claims she isn't feeling well, though, and says she thinks she'll pass. Harry can see that Ruth is disappointed. Maybe we shouldn't go, either, she says to Paul. That hurricane is out there somewhere. Paul reminds her, though, that the Weather Channel has the storm pointing more toward Louisiana, maybe even Texas, and a good day out to sea even from there.

"They can change course, and they can speed up," she mutters. But he points out that the sun is shining. How bad can it be?

Not wanting to be a poor guest, she goes along.

Paul leaves Harry the house key in case he wants to go for a walk along the beach. Fat chance, Harry thinks as he waves goodbye. He is dead on his feet; they are still backing out the driveway when he turns to head for the bedroom. Naomi is already inside, in her room.

Harry is not yet asleep, lying on his back the way he can't when he shares a bed with Ruth, because of his snoring, when he hears a tapping, so light he thinks at first he is dreaming it, and then he hears Naomi's voice.

He tells her to come in.

He can see why she begged out of the trip to Seaside. She doesn't look well at all.

Harry swings his legs off the side of the bed, and she sits down at the other end.

"Harry," Naomi begins, "my shrink says I shouldn't hold things in."

Suddenly, he is wide awake.

TWENTY-FOUR

NAOMI ASKS HARRY if she can light up. He tells her second-hand smoke holds no fear for him these days. She goes looking for something to use as an ashtray and comes back with a seashell.

When she has settled again on the foot of the bed, she says she isn't telling him this because he is her father.

"I guess," she says, shrugging, "that I just need practice telling it to someone who isn't a psychiatrist. And I don't believe I could ever tell this to Thomas."

She puts her left hand around her right wrist and guides the cigarette toward the shell on the bedspread.

Harry thinks he knows how this story ends, but he knows that Naomi needs to tell someone, and he is willing to be that someone.

"When I was a little girl," she begins, talking slowly and stopping to clear her throat, "I thought that if I worked hard enough and always made straight A's and ate my vegetables and went to church every Sunday and never lost a swim meet, that everything would always be good. And I thought Momma would always be there to protect me, to make sure nothing bad happened. She said she and God would look after me."

"Well," Harry says, "nobody can be there all the time."

Naomi shakes her head. He can feel the cold her smile transmits.

"Let me tell you how I lost my faith, Harry."

The spring of 1957 was late in coming. There would be a deceptively warm spell, then it would turn rainy and cold, then warm, then cold again.

It rained so much that the swamp rose all the way up to the railroad tracks. If the bed for the Sam and Willie line hadn't been built four feet above the normal high-water point, a serendipitous levee, Kinlaw's Hell would have spilled out all the way to Henry and Ruth's front door, all the way past Jane and Charlotte's house into the Beach Road.

On the last Friday of April, some of the high school students downriver and along Turpentine Creek were cut off by flooding, so school was canceled. Since the elementary school to which Hank and Paul went was just for the town children, they were not spared.

"But then, the day cleared off and it seemed as if the temperature rose 20 degrees," Naomi says, looking out the window. "Mom had already gone to work, but she didn't expect much business, with half of her customers bailing water from their houses, so it looked as if I had a day off. I didn't get many of those, let me tell you."

Henry Flood was at loose ends that Friday, too. It was, as the expression went in Saraw, too wet to plow. There apparently wasn't enough action at the pool hall or the store to sustain his interest, because he was back home by 11 that morning.

"I'm not sure he even meant for it to happen," Naomi says. "He might have, but I doubt it. He never seemed to plan much of anything."

Naomi tried to stay out of his way. They didn't have a television yet, but she had been given a record player for Christmas. She was in her room; she remembers she was listening to "Blue Suede Shoes." He didn't even bother to knock, simply walked in, the way he had always done. He had his tackle box with him.

"Let's go fishing," he said. It was not a request. Naomi said she took the needle off as quickly and gently as she could. Henry, in his moods, was fond of breaking things.

Naomi had been fishing with Henry a few times, but always either with her mother or with Hank and Paul. Henry knew the waters of Kinlaw's Hell better than anyone else in or around Saraw, and the children never knew where he had taken them when they got there, but the fishing was always good.

"And the times we went fishing were usually good times. He'd wake us up, cook pancakes for us, about the only time he ever cooked. He'd even bait our hooks for us when we got where we were going in that old boat of his. But this didn't seem like one of those times. He didn't seem all that jolly. Frankly, though, the jolly times made me more nervous than the rest; you knew what followed would be worse than normal, just to balance things out."

It was turning into a beautiful day. The last of the clouds were scudding away. The high water across the tracks shone like a big ocean studded with trees. There was always water there, but except for the creeks that spider-webbed through it, it usually was hidden by all the tangled underbrush.

Naomi got a sweater to wear over her dress. Something felt wrong, and she considered running in the other direction, toward the temporary safety of the Fairweather Grill, but what was she going to say? What had Henry done?

She helped him get the boat onto the bed of his ancient pickup truck, and then got in as he backed it to the edge of the tracks, from where they could slide the boat out and be right on the levee. He made sure the poles and tackle box were in, along with some banana sandwiches, a Pepsi for her and a fifth of bourbon for him.

Henry Flood had lived on the farm his whole life. He was alleged to have once taken his jonboat all the way across to the East Branch of the Campbell River, more than 20 miles from Saraw. The East Branch has no creeks leading off it that can be found on a map, but Henry got there, by water. He had to call a drinking buddy from a country store to come get him and the boat, because not even Henry Flood could find his way back across the swamp with the sun going down.

In the years leading up to end of 1975, Henry would spend more and more nights haunting Kinlaw's Hell.

He would stay out all night sometimes, possum hunting, spotlighting deer, doing whatever he wished to do. He claimed to have gotten close enough to the Saraw Lights to see Theron and Belle Crowder swinging their lanterns, although almost no one really believed that. He swore he had seen, more than once, a cat deep in the swamp that was far too big to be a wildcat.

Once he shot and killed a bear that weighed more than he did and somehow managed to get it into the boat and back to Saraw.

Henry Flood knew the swamp he'd grown up beside better than anybody in the world, better than he knew anything or anyone else.

Naomi pauses from her story to light another cigarette. Harry gets up to open a window.

"Sorry," she says, "but I don't think I can do this without my nicotine delivery system."

By the time they got into the swamp, she told Harry, it was half past noon. Naomi took off her sweater and folded it, very neatly, in the back of the boat. She soon lost count of how many rights and lefts, half-rights and half-lefts they took, how many sweet bays and loblollies they turned at. The swamp closed around them.

"It was just the kind of spring day we had all been waiting for," Naomi says. "And once we got away from the house and on the water, he didn't seem threatening. He would point out a hawk or a blue heron, or a water moccasin sunning itself. He seemed almost normal. I actually felt safe."

They'd been in there about an hour, and it was getting almost hot. The big trees that reached straight up to the sun knocked off the breeze without providing much shade.

"Now," Henry Flood said to her, and she realized he hadn't spoken in quite some time, "I'm going to show you something, and you've got to promise not to tell anybody else about it."

Naomi promised. Only one of them knew how to get out of Kinlaw's Hell.

Henry steered the boat hard to the right, where there seemed to be no exit to the little branch they were on, only leaves and Spanish moss.

"Watch your head," he told her, and then they were through the bushes and into another stream, one so tight that Naomi wondered how it could possibly lead anywhere.

But it eventually widened. They went along this new stream for what Naomi estimates now to be 200 yards, twisting and turning, riding the slow, tea-colored current for the most part. Then they came to a split, and Henry went left. They went a few more yards, through a thicket of undergrowth 10 feet high, and then, with one last turn, they were there.

Henry told her he had figured out years before that the hidden opening they had gone through earlier was the dividing line between what fed into the Saraw River and what fed into the Campbell, which joined the Saraw downriver at Newport. It wasn't a clear divide, of course, but he said that you could put a leaf down on the west side of that thicket and it would wind up floating down the Campbell River, while on the other side, the side they came in on, it would end up in the Saraw.

"Doesn't make any difference anyhow," he laughed. "They both wind up in the Atlantic Ocean. Everything winds up at the same place anyhow."

Past that last turn was the cabin. It had been made out of pine, hauled in a few pieces at a time, whatever a boat would carry, or hewn from the trees in the swamp itself. It looked as if it had been there for decades. It had a tin roof and wood weathered to gray. There were no windows. In front was a small wooden deck that didn't look as old as the rest.

It sat on the highest piece of ground Naomi had seen since they entered the swamp. Otherwise, the high water would have been up to the front door. The land a few feet around it had been cleared.

"He must have built it when he was a boy," Naomi tells Harry. "It must have taken him years. Maybe his parents or his brother knew something about it, but they were gone by then. And to my knowledge, no one in my family, not even Mom, had ever seen it. At least she never mentioned it to me, and I certainly never mentioned it to her. I suppose he maintained it over the years. Inside, I remember it had a couple of wooden ladder-back chairs, a rug made from a deer's hide, and not much else. The rear wall was the most amazing thing; it was stacked halfway up with empty liquor bottles. And there was a camera sitting on a little table next to the bottles.

"The bed was in the back."

For two minutes Naomi says nothing; it seems longer to Harry. He can hear the gulls screeching outside over hum of the air conditioning.

"Naomi?"

She shakes her head as if she's trying to clear cobwebs.

"Sorry," she says, and continues.

Henry Flood dragged the chairs out to the deck. He took out the sandwiches and sipped bourbon while his step-daughter drank her soft drink, now warm from the trip.

"Then, just out of nowhere, he turned to me and said he bet that a pretty girl like me had lots of boyfriends. But I knew it was coming, Harry. I knew it.

"He was sitting on my left, and he put his right hand down beside my bottom, not two inches away. I swear I could feel the heat from it.

"At that time, I had kissed one boy, a boy named Kenny Painter. We had gotten together at a school dance and slipped outside with one of my friends and one of his. I suppose, the world being fair and somebody watching out for the bad guys, I would have graduated to French kissing pretty soon, maybe light petting the next year. I might have let somebody get to third base by my senior year, maybe gone all the way before I got to college. Maybe met some dark, handsome Italian boy in Rome and given my virginity to him.

"But Henry Flood saved me the anxiety and hassle of all that. He did a couple of things to me that afternoon that I didn't let Thomas do until we had been married awhile."

"Naomi, I'm sorry." Harry puts his hand on the bed near where his daughter is sitting and realizes the inappropriateness of this just as she jumps.

"Nobody's fault," she shrugs. If her anger were electricity, Harry thinks, they could light the whole house with it. "But I wish somebody, some damn body, God, my mother, somebody, had been there. I know they weren't; I know I can't change it now. But I can still hate it, still mourn it. I can do that, can't I, Harry?"

He nods.

Henry Flood had stood up quickly and scooped Naomi into his arms, carrying her inside the cabin. He made it quite clear that there was no other human being for miles.

"No use calling for help," he had whispered into her ear. "And I don't want to hear no crying, neither."

"You know the worst thing?" Naomi says, staring straight ahead as the ash grows on her cigarette. "I couldn't, or wouldn't, even scream. And as athletic as I was, he could hold both my wrists in one of his. He seemed to enjoy the terror, the control. I believe he was acting out of spite and anger a lot more than any lust for my pitiful 13-year-old body.

"He made me take off all my clothes and fold them neatly on the chair, so I wouldn't come back looking like I'd just been raped, I suppose. I begged him to have mercy, and it just seemed to make him more excited. He had on these old coveralls, and he was out of those and his undershorts before I could blink. He didn't even bother to take off his shirt or socks. Very romantic, huh?

"I had never seen a man's penis hard like that before. You can't imagine, Harry, how scared I was. I was trying not to cry, because I was afraid he might beat me or even kill me. He put his hand over my mouth to muffle me. They'd never even find my body, was what I was thinking. Never, before or since, have I ever felt half as helpless. I actually did faint once, and when I came to, he was still inside me."

And so Henry Flood spent the better part of two hours using his stepdaughter as many times and in as many ways as he could manage.

"Harry," she says now, to the silence, "you can't imagine. Maybe if you were snatched up out of your comfortable stockbroker's life and dumped in some prison, then buggered repeatedly by psychopaths, it might have been the same. But even then, you would have built up some mental callouses, some higher threshold of psychological pain, just from living in the adult world. But my universe, up until some time in the early afternoon of April 25, 1957, was this fantasy world where God benignly ruled and you knew that your prince, all handsome and kind and gentle, would come some day.

"Except my prince preferred to come in my mouth, and insisted that I call him 'Daddy' afterward."

Before he let her get dressed, he took several pictures, threatening her with worse things yet if she didn't stop crying and look the way he wanted her to look.

Harry has no words. At that moment in 1957, he thinks, he probably was in his swank office at Martin & Rives, making a few more dollars, fantasizing about the new secretary, when he should have been wading through Kinlaw's Hell with a shotgun in his hands in anticipation of blowing Henry Flood's psychopathic head off, but only after a couple of shots to his knees and one to his genitals.

Afterward, Naomi says, he helped her clean up as best could be managed with a couple of old rags and some swamp water. Then it was over. They came out of the swamp the same way they'd gone in, father and daughter back from a fishing trip.

"I never felt normal after that day," she says, "not to this day. He got us back a little after 3, because he knew Mom would call me shortly after that.

"Do you know what he told me? He told me, 'If you let anybody know, I'll swear you asked for it, that you couldn't keep your hands off me. You will forget this ever happened, if you know what's good.'

"You know, people hear about girls being molested by monsters like Henry Flood and they can't believe it. We were at a party a while back, and they were talking about this man out in California who had allegedly raped three of his daughters over a period of several years. And my best friend said she couldn't imagine such a thing, didn't anybody notice anything, why didn't the girls tell somebody? She wouldn't shut up.

"But they just don't know, Harry. You think, what did I do to bring this on? And you think, God help you, that at some point you might have actually cooperated with him, might have pushed forward to meet him. And I'm sure I never heard the words 'statutory rape' until I was in college. And you're just sure that, if you aren't actually at fault, everybody will think you are.

"It seems easier, Harry, to just shut up and try to do what he said: forget it ever happened. Deep down, there's that voice inside you whispering that you're bad, that you asked for it.

"Except, of course, you can't forget it."

He raped her on two other occasions, once in her bedroom, once in his and Ruth's, despite Naomi's best efforts to stay away from him.

And then it stopped. He quit trying to find ways to be alone with Naomi.

"You know what I think? I think I got too old for him. I think 14 wasn't quite innocent and defenseless enough for the bastard."

She thought — half afraid, half hoping — that Ruth, of all people, would notice. She tried to stay away from her, but part of her wanted her mother to somehow intuit the damage that had been done and protect her.

"But she didn't," Naomi says, with real bitterness now. "Either she was too busy with that damn grill, or she just didn't want to deal with that kind of information.

"And by the time she figured it out, well, it was too late, you know? It wasn't long before Henry died. She found some old pictures or something. She told me, tried to apologize, but, what the hell. I told her it wasn't her fault. How could I really blame her?

"Except I do. I can't help it. I do."

They are quiet for a minute or more, and then Naomi looks over at Harry. Her eyes are red.

"Did she tell you?"

Harry can't lie, not now.

"But I just knew he raped you. I never knew how bad it was."

She smiles the thinnest smile Harry has ever seen.

"You still don't."

Harry thinks to himself that, promises or not, Naomi may have to hear a story herself.

TWENTY-FIVE

EVEN IN 1972, with the loose threads of her life coming together like some preordained quilt, Ruth thought, in unguarded moments, about what would have happened if she had, once upon a time, hung on to Harry Stein with both arms or, failing that, not been quite so committed to the concept of for-better-or-for-worse.

"I have promised myself," she wrote to Harry after the elections that year, "never to look back, but as I get older, my mind turns more and more to the rear-view mirror. You don't know how frustrating it was to me when you and Gloria divorced. I felt as if I hadn't done the right thing at all, after telling myself for years that I had. If I was going to give you up, there at least ought to have been some happiness somewhere. You and Gloria owed me that, Harry. Otherwise, it was a sacrifice for nothing. . ."

By the time she wrote that, the careers of Harry Stein and Ruth Crowder Flood were headed in decidedly different directions.

After the breakup, after Harry left Washington and returned to Richmond, he began what he came to think of as his Moses years: wandering around in the wilderness, never at home anywhere. The cottage in Safe Harbor became his refuge, and he would move a little more of himself there every year, but he didn't feel truly comfortable in either place. He found that a man of his age who was heterosexual, had his own teeth, made a good salary and weighed less than 250 pounds would never want for female companionship, but he never stayed with one woman more than eight months, and, usually, she left before Harry did, aware of what a dead-end street she was on.

Harry spent as much time as he could with Martin and Nancy, but he sensed, without either of them ever actually saying it, that they felt (Nancy more than Martin) some of the betrayal that had driven Gloria from him, a belief that

Harry Stein had endured his wife and children while wishing he were elsewhere. Harry thinks it would have been better if one of them would have just come out and said it, so that he could have told them how untrue it is, how much he cherishes all the Little League games and dance recitals, how much he regrets all the ones he missed.

The post-Washington years were flush times for Harry, if money was the gauge. His time in Washington had ended badly, but few knew even the barest details of how he lost his ambassadorship. He found that he was greeted back in the Richmond financial community, by peers and investors alike, as a bright star that had voluntarily come back to shine upon them once again.

How, Harry often wondered, when he thought of his long-ago career choice, did you not become rich if you were a white male, got into the stock market right at the end of World War II and followed it through the 1970s? He figured a broker had to be either an alcoholic, a drug addict or a hopeless gambler, and these were not his vices. Gloria remarried, Martin and Nancy finished college, his parents both died and left him and Freda a considerable sum of money, and Ruth was so well-off she could have sent money back to him. In Harry's darkest days, he had the not-inconsequential solace of wealth.

He followed the fortunes of Ruth Crowder Flood, like some soaring stock that once he could have owned if he'd only had the courage.

Never did he surrender, squirreled away in the back of his mind and never expressed to anyone but her, his dream of them, together.

And he drew bittersweet pleasure, like some football fan watching through binoculars from the cheap seats, in the rise of Ruth.

She had always wanted to go back to college. In 1966, with Paul already a freshman in high school, she started taking classes. The farm by then was more of a hobby, something that brought in a few dollars, worked by a man who rented it and four others nearby.

Henry grew vegetables for the grill and to sell at a roadside stand, but the main source of income was the grill itself, which thrived with the vacation traffic that caused the state to four-lane the beach highway in 1963.

The roads were full of newly-minted middle-class families headed for the ocean, the fathers steering late-model Buicks with one hand, pointing out prominent landmarks like the Fairweather Grill and moaning about how easy it would have been to buy that lot at White Oak Beach back in '55, envying the prescient ones (or the ones with money) who did so. The old, old story that Harry heard so often from the would-be wealthy, of how the poor don't get rich: What seems like a million now will seem like a hundred someday, but it still seems like a million now, and few ever discern what's going on until later.

And so, Ruth sent herself to college. It wasn't a full-blown midlife crisis; she still had to be around most of the time, just to make sure the help didn't walk off with the Fairweather Grill, bit by bit. She took a couple of courses a semester at the Newport branch of the state university and a couple of summer-school classes each year, some on campus, some by correspondence. She spent much of her waking time on schoolwork and at the grill.

Ruth's major, which Harry considered to be as worthless as a sand pit in the Sahara, was English, the same one he had chosen more than 30 years before. Why, he wrote, would you choose English? Why not business administration? Why not computer science?

"Harry," she wrote back, "I'm going at this with a good heart and all my strength." Enough said, he responded.

She took six years to graduate, finishing in the summer of 1972. She studied for her final exams while she was campaigning for the state legislature.

She was a small-town mayor with little money behind her, and even mediocre Republicans were riding Richard Nixon's coattails into office. But the incumbent, a Democrat, was retiring, and Ruth was the obvious choice to run. Her opponent, a lawyer from the city, spent more, but

Ruth had built up a lifetime of trust and good will, even among many who had fought her over integration.

And, she had the support of the *Newport Times*, the only daily newspaper in the county. The editor had gone to high school with Ruth. Over the years, he had lunch with her perhaps twice a year and called her from time to time to get her read of issues. Bobby Guy was a liberal, by Pembroke County standards. He picked his spots, and when he endorsed Ruth Crowder Flood, it made the difference.

"Where would I be, Harry," she wrote that year, "without old friends?"

And so, it was a good time for Ruth, Henry Flood notwithstanding. In the same year, her first grandchild, Geneva Grace, was born, she received her college degree, and she was elected to state office. Hank was coping better and was able to take a couple of correspondence courses a semester. And Paul was back from Vietnam, unscathed, married and going to North Carolina State on the GI bill, despite Ruth's protestations that she should be paying his way.

"You know," she wrote Harry that summer, "I feel bad about Paul. With all the uproar that always seemed to hover over this place like a thundercloud, Paul just sort of got lost. It was because he didn't need the attention, but just because you don't need it doesn't mean you don't want some once in a while. Sometimes, with all the squeaky wheels in the Flood household, little Paul just got overlooked. It isn't fair, how your reward for not being a bother is being ignored. Oh, I wish I could go back and do some things differently."

Don't we all, Harry wrote back.

Paul enlisted in the Marines immediately after high school in 1969. Ruth was dead set against it; she and her friends could have gotten him into any National Guard unit he wanted. Better yet, she told him, why not go to college and wait it out? Or the Navy or Air Force — even the Army would be better. Very few were willingly going into the Marines in 1969. There were the brave and the foolhardy, and the ones who, without thinking, did what their fathers had done in 1942 and their grandfathers had done in 1917.

Harry remembers stories about Marine recruiters reduced to showing up at Army induction centers and going through, like jackals stealing bits and pieces of the lions' prey, snatching every fourth or fifth boy. Draftees under the mistaken impression that their luck couldn't get any worse were tagged for Parris Island.

But Paul wanted the Marines. He was the third child, trying to carve his own niche. He had been a B student, strong in math and science, a boy who never read a book unless it was assigned. He was a tenacious athlete, but he knew in his heart that Hank would have been much better. He was nearly as sick of that knowledge as Hank was.

Henry Flood, the old Marine, was all for it. Hank had never been a serious consideration for the draft, and Henry would sometimes, when he had been drinking, remind him of that. Henry at last had someone in his family aiming for the one occupation at which he had truly succeeded. And he had some basis for doing the final, unforgivable thing an old hero can do: He bragged. He told stories he'd kept corked inside him for years. And kept telling them.

"Harry," Ruth wrote, "when he first told a bunch of his cronies at Payton's Billiards about what it was like going into those holes, not knowing whether there were Japanese in there or not, everybody stopped and listened. Nobody had ever heard him tell those stories before. Even drunk, he wouldn't tell them.

"Roy McGinnis was there, and he told me nobody said a thing at any of the six tables, and you could see people edging closer so they could hear. Next day, it was all over town, and I think it was good. It reminded people of what Henry Flood was, and what made him how he is now.

"But that one telling, or maybe Paul going to another jungle in another war, opened up some kind of dam, and now he can't stop talking about it. He'll take his medals out, the ones he's had put away for years and guarded like I guard your letters, and show them to people, and sometimes he forgets he's already shown them. He tells the same stories over and over, and they are starting to stretch a little bit, the way stories do sometimes. He's started getting interested in the American Legion and the VFW. He used to shun those people, said they were just a bunch of braggarts and blowhards.

"The sad thing is, a part of me doesn't want to shut him up, even when he's boring me, even when I can see other people trying to find some excuse to get away. You see, it's the only time in years that I've seen him really happy, the way he was when we were dating and for a while after we were married."

Ruth worried herself sick over Paul. "God forgive me," she wrote, "but almost as much as death I fear him coming back like his father."

Paul saw many others get killed, and he did some killing himself. He doesn't talk much about Vietnam now, but to Harry's eyes he doesn't seem to have suffered much if any for his days in the jungle. Harry believes there are some who do, in spite of everything, become better for having their lives placed in daily jeopardy at an early age.

In World War II, Harry had fought alongside lawyers and plumbers, accountants and farm boys. Paul's platoon was mostly peopled by the ones who couldn't get out or the rare ones who didn't exercise that precious option. That's what Vietnam was, for Paul and for Harry's own Martin — optional. Harry's war was as compulsory as breathing.

If every mother's son had been fair game for Vietnam, Harry has argued more than once, the U.S. might have won, might have dropped the Big One and had a confetti parade down Fifth Avenue.

We'd still have been wrong as hell, he thinks, but at least we might have won.

Paul came home in 1972 somewhat older than his chronological years, ready for college, and married.

"Paul has married a Vietnamese girl," Ruth wrote that spring. "At first, I was taken aback, but who couldn't love Tran? She won my heart right away, although I am afraid she does too much for Paul. She has lost most of her family to that damnable war. If I'd lost all she has, I'd be locked up in a room somewhere, no windows, just me and my strait-jacket. But she just goes on, learning English, smiling, working until somebody makes her stop."

Paul majored in computer engineering when few others were. His fortune, after all the years of Henry Flood's terrorism, of existing in the shadow of his big brother and big sister, of tiptoeing past land mines and working his way through college while married to a woman who depended on him for everything in her strange new world, was made rather quickly.

He seems to Ruth to be unfazed by either Vietnam or his early life. There are no traumas for Paul, no flashbacks to little Susanna's death or friends' heads exploding from sniper bullets.

"Momma," he said once, "if I ever take the time to sit back and think about everything, maybe I'll have myself a nice little nervous breakdown."

He was laughing when he said it.

Ruth says Paul is the Flood family glue, although Harry argues he is only Son of Glue.

As for Tran, she has changed little in the 23 years Ruth has known her. She abides little nonsense from her children, but it is obvious she would chew her arm off to save either one of them from harm or pain. Voices seldom have to be raised at Paul and Tran's.

Harry envies them their courage and judgment. Often he thinks that Paul and he were faced with the same dilemma: A young man, a soldier, in a strange land meets and falls in love with a woman who is so different from anything in his previous life that he doubts his instincts, hesitates to do what he feels is right, teeters there on the edge like a baby bird peering out over the lip of the nest.

Once Harry asked Tran, in a rare moment alone, if it wasn't hard, coming to another country where she didn't know the language or the culture, leaving everything behind.

She looked at him as if he were a child asking why water is wet or the sky is blue.

"I don't have any choice," she said. "What I have back there is gone. Only one way for me to go."

And then she went back to cleaning the kitchen counter, which to Harry already looked extremely clean. She was humming a tune he didn't recognize.

TWENTY-SIX

TUESDAY NIGHT, RUTH and Harry stay outside until after 11, cool but not cold in their sweaters. Harry tells her that they must look like a couple of old geezers on the deck of a cruise liner.

He is amazed at how energized he is — relatively speaking, of course. The days when Harry Stein could dance and party all night and then work the next day are so far gone that he believes sometimes he must have stolen another man's memories. He doesn't like to tell stories from those salad days any more, because he is afraid that the listener, if he didn't know Harry then, will see a sad old man trying to impress those who still possess what he might or might not have once had.

Ruth turns and catches him staring at something she can't see.

"What?" she asks. "What're you thinking about, Harry?"

He shakes his head and tells her it's nothing of great importance, just ruminations on a life pissed away.

"Hush," she says. "You have not peed your life away."

"Ruth, you cannot interchange pissed and peed in that context."

"I can if I want to. I can't help it if I haven't had the benefit of a lifetime of foul language. It's hard to teach an old dog new cusswords."

Harry laughs, and is hit with a stab of pain. He wonders if God is punishing him for filching a last mouthful of enjoyment from life's great buffet.

"Are you OK?" He and Ruth are holding hands, and he realizes that he has been squeezing too hard.

"I'm OK. Not great, but at least OK. Don't let go; your warmth feels good."

"Have you taken your pills?"

"Enough to sedate King Kong," he says.

Harry has not minded at all basking in Ruth's late-blooming glory these past few years. Usually, he accompanies her to Raleigh when the legislature is in session, and until recently, he enjoyed more than his share of free food and drink at the lobbyists' parties.

There is usually something to keep him entertained there. He'll waste an entire morning in a bookstore; he's fond of ones that smell of old paper instead of coffee. Sometimes, he just wanders the campus at Duke or Chapel Hill, perhaps spending an hour or two under one of the old trees that are held up with wires (and remind him of himself), reading a book or tracking the market.

He did have a few favorite bars in the Triangle area, but his doctors have for the past four months absolutely banned alcohol. He has gotten to know some of the coaches at North Carolina State and UNC, and they usually let him hang around at basketball or football practice. In exchange, he gives them tips on the stock market. There is an assistant basketball coach who was able to buy a new Acura mostly on what he claims he made on an up-and-coming computer stock. He calls it "Harry's car." Harry told him he shouldn't have sold so soon. And, he swims at the YMCA.

Ruth has said this will be her last term. She would like the opportunity, she tells Harry, to emulate him and do nothing except waste time. "It isn't as easy as you think," he warns her. "I've had almost 20 years of practice."

They talk about the inconsequential. Finally, Harry sees an opening.

"I've had a wonderful time," Ruth says. "Paul and Tran are so sweet to do this. I am so lucky to have such a loving family."

"So," Harry asks, "how are things with Naomi? Better?"

A frown. "I don't know, Harry. I guess so. She still seems so edgy when I'm around, nervous as a cat."

"I had a talk with her this afternoon."

Ruth looks over at him. From the corner of his eye, he can see her frown.

"I thought maybe so," she says. "About what?" Her inflection rises on the last word, a perceived weakness she usually avoids.

"About her and Henry."

They are both silent then.

While Harry was rotting comfortably, dividing his year between Richmond and Safe Harbor and dating women who were all approximately the same age but, from Harry's vantage point, seemed younger and younger, Ruth was making her mark.

And enduring Henry Flood.

As she and the Fairweather Grill prospered, Ruth tried to include Henry in her life, but by the 1970s, she came to see that the most she could hope for was that he would not scare the customers away.

Finally, by mutual consent, he quit coming to the grill altogether. Even when he was drunk and looking for trouble, he would avoid it. Ruth appreciated this consideration, and she made sure that Henry had enough drinking money.

A better person, she told herself later, would have sent him somewhere to dry out. But she knew that he wasn't much if any better sober. Sometimes, when he was drunk, he seemed temporarily happy.

No one at the VA hospital or among the many doctors to whom Ruth sent him ever really stopped the headaches, and old shrapnel was causing other pain to join forces, an army growing ever stronger.

She wished sometimes that she could be inside Henry's body for just one minute, to feel the pain. Then, she thought, she might appreciate it more and be more sympathetic.

Ruth, from the grill and her investments, was becoming prosperous. Henry would never find out about the Richmond money, and Ruth made sure he never knew exactly how well her stocks were doing.

What Henry finally seemed to do, to Ruth's relief and sadness, was surrender. By 1970, Paul was gone, but Hank was far too strong to absorb any more physical punishment from his father. Ruth had her own defenses. Henry soon found that his wife didn't mind having him thrown in jail if the occasion warranted it, and that, unlike other women with less clout, she had the sympathetic ear of the sheriff and the local judge. And she was willing to endure the embarrassment of having all of Saraw know that her husband was in jail again.

"Harry," she wrote, "what do you think is more embarrassing: to have your Sunday School class know your husband is in jail, or to have to lie about a black eye when everybody knows you're lying?"

After a few nights in jail, including one episode in which he had to be beaten into submission by a couple of deputies, Henry began finding ways to keep his devils away from Ruth.

Since Harry's fall from grace, Ruth had suspected that her husband knew about the letters and sensed Randall Phelps was still lurking somewhere, ready to take away his only thin link to sanity.

He would cry sometimes and beg her forgiveness, plead with her not to leave him. He would turn over new leaves and be a changed man until the next "spell."

What Harry Stein wanted, after 1966, was for her to leave him. He knew she would be happier without Henry Flood. "What do you owe him?" he wrote once. He had married her, Harry conceded, but wouldn't any of a dozen others, equally handsome and steady as a rock, have done the same?

"I want you," Harry wrote, more than once, and described this want in great detail.

"I want you, too," she responded once. "I think of you when I am alone in my bed at night, alone even when Henry is here. I think of you and me, in that hotel room at White Oak Beach, on the railroad tracks, everywhere. I think of all the things we did . . ." Her letters, more demure in the earlier years of her marriage, were now racy enough, when the subject was desire, that Harry would have an erection reading them.

But she wouldn't leave Henry Flood.

"Where would he go, without me?" she asked in a letter not two years before Henry died. "What would he do? I promised, Harry. I don't mean it to seem sanctimonious, but Henry Flood is my husband, the one who asked me to marry him, the one I said yes to. If he was a sane, solid man and I found out one day he'd been having an affair with his secretary, that would be different. I might not forgive him that. But Henry Flood cannot help himself."

Later, she would feel differently.

"Probably, the best thing I could have done would have been to just pack up the kids and leave," she would say then, after she'd told Harry how it all ended. "Maybe then he would have gotten help and all this could have been avoided."

Eventually, the rest of the family comes outside, except for Naomi, who's already gone to bed.

Paul tells them that there has been a "weather development." Ruth, half asleep, jerks her head toward him.

The storm might turn in our direction, he says, but it won't be a factor until mid-afternoon tomorrow at the earliest.

"We've got to have Momma's party tomorrow; it's her birthday," he says.

"Can't we just light a candle or two at midnight and be done with it?" Ruth asks plaintively.

"Can't do that at night. The fire department might see all those candles and think the house is burning up."

Ruth shakes her head and laughs along with the rest.

Before they go to sleep, Harry asks what he's wanted to ask since the afternoon.

"Ruth, can't I please tell her? She needs to know. It'll help; I'm sure it'll help."

Ruth turns sideways, away from him. She is shaking her head. She puts the pillow over her ears so she can't hear him any more.

TWENTY-SEVEN

Nov. 27, 1975
Saraw, N.C.

Dear Harry,

Please excuse me for not writing sooner, but I am sure you will understand when I tell you the reason.

Henry went into Kinlaw's Hell three weeks ago yesterday, and he never came out.

They found his body eight days later, near his old camp. Roy McGinnis went with the sheriff and identified him; he said Henry's body was lying next to his boat, in front of the cabin I've never seen and never want to, where he always went when he had to get away.

There are people around here who are sure Henry was burying money at his secret hideaway, like some pirate, and now that someone knows where it is, I expect the swamp will be full of fools looking to get rich off Henry Flood's hidden treasure. I don't think I have to tell you, Harry, that unless Henry found a way to get into my investments or savings account since my last statement, it isn't likely he's been burying a lot of money in Kinlaw's Hell.

They said it was probably a heart attack. . . .

Steady, Harry, he counseled himself, actually saying the words. Steady, steady. It can't be this easy. If she had really wanted you, she wouldn't have waited for Henry Flood to die.

The day before, he had broken up with a woman approximately half his age. He couldn't believe that his life had been reduced to "breaking up," as if he and his female companion of the day, week or month were high school sweethearts instead of a couple of opportunists. This one, an artist, had been with him four months. She was a little less interesting to him than the one before, and, as best he could remember, that one was less interesting than the previous one.

He had read the letter walking back from the mailbox that cold, dark Long Island morning. By the time he got to the front door, his hands were shaking.

His first inclination was to pack a few essentials, catch a train to the airport and fly to Newport, rent a car and drive directly to Ruth's house, where sympathy cards still lay on the kitchen table. But he talked himself out of it. He was too close, he told himself, to ruin it by doing something heedless.

Instead, he did something that, by his and Ruth's rules, seemed almost as rash.

In all their years apart, he had never called, never broken the spell that he came to feel was cast by the written word. As long as their life was on paper, it was still somehow 1942, a year when he and the world were relatively young. By writing, he felt a small part of him stayed back in Saraw, with the hope of making everything turn out right. On paper, he could still be 23.

So, even with Henry Flood some three weeks dead, Harry agonized over making that call. He saw himself as some cartoon character with a devil whispering in one ear and an angel in the other, except both were the same, and he couldn't decide which one to heed.

First he dialed information and got the number, available for the asking all along: H.B. Flood in Saraw, North Carolina. Just 11 numbers away.

Then he ate lunch, barely tasting the cold sandwich. He tried to watch television. He took a walk to the pond on the back of his property.

Finally, just after 4:30, he called Ruth.

The phone rang four times, and he was going to hang up, relieved, when she answered.

He knew her voice, though they had only talked once in all those years. It hadn't changed so much, he thought. It was still Ruth.

She said hello twice before he could speak.

"This is Harry Stein," he said, afraid her life was full of a variety of Harrys these days, so many Harrys that she would need further identification.

"So it is," she said after a long pause. "Harry Stein. Harry Stein. What a strange world it is, that I'm talking to Harry Stein."

He could not read her mood. He certainly did not feel free to speak his heart.

They talked about the weather, Harry digging his nails into the meaty flesh in his other hand as he found himself babbling about frost and fog. He pretended sorrow for Henry's passing, and she accepted his condolences without comment.

By this time, Harry was sure he had made a mistake.

Ruth had lost both her aunts the previous summer, within a month of each other, and for this loss Harry expressed genuine regret. He remembered their unwarranted kindness that long-ago winter.

"So," he said, thrashing about for a way to keep the link alive, "what's next?"

"Oh, I don't know, Harry. I don't know. The grill and politics keep me pretty busy. And Hank's still here. We look after each other. And we're moving."

With her aunts dead, she intended, as soon as she could, to return to the house where she had been born, where her parents and then her grandparents raised her.

"Maybe you'd like to come up here and get away from everything for a little while," Harry said, too much forced nonchalance in his voice. Please come, he willed. Please come.

There was a short pause.

"I don't know, Harry. I can't get away right now. There's too much going on — Christmas, getting the estate settled, just getting my life back together."

"Well, maybe later then."

"Yes. Maybe later."

All those years, all the letters, seemed to Harry to mean nothing at that moment.

He kept the conversation alive awhile longer, hoping for hope.

"Well," he said at last, full of false cheer, "maybe I'll come see you, then, give you another surprise visit."

"Yes," she said. She sounded distracted, but the phone line was becoming scratchy, conspiring against him. "That would be nice, Harry. That would be nice." Her voice trailed off.

Shortly after that they said goodbye. Harry drove into East Hampton and drank away a few hours of the endless northern night, brooding, examining every word she'd said, every word he'd said.

At one point, he leaned forward, unable to resist the urge, and banged his head on the wooden bar, twice. The bartender cut him off, and he went back to his cold, dark home.

He didn't write for two weeks afterward. He remembers that December now as a time of insomnia and long walks, broken by a short visit to see his children and grandchildren. By the time he got her next letter, the one he wasn't sure he would get, it was New Year's Eve. There was a return address, something Ruth had never employed before, in their clandestine days. He saw that she had returned to the home of her childhood.

"I'm glad you're still my friend, Harry," she began. "It was so strange hearing you on the telephone. Forgive me if I sounded distracted. Believe it or not, I have wanted, more than once over the years, to call you, sure that you could talk my blues away. But there was always something holding me back, some feeling that calling you from some pay phone or from Mercy's would spoil it all. I don't know. Maybe we're meant to just keep on the way we've been. You seem to have a good life up there. And an impartial observer would have to say things are going well for me down here. . . ."

There wasn't much hope in that letter for a man who saw his one last chance to alter the past slipping away. But there was enough.

Harry didn't really think innocence could be regained; he knew that nothing duplicated was as good as the original. But he was willing, at this point, to try almost anything. The idea of Ruth, all of Ruth, had slipped into his brain in the last month, and he knew he couldn't live on letters any more.

And so, he packed all he could into the trunk and back seat of his BMW that New Year's Eve. Then he locked the door and left. He stopped at a liquor store and bought a bottle of Moet et Chandon, a Styrofoam cooler and five pounds of ice. After that, he headed west and south, into the unknown.

He knew she could tell him to turn right around and go back to New York. She owed him nothing more, really. Still, he had to try.

It was nearly dark by the time he left. Almost anything would have been smarter than driving, he knew later, when he was rational. To get from Safe Harbor to Saraw required getting past New York City, and then the trip was just getting started.

Two hours past the city, nothing about it made sense to him, as he hummed along in 1975's last hours, listening to reality's mean whispers. She'd probably send him back, or at best tolerate him for a few hours. He might be appalled by the inroads time had made into his dream, and what would she think of Harry Stein at 56? They would be as tongue-tied as they had been on the phone five weeks before. He should have called first (but then she might have said, Don't come). He should have taken the train (but that was next to impossible on New Year's Eve). He should have flown (but he was still spooked by the Eastern crash at Kennedy a few months before). He should have, he told himself, forgotten the whole damn stupid idea.

"Philadelphia Freedom" had been big on the radio that year, and he heard it at least 10 times in the 13 hours between Safe Harbor and Saraw. Even now, Harry can't hear the song without a sense of excitement and foreboding.

He had a late dinner at a state-run hamburger joint in Maryland, popped two more No-Doz, filled the car up with gas and headed back into the night. He drove through Richmond, where many of his family would be at one party or another, without slowing down, the clock in the old train station beside the interstate eyeing him at car level. Somewhere in Southside Virginia, 1976 began. As he crossed under a bridge near Emporia, a shotgun blast from overhead greeted the new year and gave him a free half-hour of adrenaline.

He left the interstate sometime after 2 and realized he was exhausted. This was the longest drive he'd ever made in his life, and there was at least a three-hour stretch of mostly two-lane road between him and Ruth.

At the exit, he pulled into a Texaco station that had shut down for the night. He parked the car and went to sleep sitting up behind the wheel. He knew that if he lay down he'd be out until some irate mechanic or state trooper woke him sometime after dawn.

He did not even know he was asleep until he was awakened by the car horn after his forehead fell against it. He looked at his watch, its hands glowing in the dark like fox fire. 3:30.

He found enough change to buy a Coke from the vending machine outside, then washed down two more No-Doz and drove the last two-and-a-half hours into Saraw with the driver's-side window rolled halfway down to keep him awake. Two miles outside town, on the edge of Kinlaw's Hell, he passed a blur in the road and was two hundred yards away when he realized that it was some farmer's mule, solid as an oak tree, standing dead center on the white line, parallel to the side of the road. Two more feet, Harry thought, and I'm dead. He felt it was either a good sign or a bad one, but it surely was a sign.

He tried to convince himself that it would soon be light, or that the mule would wander off the road on its own. But Harry, if not religious, was at least superstitious, and he knew it was no day to let good deeds go undone. He turned his car around, hating the idea of going anywhere except forward, and parked beside the animal, which was standing as still as a statue. The mule was not easy to shoo, but after 10 minutes of clapping his hands and throwing rocks and pine cones, Harry managed to get it off the road and past the ditch, temporarily out of harm's way.

Returning from his good deed, he found that his car wouldn't start. The BMW, as stubborn as the mule in its refusal to obey Harry's pleas and threats, had been ridden hard and was willing to go no farther. There was nothing to do except walk.

It was not a bad morning for a walk, Harry conceded. After Long Island, it felt almost balmy with his heavy coat on; it was just chilly enough to clear his mind. He took the champagne from the cooler and finished his journey.

He soon crossed the northern tip of Turpentine Creek and passed the optimistic city-limit sign — "Welcome to Saraw. A Town on the Move." Here and there, a light, perhaps not yet doused from the night before, broke the darkness between Harry and the swamp. It was 7 by the time he reached the town itself. He had been there once in 33 years, and it occurred to him that, while his memories of Ruth were enduring, he had only the most vague sense of where, specifically, she lived. He remembered it was on the west side of the Beach Highway, and he knew it was north of the river. Saraw had not grown much, in spite of the sign, but it had grown enough to confuse Harry momentarily.

Just when he thought he must have taken a wrong turn, somehow, or dreamed it all, he saw the church. The first light of the new year caught the tin of its steeple, in front of him and to his right, a Presbyterian beacon to guide Harry Stein.

He climbed the church steps, lugging his champagne, to where everything began. There he sat and watched day seep down the pillars of the sanctuary, then cover the frosted ground. Finally he saw it illuminate the old Crowder place, Ruth's house, not 200 yards away.

He leaned back on the cold stone to rest for just a moment, to wait for full light and get his second wind.

In his next moment of consciousness, she was there, over him like a dream. He thought he might have died, looking up at Ruth with pastel-bordered morning clouds scurrying past in the background.

"Harry? Harry Stein? Is it you? Have you lost your mind?"

Yes, yes, yes, he thought, I probably have.

He told her, his mouth feeling as if it were full of cotton, what exactly had brought him to Saraw, what he meant to do, how happy he could make her if she would let him. He did not say it smoothly, but like a man who is about to find out how the rest of his life turns out, who needs food, sleep and the right answer, in reverse order.

Ruth was wearing a red jogger's suit and large running shoes that made her look so capable and modern that Harry wondered if his dream wasn't already beyond him. But she was still beautiful, backlit by the sun, some gray in her blonde hair, a few wrinkles but otherwise an amazing likeness of the young woman he had last seen in that train-station cafeteria in 1954. She had been on her morning walk, and the first thing she saw when she turned the corner onto the lane was Harry, laid out on the steps as if dead or drunk, a bottle of champagne sitting beside him.

Harry Stein, his dice rolled, his cards played, his hash about to be settled, sat up and looked at his watch. 10:30.

"Help me," he said, because he could think of nothing else. He held out his right arm. She bent and took his hand, and he rose unsteadily to embrace her. They fit each other when they hugged, as they once had. And she still smelled like Ruth. Once, in Safe Harbor, he had spent two weeks with a woman who had no discernible charms other than the fact that she smelled like Ruth Crowder.

Ruth had not expected this. She had spent December convincing herself that it was her self-imposed punishment to stay in the house of her childhood and grow old gracefully, dryly, if fate and the authorities allowed her to do even that much. She couldn't allow herself to think of sinful extravagances such as Harry Stein. She was not allowed that, she told herself. She didn't deserve that. Not if there was a God.

But Harry looked so good to her, even in his unshaven, bleary-eyed, rumpled current state. When he held his arm up toward her, as if in supplication, she could not turn away.

In Ruth's arms, Harry started to cry, something he had not done even on the cold, bare nights after Gloria left. Ruth led him back to the house, where they began to talk. Harry chilled the champagne, and they drank it all at the kitchen table before noon, out of two coffee cups Ruth pulled from the dish drain, with the grandfather clock ticking the morning away down the hall, its bells the only thing to remind them that time had not stood completely still.

They didn't stop talking for a month, and even then, neither of them felt even mildly sated. Ruth noticed that she was constantly hoarse that January, but there was so much time to make up, so much to say. She had an irrational fear that she would awaken and find Harry gone, as if it had all been a dream, and she wanted as much of him as possible before that happened, in every way possible.

At first, Ruth told Hank that Harry was an old friend, and Hank was kind enough not to ask any probing questions. But gradually, in a few days, the truth was too obvious to hide in even a large house.

"Momma," Hank said to her at breakfast one morning, before Harry came down and before he would officially move into Ruth's room, "I think it's time you and I had that talk. About the facts of life."

She tried to keep a straight face, but she couldn't, and neither could Hank.

"People are going to think you're crazy, Momma," he said, shaking his head, still smiling. "They're going to run you out of the church."

So she told him who Harry Stein was. By the end of the week, she had told Paul as well.

Ruth waited another week to tell Naomi that Harry had returned to the scene of the crime. When Naomi made a rare, unplanned trip from Denver to Saraw a few days later, Paul and Tran came down from Raleigh, and they were all together, asking questions at first awkwardly and then with the kind of frankness that Harry usually encountered when the Steins got together.

"So," Paul said when he was introduced, "we finally get to meet Randall Phelps."

While Naomi was there, Ruth and she went for a long walk one afternoon. When they came back, they both seemed to have been crying, but neither would talk about it afterward. The next morning, Naomi went back to Denver.

Harry, once he returned, did make Ruth happy. These days, he is warmed by that thought. Weighed against the pain in which he has participated, he has made one person more or less permanently happy (two counting himself), even if it did take him 33 years.

"Why didn't you act more interested?" Harry asked Ruth once they had slowed down enough, in bed and out, to analyze things. "I almost didn't come. I was so afraid."

She rolled over on her side and pulled the kimono over an exposed breast.

"I don't know," she said after a pause. "I worried that nothing could beat what we had. You came to mean so much to me, Harry, and my experience with men in the day-after-day flesh and blood has not been so good. I thought maybe Harry Stein and I would both be better off if we kept going to bed with memories. And then, after Henry died . . . Well, let's just say I thought everything was over."

"What if I hadn't come, though? What if we had missed this?"

Ruth frowned.

"If you hadn't come down, I wouldn't have known what I was missing. If you had stayed up there, in my dreams, we would have always wondered, but we would have survived. If you don't know what you're missing, you don't miss it."

"Speak for yourself," he said, as he pulled her body on top of his.

TWENTY-EIGHT

THIS TIME, IN Harry's old, old dream, Sergeant Stevens' face has been replaced by that of grinning Henry Flood. When he awakes, breathing hard, he has kicked the sheets off his side of the bed.

The wind isn't howling or shaking the windows, but he can hear it now. Something has changed.

Harry's pain, his semi-constant companion, is back, and he wonders if its absence won't presage something worse.

He slips out of bed as quietly as he can, goes to the bathroom to relieve himself and take more pain medicine, avoiding the mirror, then shuffles into the living area. By the various small illuminations — microwave clock, VCR, a night light by the kitchen counter — he can soon make his way to the room's most comfortable chair.

He is settling into it when he sees one more small light, from the tip of a cigarette on the deck.

With the wind up, Harry knows it is bound to be chilly outside, and he wants to stay where he is, hunkered down and quiet as a mouse, hiding from the pain.

He weighs everything, again. He is relatively certain that Naomi needs to know what he knows. He is almost as sure that Ruth will not forgive him for telling.

Thirty years of Ruth's censure would be hard punishment, but Harry is thinking, this night, of a depressingly smaller number. He uses most of his strength to remove himself from the chair, then limps toward the deck.

He can smell the salt spray as he opens the door, just like at the ocean. Naomi doesn't seem surprised to see him, almost seems to have been expecting him. By his watch, it's almost 2:30.

"Couldn't sleep," Harry explains.

"There's a lot of that going around." She smiles, putting her cigarette on the lip of the ashtray. "Is the pain really bad?"

"Nah," he lies. "It beats the alternative."

She tells him he'll be around for another 20 years, and he lets it pass.

"Do you have insomnia a lot?" he asks, thinking to himself that it's late to be asking his daughter that.

"Just when I'm around Mom," she says, taking another puff. "No, that's not right. I'm just being an asshole. Just all the time. I'm trying to stay off those damn sleeping pills, but there are nights when I just lie there, looking at those little green numbers flipping over. My mind'll hop from Gary to Grace to Thomas to Mom. On a really bad night, I'll even go back to Henry Flood. Guilt, anger, worry.

"You know what calms me down sometimes? God, I shouldn't be telling you this. But if you can't tell your old dad, who can you tell?" She smiles her usual way, her mouth twisted a little to the right, as if the act of smiling causes her pain. She stubs out her cigarette on the rail, hard. "What does it for me is this: I imagine that I'm at that cabin with him. When he reaches down to 'help' me take my panties off, I grab the crowbar that was lying beside the cot. I'm sure that crowbar was there, Harry, that I haven't just invented it. And I hit him over the head with it, over and over again. He's begging me to stop, but I keep hitting him. I revel in his suffering.

"That works sometimes. Sometimes, though, I even turn that into angst. Why didn't I hit him? Why didn't I kill the bastard? Why didn't I try to escape? I was a good athlete, a good runner. Even if I hadn't killed him with the crowbar, I could have run into the woods, somewhere. Starving to death would have been better, dying of snakebite. Why. . .?"

Harry puts his hand to her lips, and she is silent, waiting.

"I have a story to tell you," he says, "one that might help you get some sleep."

Five years after what Harry thinks of as his redemption, he and Ruth went for a walk one day along the ancient railroad bed where the Sam and Willie once ran. The linear park that replaced it, largely the doing of State Senator Ruth Crowder Flood, is a perfect path for jogging, biking or just, as she describes it, putting one foot in front of the other.

They would go south, most days. The park picks up the Saraw, with its dark water and low-hanging moss, half a mile from the Crowder house.

Once in a while, though, for a change of pace, they would go north, where the old railbed is the boundary of Kinlaw's Hell. Here, the view is not quite so spectacular — bays and low-lying shrubs, tall, angular pine trees like underweight sentries guarding the swamp, loons mourning in the distance.

Sometimes, they walk late in the afternoon, especially in the summer, and occasionally they return home after dark. On those days, they never go north, where the Saraw Lights, once the ghosts of Ruth's doomed parents, have imitated late-20th century life and downsized. Now, people swear they see only one light, and the light they see is Henry Flood weaving around in the distance, trying to get home.

That morning, five years after his return, on one of their infrequent walks north, Harry looked over and saw the back of a house he had passed often on the highway — the old Flood place.

After Henry's death, Ruth gave the house and the land to Henry's younger sister in Laurinburg. The sister in turn sold it to a family named Hedgepeth, which soon moved onto the property five double-wide trailers housing almost every Hedgepeth in Pembroke County. Ruth had not set foot on the land since she moved out.

Harry had often wondered about the place where Ruth and Henry Flood lived, what it looked like on the inside, whether he could discern the scent of something that would tell him more about the years he missed. But Ruth always demurred, and Harry never pushed it.

Now, though, it was right there beside them. Harry could see small, ragged children playing next to the closest trailer. He asked Ruth if she wouldn't like to see what had been done with the place in which she had spent the majority of her adult life. She said she would rather not, in a tone that indicated that she would rather be in hell.

After that, Harry would push the issue every time they passed the house. It became a contest of wills.

Finally, one morning in the late spring of 1981, Ruth gave in.

That day, she stopped dead on the path, so suddenly that Harry was a few steps beyond her before he realized she wasn't with him.

"OK, Harry," she said, "you want to see the damn farm? Let's go see the damn farm."

He followed in cautious silence as they eased down the bank to a path through the weeds that led toward her former home.

Dogs of indecipherable pedigree barked their arrival at each mobile home they approached. It looked to Harry as if German shepherds and dachshunds, terriers and Labradors, chows and Chihuahuas had found a way to mate with each other. Ruth told them to hush, and they did. She waved a greeting to one young overweight mother who was hanging out her wash. The mother tried to speak with a clothespin in her mouth, then was distracted by her 2-year-old, who appeared to be trying to use his big-wheel to run over his baby sister, lying on an old Army blanket in the side yard.

They approached the main house from the back. Ruth walked up and knocked on the kitchen door, and a woman who appeared to Harry to be approximately 80 years old answered. She apologized for not having her teeth in yet. Ruth called her by her first name, Cora. She introduced Harry, then asked if they could wander around the farm so she could show him where she had once lived.

"Wonder all you like," Cora said with a toothless smile Harry would just as soon have not seen. "Wonder away."

Cora Hedgepeth turned to him.

"She's a good womern," she said, barely intelligible without her dentures. "I always vote for her."

Ruth thanked her for that and declined an invitation to see the inside of the house.

Walking across the yard, she said to Harry, "I don't think I'm up to that right now. Besides, I've got something else to show you."

"How old is Cora Hedgepeth?" he asked when they were a polite distance from the house.

"She and I were in school together."

"Well, I'd definitely advise you to keep the teeth. I never realized what a vital fashion accessory they were."

He had hoped Ruth would smile at that. She didn't.

The farm was typical for the area. There was an abundance of outbuildings of various sizes and uses. An old "carhouse" was employed mainly to shelter the weathered remains of a 1965 Mustang that someone still thought he would restore someday. A chicken coop and the wire fence around its yard were leaning, decaying. A pair of tobacco barns, one listing badly, were used mostly to store old, never-to-be-used-again furniture. What once was a smokehouse lay in ruins, its boards now used for kindling. A safe distance from all the rotting wood stood rusted-out 50-gallon drums, in which trash was burned.

Ruth led them to a smaller building that stood, barely, besidc the smokehouse's remains.

Its windows were clouded over with years of dirt and cobwebs, and there was a wooden latch on the one door, accessible by stepping up on a two-tiered arrangement of cinder blocks that had replaced the original pine steps. Next to the latch was a piece of metal where a lock once had been.

Ruth opened the door and Harry followed her inside, hesitantly. His deep dislike of spiders and snakes already was legendary around Saraw.

The room still held some of the previous night's cold. Unlike the other buildings, it had a concrete floor.

"This was Henry's workroom," Ruth sighed, speaking at last. Her right hand was shaking slightly, and Harry began to finally realize how much it had taken to get her here.

After five years, it still housed most of the tools needed by a farmer who couldn't afford carpenters and handymen. It had the metallic, rusty smell of old nails and saws and rasps and a hundred other tools whose uses were inscrutable to Harry.

Two benches had been built into the walls, and a couple of chairs sat in the middle of the open area.

"Sit down, Harry," Ruth said. He started to protest; the chairs didn't look as if they would hold an adult, and he was certain that the room could produce at least a couple of respectable chicken snakes. But Ruth sat, and he saw that he didn't have any choice.

"Look under there," she said, nodding to a place where two rows of four drawers each were set back a few inches beneath one of the benches. "I thought they might have thrown that thing away.

"It was the third drawer down on the right-hand side. That's where I found it."

Harry pulled the drawer open slowly, uneasily, sure something live was inside. But the drawer was empty. It smelled of ancient wood and something he couldn't place.

"Oh, there's nothing in there now. Nothing for more than five years now. I burned everything."

By 1975, Ruth and Henry Flood had come to an understanding. It was similar, she wrote in a letter that year, to the one reached by North and South Korea. He was 60; she was 50. Their marriage was now a truce broken only by a rare uprising. Henry appeared to Ruth to be more at peace than he had been in years, and if his disappearances into Kinlaw's Hell increased in frequency, then maybe there was cause and effect. Whatever the cause, she was grateful.

And, the legislature kept her busy most of the time she wasn't running the grill, which she was more and more leaving in other hands of varying capability. In the winter and spring, she would be gone to Raleigh for weeks at a time, only returning on Saturdays and Sundays, when she could get away then.

Everything else seemed to have fallen in place. Paul was graduated with a degree in computer engineering. Hank was becoming an excellent carpenter in a place where people knew him, made allowances for shortcomings and judged him on his work. Naomi had just given birth to her second healthy child.

"I thought everything was fixed at last," she said with a sigh that day in Henry Flood's shed.

Then, one Monday in mid-October, she came home early from the grill, sick with a low-grade flu. It was a teachers' workday, and she saw children out everywhere playing in the Indian summer sunshine and wished she felt well enough to enjoy it. She promised herself to take more time off on account of nice weather.

When she got home, she saw no sign of Henry. His truck was not parked in the driveway, but that was not unusual. Probably, she thought, he was using such a fine fall day to do some fishing in the swamp. She was in the bathroom, looking for the Pepto-Bismol, when a flash of movement out of the window caught her eye.

The window faced Kinlaw's Hell, and from it, she could see Henry out by the railroad tracks, pushing his boat onto the back of his truck. There was someone with him.

When he was through, he and the other person, younger and smaller, got into the truck, and he drove it up into the back yard.

The other person got out, and Ruth saw that it was a girl named Angela Spooner, whose family lived three drive-ways north.

"Angela was about 12 then," Ruth said, looking over at Harry. "She was a bright-eyed girl, thin and mischievous, with long dark hair and beautiful skin. I saw Henry lean over to say something to her, and then he did something strange. He slapped her on the butt, not like you would slap a bad child, but like you might slap a girlfriend. A playful slap.

"And then the girl turned suddenly, and she saw me there in the window. The look on her face, Harry. My God, the look on her face. It was part bewilderment, part shame, part blame. And the blame part included me.

"She walked away, toward her mother's house. The way she looked had reminded me of something, and it troubled me the rest of the day. When it hit me, I was in bed with him that night. He was already asleep. I had to tiptoe to the bath-room, where I threw up."

Ruth paused for a few seconds, and Harry thought she might not be willing or able to go on. She seemed short of breath. Finally, she spoke again.

"One of Henry's good points, or so I thought, was that he would, when he was in the mood, take kids hunting or fishing. Even after Hank and Paul were grown, he would befriend children from the neighborhood. Sometimes he'd take several of them for a hike into the swamp. Sometimes he'd take a couple in his boat, sometimes just one.

"Sometimes he'd take girls. Sometimes he'd take boys. Nobody thought anything about it. Everybody fishes around Saraw."

Ruth said she waited for Henry to go into the swamp again, which he did two days later. This time, he went alone, and she went hunting.

She knew he considered the shed to be his private territory. It was the only outbuilding that had a key.

He didn't know, though, and never did, that Ruth had a key, too.

"It never set well with me to be locked out of anything," Ruth said. "One night, I had to come get him at the pool hall when he had gotten out of control. He'd hit one of the Morrissett boys with a cue stick. Well, he wouldn't listen to me, wouldn't calm down, and so I had him locked up.

"They gave me his keys so I could take the truck home. The next morning, before I came to get him out, I went by the hardware store and had them make a duplicate of one key.

"It tickled me, to tell you the truth, that I had the key to Henry's little one-man boys' club, but I never thought I would use it. It just made me feel good to know I had it in my purse.

"That day, though, it felt like fate to me, having had that key made."

As soon as Henry Flood was out of sight, she went to the shed and unlocked it. It took her less than 10 minutes to find what she was looking for.

"It had a lock on it, too, and the same key fit that. It was the only drawer that was locked."

Ruth didn't give Harry many details about the pictures. They had been the cheap, instant-camera type. They were all of girls, mostly very young, most of them with few or no clothes on.

At least six girls had been photographed, and she recognized five of them. The pictures must have been taken over a period of many years, because at least one of the girls was, by then, 32 years old.

Listening to Harry's story, Naomi has gone through a couple of cigarettes. For two minutes, she has barely moved, and her unblinking eyes seem now to be fixed on some spot behind him.

The story is taking its toll on the teller, too. The pain medication has kicked in hard, and Harry is aware that he is starting to slur his words slightly.

When he tells Naomi about Ruth recognizing the girls in the photographs, she shakes her head from side to side, over and over. Harry jumps at the sound of the sliding glass door opening behind him.

"You told him all this," Naomi says.

"Yes," Ruth answers.

"Anyone else?"

"You know better than that."

Ruth is giving Harry the kind of look he imagines Jesus must have given Judas. She shakes her head and sighs.

"I think I'd better take over from here, Harry. You've done enough damage for one night, and you look like you could use a break."

He hopes he hears a drop of forgiveness in her voice, but what the hell, he thinks. Pancreatic cancer is never having to say you're sorry.

"You'll thank me for this someday."

She looks at him just for an instant, whispers "maybe," and turns back to Naomi, who is sitting forward, elbows on her knees, face hidden by her hands.

Ruth sits beside her. She puts one arm and then the other around her daughter, enveloping her. Naomi tries to get away, but Ruth won't let go, hanging on with the ferocity of a mother who sees her child trapped beneath an automobile and lifts the entire car on love and adrenaline. She's angry to be forced into this and she's damned if she's going to leave it half done. There is no tentativeness in Ruth's actions, no escape for Naomi. It is all done so quietly that no one else in the house is aware they're even awake.

"Okay, baby," Ruth says, "like that man on the radio says, now for the rest of the story. Wouldn't you like to know how Henry Flood spent his last day?"

TWENTY-NINE

RUTH CROWDER FLOOD had never dispatched anything larger or more sentient than a chicken.

And after she did what she did, she would play it over in her head a thousand times.

"It just seemed easier, Harry," she said, that day in the shed. "Easier on those girls, although they'd have to be the judge of that. Easier on our sons, easier even on Henry. And I admit it: easier on me, too. Justice or revenge, I don't know. I regret a lot, but God help me, I don't regret killing Henry Flood."

After Charlotte and Jane died, Ruth employed a maid to come in every other week and hired an ancient black man to mow the grass and take care of the yard work. She kept the electricity turned on.

The aunts had left the house and most of their money to Ruth. Roy McGinnis advised her to sell the place. He told her it never would be worth the expense required to bring it up to late-20th century standards. The tin roof needed replacing, there was substantial termite damage, it still had oil heat and was cooled by two window air-conditioners. It needed aluminum siding over the old, paint-thirsty wood.

"Well," Ruth told him, "it might not be worth it to you, but it's worth it to me."

Occasionally, she would go over to her childhood home. Sometimes, she would just sit on the porch and rock. Sometimes, she would rummage through the plunder rooms, perusing the postcards, magazines, letters, jars, clothes, toys and other detritus that had settled there over a century.

She didn't like throwing things away, not even the arsenal of medicines covering every shelf of the bathroom cabinet.

Jane had suffered angina attacks for years. Her condition grew progressively worse, and she had died of a heart attack in mid-July. Charlotte had a stroke and died during the night a week later.

In their latter years, Ruth sometimes would fill the aunts' prescriptions. One day, the pharmacist had noticed the digoxin had disappeared faster than it was supposed to. He had warned Ruth that the same thing that was good for the heart in small doses could kill in larger ones.

Ruth found that Jane had simply spilled some of the pills, and she didn't think of it again until after she decided to kill Henry.

She remembered what the pharmacist had said two years before, and she remembered seeing the digoxin, sitting on an overfull shelf in the aunts' bathroom cabinet, within the last month.

She went to the main library in Newport, where she was less likely to be recognized. On the way home, she stopped by the aunts' house and took the nearly-full bottle of digoxin.

Henry Flood went into the swamp to hunt or fish every few days, deep into the fall. He could stand the cold; even in December sometimes he would stay overnight.

His drinking had increased over the years, and by 1975 he was in the strict habit of taking two fifths of Jim Beam with him into the swamp, summer or winter. He would throw the cap away when he unsealed the bottle, because by that time Henry Flood seldom dealt in bourbon units of less than a fifth.

His "traveling bourbon" he kept stored in the basement, lined up like soldiers at attention along the wall. To Ruth's knowledge, he always took the bottles on the left, sliding the rest over to take their places. He kept half-gallons of a more expensive brand upstairs for daily use, never mixing that with the Jim Beam in the basement. He would sometimes drink four fifths a week. Usually, Ruth didn't mind. Henry tended, in his last year, to get more mellow after a few drinks. Without liquor, he became fidgety and more combustible.

It took Ruth three weeks to put her plan in motion.

Henry had gone into town to shoot pool and tell war stories that November Monday morning. Ruth stayed home, calling the manager at the grill and telling her she would be there sometime before noon. Hank had already left for his carpentry shop near the old mill.

Ruth unlocked her private trunk, with 33 years of letters inside, and took out the little pharmaceutical bottle. She went to the basement shelf and removed the second fifth of Jim Beam from the left. She opened it, tearing the seal as little as possible.

"What I was counting on," she told Harry, "was that Henry wouldn't notice a little thing like a broken seal when he got to that second bottle. I thought I knew Henry Flood rather well by then, even after what I had found out, and I believed that, somewhere deep in Kinlaw's Hell, he was not going to ponder long about the seal on that second fifth of bourbon when the first bottle ran out. If it was bourbon, he was going to drink it."

She crushed the digoxin, everything in the nearly-full bottle, into powder on a paper plate. Then, she poured the fifth of bourbon into an empty Mason jar and put the powder in with it. She mixed it. Then she strained the bourbon back into the original Jim Beam bottle and sealed it. It took her less than 20 minutes.

Two days later, Henry pushed his chair back from the breakfast table and went to get his shotgun and shells.

When Ruth left for work, he was still in the basement. She resisted the urge to go home at lunch that day and see if her plan was working. When she returned at her normal time, just after 6, Hank was upstairs in his room. Henry's truck was gone; she was sure that it would be at the end of the rut road next to the old railroad bed, and that Henry and his boat were by then somewhere deep in Kinlaw's Hell.

She went into the basement, afraid he had taken the bottles, afraid he hadn't. On the wall, where 10 fifths of Jim Beam had sat two days earlier, there were eight now. None of the eight had a broken seal. That evening, she couldn't get a song out of her head that they had sung when she was a child: "Ten little, nine little, eight little Indians. . ."

"Do you know what worried me the most?" she asked Harry, sitting down again in the shed. "I was afraid he had some pictures of those girls out there in that cabin. I was afraid they'd find the cabin when they found him, and that everyone would know anyhow.

"I know I should have been more afraid of getting caught, but that didn't worry me. I didn't really think, then, about how bad it would have been if they had done an autopsy."

She knew, though, that she had left stones unturned.

"Those were the longest eight days of my life," she said. "All day Thursday, I expected to see a police car come driving up to the grill to arrest me. The more I thought about it, the more obvious that broken seal on the bourbon bottle seemed to me. It would jump out at him out there in the swamp. He'd take it back into town and have it analyzed, and that would be that.

"Then, when neither he nor the police had showed up by Friday morning, I started dropping hints that I was worried, that he didn't usually stay out two days this time of year, and so on.

"By Friday afternoon, I had gone by the house one last time, and then I called the police and told them Henry Flood was missing in Kinlaw's Hell. And for the next six days, I worried about what they might discover when they found his body, about whether a police officer could just look at somebody and tell that they had been poisoned, about whether he'd be at the cabin and what else would be there."

By the fall of 1975, the trees around Henry Flood's cabin in the swamp had grown high enough to form a canopy and make it all but invisible from the air, the way Henry wanted it. This worked neither for nor against him, because he would have been long dead even if they had found the cabin first thing on Friday.

It took them six days. Two swampers freelancing for the sheriff's department saw the buzzards circling, and they eventually found the nearly-invisible opening that led them through to Henry Flood's cabin.

Henry had managed to open the cabin door. He was lying there, half in and half out. A nearly-empty bottle of bourbon lay on the ground. It appeared to have fallen from his hand and rolled onto the dirt, where most of it had spilled, staining the white sand. The rats had found him even before the buzzards.

The sheriff and most of his deputies found their way to Henry Flood's cabin, mostly to marvel at what one man had built, by himself, hidden so deep in Kinlaw's Hell that only a dead man's body could give it away. Even after they got there, some of them got lost trying to canoe out and had to be rescued by helicopter.

Nobody seemed very interested in going back to the cabin to dust for fingerprints or look for evidence. Anyone who knew Henry Flood knew he had drunk enough to kill 10 men, that it was only a matter of time until something caught up with him.

"Do you know the most peculiar thing we saw there?" the sheriff had asked Ruth, who told Harry she stopped breathing at that point. She had already told the sheriff she had no desire to see Henry's cabin, either before or after he died. "He had saved all these empty bourbon bottles. He had 'em stacked up along one wall, about eight rows high. He had almost filled up the entire wall with empty Jim Beam bottles. Can you imagine such a thing?"

Ruth said she could.

The only other thing of note they had found, he said, was an instant camera, which he would have someone send to her. She held her breath, but the sheriff said nothing about any photographs.

He told her that one of his deputies had poured the rest of the bourbon out and stacked that final bottle next to the penultimate empty, the fifth Henry had drunk first and the last one he would ever finish.

"I guess he'd have wanted us to do that," the sheriff said, and Ruth didn't say anything.

Paul would come back for the funeral. Naomi wouldn't.

"I asked Hank to call her," Ruth said. "I wasn't up to speaking to her just then. Hank got upset with her for saying she just couldn't get away right then, but I knew this was one funeral she wouldn't be coming to. I tried to smooth it over with Hank, told him that Naomi had some bad memories about this place that she might never get over. I did get her to write him a note later."

After Harry Stein came back to Saraw, she worked up the courage to tell Naomi that she knew, too late, what Henry Flood was.

"You know, though," she told Harry, after she had finished, "there's a part of me that thinks I'm still going to be called to justice someday. The way forensic medicine is progressing, I have no doubt that they could dig Henry Flood up right now and prove he'd drunk enough digoxin to kill him. And somewhere back in Kinlaw's Hell, there's a cabin with a few hundred empty bourbon bottles in it, and one of them probably has enough digoxin residue to put me in the state penitentiary for the rest of my life, if anybody ever found it and knew what to do with it."

She looked over at him.

"But that's only right. It's good for me to live with it, to look out my window and know my undoing lies there, mocking me. I don't visit Henry's grave any more, and I don't go into that swamp. My minister would say I'm doomed, maybe in this life and surely in the next. I don't know if that's true. I've sliced it every way you can, and I still don't know.

"Some things, Harry, you just have to live with."

By then, her eyes were swollen.

"Damn you, Harry Stein," she said. "Damn you for pushing me until I told you that story. I had sworn nobody would ever hear that story. What if I tell somebody else, or you tell somebody?"

Harry, though, has had no regrets about forcing the story from her. He doesn't believe anyone is strong enough to keep a story like that inside forever. Not even Ruth.

He has never mentioned it again, after they left the old shed and put the wooden latch back in place, and neither has she, not until this dark morning.

Ruth feels surrounded, by her daughter and her past. She has just told her story a second time, 14 years later, on the deck of a Florida beach house, on the morning of her 70th birthday, with a stiff Gulf breeze trying to drive the three of them indoors. They refuse to leave, though, because each knows this might be the only place, the only time, the one correct temperature and barometric pressure for this particular story. And even Ruth realizes that it has to be told.

She could have told Naomi how Henry Flood died, she supposes. But it seemed to her a kind of protection for her daughter, who shouldn't have to know that her mother killed her stepfather, shouldn't have to keep that kind of secret her whole life.

Now, though, it is told.

Naomi finally speaks, her voice trembling.

"So, Hank and Paul don't know anything about this, about any of this?"

Ruth shakes her head.

"I just can't believe it. How could you do that?"

"If you could have, and gotten away with it," Ruth asks her, grabbing her face and forcing Naomi to look at her straight on, "wouldn't you?"

THIRTY

Paul Flood was not a careless man.

On Tuesday night, just in case, he had made sure that the minivan was filled with gas and the flashlights were well-placed. He even turned the vehicle around so that it was facing the road, only scant minutes from the bridge and the relative safety of the mainland.

Once across, he knew a back street that connected with a county road farther inland that led across the swamps to a state highway, placing him and those in his charge a full 10 miles from the coast before the first threat of major traffic delays. We shouldn't even have to run for an emergency shelter, if it comes to that, he told Hank and Harry. He figured they would be able to drive straight to Atlanta, then come back later to gawk at the damage.

Should the storm hit (and Paul possessed the skepticism of someone who has spent a moderately breezy night sleeping on a gymnasium floor because he'd been bluffed out of his comfortable home), he would be more than ready. He had set his alarm for 5 a.m., just in case.

Paul was positive, sure to his no-nonsense, science-and-math bones, that he knew when to leave. He wouldn't be with the old ladies who cut their vacations short for no good reason, and he wouldn't be one of those heroes trying to surf a hurricane. There was a certain grace in timing, he felt: not too early, not too late.

His plans would have thwarted the first surprise that greeted them Wednesday morning.

At 11:15 the night before, the television weather report had "situated" the storm 180 miles out to sea, meandering toward a position west of Mobile, barely moving at all, with top winds of 95 miles per hour. In the face and voice of the local reporter, a young woman barely out of college who still had trouble differentiating Utah from Colorado on the weather map, there was disrespect.

"Jim," she had told the anchor, "I think this storm is a little bit of a sissy."

But by 4:30 a.m., the hurricane apparently had decided to reinvent itself, something Theron and Belle Crowder might have appreciated.

Without warning, it had begun moving forward at 25 miles an hour, and it had swung like a magnet, like a bull to a red cape, toward the part of the Florida Panhandle that contains Sugar Beach. Its wind speed increased to 120 miles per hour and would reach 140. It was, before anyone could think about preparing for its undependability, on a course that would have it making landfall 10 miles from Sugar Beach, before 9 a.m.

This hundred-to-one shot Paul was prepared for. But he hadn't counted on the other surprise, the one that would turn self-sufficiency into negligence.

Across the sound from Sugar Beach is the mouth of the Wewahitchka River. The sound catches everything that the Wewa sends down: red clay from the Georgia foothills, pesticides, tree limbs, the discarded and drowned. The sound reciprocates by sending a variety of items back up the Wewa: small pleasure boats, larger commercial vessels, barges to haul pine wood back down to the Gulf and the big world beyond.

Sometime after dark the evening before, a tugboat had maneuvered a barge many times its size into the sound, seeking to wait out the weather, see which way the hurricane was going, then continue on up the Wewa to Bonner, Georgia, where harvested pine trees awaited.

The barge was sitting idle and harmless in the quiet shallow water behind the island, one of dozens that would bide their time overnight there in any given year, weathering large and small storms. If the hurricane took a turn toward Sugar Beach, Wewa Sound was as safe a place as any for a barge and a tug.

The tugboat's crew was catching a few hours' sleep. Someone was later alleged to have been on duty at 4:30 that morning.

The water sometimes sends its warning even before the wind does, to those paying attention. And the Gulf was showing Harry, Ruth and Naomi some uncharacteristic muscle by the time the three of them went to bed in the predawn, making promises to talk more later. Harry wondered if the promises would be valid in sunlight.

The pounding surf did not really register. Ruth later would realize that she was, in her distraction, equating it to the ocean waves to which she was accustomed.

Around 4:30, Harry collapses on their bed and assumes Ruth will follow soon, overwrought as she is.

He closes his eyes, just for a second.

Harry figures he must have been asleep for only a few minutes when he hears the horn's relentless, maddening blast. At what seems the exact same time, Paul bangs on their door.

"Get up! We've got to go."

It's as loud or urgent as he has ever heard Paul.

"Oh, God," Ruth says, wide awake. "Oh, my God."

She is dressed and out the door in the time it takes Harry to sit upright. He feels as if he would like to throw up and then go to sleep for a very long time. That he has time to do neither is soon evident.

Normally, the barge would have been in no danger of losing its mooring.

But Harry and Ruth have drifted beyond normality, into a world where men who have worked too many hours think they deserve to rest rather than stand watch, where taxpayers see no sense in building a second causeway over a body of water until it is ready to devour them, where hurricanes change their minds.

When the barge breaks loose, it is a quarter-mile from the causeway, closer than it should be. In a calm sea it wouldn't matter, but in a calm sea, it never would have lost its mooring in the first place.

Paul knows there is trouble even before the alarm sounds. The slow-motion collision, the discordant, ghostly grinding of barge metal with bridge metal, followed by the crashing of something heavy into shallow water — he hears it all.

And he doesn't need The Weather Channel to know he has erred, in a position where his pride has left no cushion for mistakes. The sound of the wind and the surf tell him all he needs to know.

Now, he's going through the house, not running but with hurry in his steps and his voice, rousing everyone. Hank and Naomi have to come for Harry and help him out. He sees Ruth standing there, waiting for him, wringing her hands.

Harry sees that they are in various stages of dress. Ruth is wearing her nightgown; he's still in his old-man's pajamas. Naomi, Tran, Paul and Hank have on a mixture of daywear and nightwear, whatever they could find quickly by the illumination of the hallway light. Stephen and Leigh, the most mobile, quickest to reach full consciousness, have T-shirts and jeans, even shoes.

Leigh asks her father again what's the matter.

"It's the causeway,' he says. "I think we need to leave now."

They want to know more, but Paul isn't talking.

"Ruth?" Tran says. She's been silent until this point.

Ruth looks at her, mute.

"Happy birthday."

Ruth just nods her head. The others laugh, all except Paul, who tells them to hurry up. He shoos them out the door, trying hard not to show panic. They spill into the van, Paul last, keys in hand.

The engine doesn't start on the first try.

"Oh, please," he says it like a prayer, and the second time it catches.

They head down the street to the cottage's rear, parallel to the Gulf and the sound, and Harry knows there's a problem before they even reach the road leading to the causeway. Fuzzy red stars shine out at them from ground level up ahead through the foggy, soupy air, some of them twinkling on and off as drivers momentarily take their feet off the brakes.

They are stuck in a traffic jam 100 yards from the left turn that, in another 100 yards, they expect to lead them to permanently dry land. On an island which Harry figures can't contain more than a few dozen people by this time, they are in gridlock. Ahead, people are blowing their horns, as if some Sunday driver, some lost tourist, is the cause of their delay. Endlessly, tirelessly the alarm continues bleating. It seems to be coming from the tug.

"Shut up!" Stephen says, putting his hands to his ears, speaking for them all.

Paul pulls off the street, gets out and starts running. Hank goes with him, taking a step and then stopping to tell them he will be back. After a few seconds, Naomi follows.

In the car, the rest sit in their abandonment and wonder. In the distance, higher than the brake lights and out in the sound, they see other, larger lights. They can hear angry, desperate, foreign voices, too far away to understand, even if they knew the language.

In a few minutes that seem to Harry like an hour, the three of them come back. They're arguing, then grow quiet as they reach the minivan.

Inside, Paul tells them the extent of their problem.

Where the barge hit, it tore a section that Paul estimates to be at least 150 feet long out of the center of the low-slung causeway.

"Normally," he says, "it wouldn't be much of a swim."

Normal it isn't, Harry thinks, and he knows he doesn't have to remind Paul that Ruth could not swim 10 feet on a sunny day with angels throwing rose petals on the water in front of her. And the 1935 Virginia state breaststroke age-group champion wonders if he could do a lap in a pool right now.

Harry can barely keep his eyes open. He should be energized by fear and desperation, but he can't seem to raise any adrenaline. In saner times, he supposes he might be asking someone how far to the nearest hospital. He feels that some unwelcome corner has been turned, and the door at the end of the tunnel has Worse written on it.

Hank reaches over and turns on the radio. The stations still operating are full of laconic yet somehow urgent voices: ". . . residents of lower Bay County should evacuate immediately . . ." ". . . took an unexpected turn and has picked up in intensity and speed, with landfall now predicted for between 8:30 and 9 a.m., Eastern Daylight Time . . ." ". . . winds that could reach 140 miles per hour. . ." ". . . somewhere between Bay Shores and Sugar Beach . . ."

By the time Paul starts the van again, it's past 6. In the line up ahead, there's chaos. It won't be light yet for more than an hour, so most of what can be seen are outlines, but they can tell that the occupants of two of the cars are fighting. Men, women and children have all poured out of two other vehicles and now wrestle with and gesture at each other in the chill and wind like some primitive tribe trying to dance the storm back to sea.

"Shit," Paul says, and the rest are quiet.

Some of the stranded are doing U-turns in the soft sand and heading back to their cottages. Some have left their 4-wheel drive trucks and are walking and running in the direction of the severed causeway.

"Well," Paul says, and he sounds a little more collected, "we ain't going to figure anything out sitting here." And he backs up and turns around.

The next thing Harry knows, Ruth is waking him, back at the cottage.

Paul leads them inside. They go silently and all settle in the living room.

"Are you OK, honey?" Ruth asks, and Harry realizes he is leaning against her. He can't seem to wake up.

He squeezes her hand with as much strength as he has and tells her he's fine.

Paul, Hank, Tran and Naomi try to attack it logically: They can either try to ride the storm out in their cottage or they can try to get across 150 feet of choppy water.

"It looked to me like part of the road was still there, just broken off," Naomi says. "Maybe it would be like two short swims instead of one long one."

Paul and Tran, it turns out, have four life-jackets. They try to figure how those go into eight people, then look to Paul, who is, despite everything, still the reigning expert.

"I just can't see it," he says, slowly and deliberately. "I know Naomi could make it, and maybe some of the rest could, but . . ."

"Then what you need to do is leave the ones that can't swim back here," Ruth says. Ever the pragmatist. "Harry and I have a better chance here than we do out in that water."

This is violently vetoed, even though to Harry it makes sense.

Paul goes outside. The wind is getting stronger, slowly but inevitably. An aluminum lawn chair from a house somewhere down the beach flies onto their deck, barely missing him, and crashes into the side railing.

When he returns, he says he thinks the cottage will hold, but he calls Stephen outside to help him with something. They come back with the small, bright-green boat they store underneath, next to the pilings; they use it for fishing in the sound. And he has the four life-jackets. They have to turn the boat sideways to get it into the living room, where it looks ridiculous and ominous.

"Will we need that?" Naomi asks, what they're all thinking.

"No," Paul says, "but it's like wearing your seatbelt. You want to be sure."

No one else says anything.

They find a radio station across the sound that is still on the air, and they are told what they already know: Sugar Beach is cut off, not a tethered link to mainland America anymore but the independent entity it was until the bridge was built 20 years earlier, proud, free and vulnerable.

The station reports that a rescue operation is being attempted. On that thin hope, they leave again, get back in the minivan, now swaying in the gusts of wind, and try the causeway a second time. They get closer, to the bridge road itself, where they park and walk to the sundered edge of the pavement. It is broken cleanly and falls off like a tabletop. There, most of the island's remaining population is standing and pacing. One woman in front of them is screaming loudly enough to be heard above the howling wind. Two men are holding her, to keep her from diving in. Another woman, her voice quavering, tells Ruth, leaning and shouting into her ear, that the screaming woman's husband tried to swim across. They both did, but she turned back.

"They could swim good," the woman says, then turns her eyes back to the blackness and water. Harry knows it's near dawn, but he doubts that the dark will lift anytime soon.

Across the way, on the bridge, someone has managed to produce a light like the ones highway crews use at night. It only succeeds in blinding those on the island. In the intermediate distance, what appears to be a charter boat is bouncing around, bobbing up and down in the waves. It seems to be meant for their salvation, but Harry can see that it is making no progress at all. Several men have elbowed their way to the front of the crowd, urging the boat on, sure to be first in line if it happens to reach the island.

They never see the wave that combines with the wind to flip the small boat, and Harry will never know what happens to their would-be rescuers. The boat, under no one's control, smashes sickeningly against the almost-submerged ruins of the causeway's center span.

Harry can see that their chances of getting across are diminishing by the minute. Only one of their group would be an even bet to make it; Naomi doesn't mention this, and neither does anyone else. By half past 7, when they turn back, they all know they will be in the cottage when the brunt of the storm hits.

To Harry, it is almost a relief to leave the panic and return to what he thinks of, in an attack of morbid humor that makes him almost giggle, as their last resort.

Others follow their lead. Those who are left greet this day, darker still than a half-moon night, with dread.

Paul and Hank haul the life-jackets back up the stairs to the living room when they get back to the cottage. Inside, everyone tries to dry off and get warm. Tran thinks of breakfast, something to get them through a hurricane, but then the power goes off, and they are reduced to peanut butter, jelly, bread, orange juice and soft drinks. They take their meal on the floor, as far as possible from the windows Paul and Hank have tried, belatedly, to cover.

Paul sits down next to Ruth.

"Momma," he says, "I'm sorry. But we'll get through this. We aren't going to let anything happen to you."

Ruth pats him on the knee. Neither she nor Harry has any appetite. Harry slips away for more pain pills and then returns.

He has somehow nodded off when the storm hits full force. He is dreaming, and the howling that was him, wartime Harry, wrestling with Sergeant Stevens, is the hurricane, upon them at last.

He rubs his eyes and looks at Ruth beside him. She is pale, and her hand feels cold as ice, even compared to his. Harry notices that his ears have popped, and there is a briny smell even inside, as if the wind is blowing salt through cracks they can't even see.

"Well," he says, just to say something, "we'll ride this thing to Mexico if we have to."

Neither of them is in a mood for lightness or brave chatter, though. Harry is surprised, when he can rise above his own fear and pain to think about it, that Ruth isn't running around in circles, stark raving mad.

For an hour and a half, until sometime after 10, they sit in the near-dark, saying nothing, afraid to let the storm know they are there, hiding from the bogeyman like frightened children, trying to ride it out. Water is running down the inside of the walls, coming in sideways under the molding. The roof groans for mercy.

Nobody wants to see what's outside, and nobody wants to turn the portable radio back on. Harry sees that Leigh is crying, and he thinks Stephen might be, too. Hank, trapped in a small space with seven other people, seems to be concentrating on something in the far distance that only he can see. Naomi is too nervous even to smoke.

Then Tran remembers. She gets up and scurries into the kitchen. Paul is about to go after her, to see what's wrong, when she comes back in, bent low in case the window is blown out, carrying something in front of her with both hands.

The cake.

Ruth's birthday cake has 70 candles on it. Tran has in her pockets kitchen matches and a knife. She lights three of the candles before giving up, and they all quietly urge Ruth to blow them out. She manages, through her tears, to wetly snuff them.

Tran cuts a piece for each of them, and they sing "Happy Birthday" just above a whisper, so the storm won't hear them.

They are eating birthday cake when the wave hits.

THIRTY-ONE

Harry would never know how high the wave was, but the room became noticeably darker in the half-second before it hit.

The cottage pilings are six feet high, and the building itself is another eight at least, so he figures, in the time he has to figure anything, that it must have taken a wave of 20 feet or so to snuff their already-meager light.

The impact blows out every window facing the Gulf, and water is rushing in all around them. The impact has loosened the bond between walls and roof, and in another 20 seconds there is no roof. The whole structure is partially loose of its pilings, tilting at a 20-degree angle. The cottage is moving, sliding. All the water is draining to the western, lower end of it.

Paul screams for them to get outside, on the deck. Harry wonders if this is such a good idea, but he is beyond questioning authority. Stephen has grabbed the life jackets, and Paul is trying to wrestle the boat out with him; he seems to Harry to be engaging in some kind of awkward waltz with it.

They are forced to get on their hands and knees, as flat against the wind as they can manage, willing themselves unseen the way they tried to make themselves unheard when they were inside. Paul and Tran get life jackets on their children, and Naomi and Hank manage to put one on Ruth, who seems to Harry to have turned to stone in her shock. She seems to have aged 10 years in this one morning. Paul passes the other jacket to Harry and tells him to put it on.

He says no, give it to Tran, or to Hank.

"Put on the goddamn jacket and shut up!" Paul screams over the wind and the waves. Somehow, with Hank's help, Harry succeeds in doing this. Old people and children first, he thinks to himself.

They have no chance; Harry can see that. He glances

back just as the cottage slowly separates from the deck, crumpling into the surf in slow motion, soon to be reduced to individual boards and shingles, then into smaller pieces. He imagines that eventually the cottage will be bits of colored sand under the feet of fearless future children.

But they do not sink. Somehow, perhaps from the old-timers he listens to at bait shops and the dock, Paul is aware that a deck can float.

The wave and its smaller afterwaves have driven Gulf water across to the sound. The barrier island of Sugar Beach was formed by another, nameless hurricane in the 1850s, and now the sea appears to be reclaiming it, reuniting with Wewahitchka Sound.

The deck, though, floats.

The eight of them cling to each other, to railings, to anything with a grip. Harry wonders if God is trying to find out how much they want to live.

At one point, Ruth is washed halfway off their deck-raft. Harry is afraid she will die of fright; she can't even scream. The worst part, though, is that he is beyond being able to help her; he can only watch her terror while Paul and Hank drag her back on board, saved momentarily from her worst nightmare.

After her rescue, Ruth and he lie flat against the storm. He reaches out and grabs the hand he couldn't reach when it mattered, and she closes on it so hard that he is sure he has broken a finger, but he has no intention of letting go, ever.

Harry has no idea how long it lasts. Paul is rolling around on the deck, trying to make sure there are still eight of them, a border collie obsessively herding his charges toward safety. The small green boat is long gone; none of them even remembers its departure.

There is no sense of direction, just wetness around and above as much as beneath, a gray continuity, a howling that fills all the space in their brains. Harry, with what strength he has left, howls to match it, and when he looks over at Paul, he's howling, too, but now they are drowned out completely, pantomime screamers. It's as if the wind is blowing the sounds back down their throats. Salt water burns his mouth, his nose, his eyes.

In a brief respite between bursts of wind and long, rolling waves, Harry sees something different: a swatch of red in the distance. He recognizes it and points it out to Paul. They must be moving westward, toward the one thing that stands out against the gray: the crimson roof of the Sugar Beach Inn.

Then, long after Harry has given up on the concept of breaks, when he has been hanging on for what seems an eternity out of sheer habit of living, it stops.

The calm is on them almost as quickly as the wave was. They have to remind themselves to let go a little. Now, instead of being at sea on the deck of Paul's splintered cottage in the middle of a Force 5 hurricane, they are merely at sea on the deck.

"The eye," Paul says. "It'll be back."

Harry doesn't want to know how soon. He is so tired, but he is allowed no rest.

They are drifting to the west. He can see that the Sugar Beach Inn is much closer than it was the last time he looked, so close that they can see individual people on the porch that overhangs water where the beach was a few hours ago. He can make out voices in the distance. Looking around, he sees the roofs of at least two cottages farther out in the Gulf. Clinging to one of them, several hundred yards away, is a woman, straddling the top of the roof. She appears to be naked.

The beach itself has changed completely. There seems to be a channel between Paul and Tran's cottage and the inn, the only structure still standing on the west side of the island.

The Sugar Beach Inn was built on enough fill dirt to place it 10 feet above the rest of the island, an edge the inn needed on this day. Some of the stranded islanders might have figured this out, Harry thinks, or perhaps everyone on the porch, calling to them through the gray mist, is a grateful guest.

Harry looks around at the rest. All of them are bleeding; no one has on anything resembling full clothing. Ruth and Leigh have lost their blouses, and now that the eye is upon them, they have the luxury of embarrassment. Stephen has one shoe on and is holding his leg. He and Hank have wicked-looking cuts on their arms.

Paul is looking at the Sugar Beach Inn's bright-red roof.

"We have to try for it," he says, and no one disputes this.

They are almost even with the building, perhaps 100 yards east and 200 yards out. Beyond that is open Gulf, and Harry knows they won't be in God's eye much longer.

"The water shouldn't be too deep here," Naomi says. She's been swimming farther out than this.

But when she was swimming, Harry thinks, the Sugar Beach Inn was on dry land. None of them can envision the present depth of the water between them and the inn.

The respite from all the wind and noise makes Harry sleepy. He is beyond pain and beyond caring. Still, though, they won't let him rest.

There is little time for a plan. Harry guesses Paul's strategy is that surely, this time, they are bound to catch a break. Murphy's law in reverse: Everything that can go wrong won't go wrong.

Naomi tells Ruth she will swim beside her, that she will lead her until Naomi can feel the bottom with her feet.

Harry isn't worried about Paul, or Tran. They are both excellent swimmers, and they plan to escort Hank and Leigh to safety.

Stephen, though, concerns him. The top freestyler at his school, he's already given his lifejacket to Hank and will stay with Harry, floating and dogpaddling beside him, urging him to shore. But the way he's holding his leg, Harry is sure he's suffering from more than the deep cut that is starting to bleed in the saltwater.

Stephen swears he can make it, though. Paul asks him if he is sure, and the boy says yes. The look they exchange, hanging to the side of the floating deck, is one that passes between fathers and sons who have camped together, sailed together, taken small risks for large profits. It is the look of fathers and sons who will be friends. Harry can tell, in that one look, that Paul doesn't fuss over Stephen. Harry wishes he could see, once more, his Martin.

He is sure Stephen will make it, buoyed by Paul's confidence if nothing else. He only has to avoid getting tangled up with ancient flotsam, Harry realizes, only has to keep from being dragged down by the death grip of desperate, shameless, selfish, hopeless old age, willing to take youth with it to the bottom on the outside chance of living five more minutes.

His eyes meet Ruth's. She looks so worn that Harry wonders if she will ever get back what has been lost this morning, even if she makes it to shore. She's still vomiting seawater, and she says nothing when she catches her breath and looks back, but from that look Harry sees that he must look worse than he feels even. Harry and Ruth shake their heads in unison, lying on their deck-raft, hoping for strength, and Harry surprises himself by laughing. Ruth tries to smile but can't.

Harry suddenly realizes that the pain has eased, but he is feeling nothing much else, either, except some regret. What he wants more than anything is a nap. They won't let him sleep.

They leave their raft when they have no other choice, with the inn and safety about to slip past and the storm returning. Naomi and Ruth go first, Naomi jumping in and then pulling her mother in with her. Naomi is swimming a side stroke, holding Ruth's life jacket with her free hand, talking to her as if she is trying to calm a wild bird trapped inside a house. Ruth's panicky paddling succeeds mainly in splashing more water into Naomi's eyes.

Next comes Paul, guiding Hank. Something Paul told Harry one time bobs to the surface of his memory. Paul had said swimming was the only sport at which he was sure he could beat his brother, probably because Hank couldn't bear the momentary terror of being completely underwater. Now, Paul is trying to jolly his brother along and avoid a full-scale panic attack in the water by a large, powerful man.

Tran swims beside Leigh, speaking to her in a language Harry has never heard before but which the girl seems to understand. She nods and paddles forward confidently in her life jacket.

Stephen and Harry come last. Harry manages to roll off the raft; he had just as soon stay, to see where they wind up, but they won't let him. His hands don't seem to work; he is having difficulty hanging on to the orange collar that lets him float in this unfriendly sea. His swimming days seem to be over.

The others are in front of them when Harry realizes, through the mist of his self-absorption, that Stephen is in trouble. Whatever he has broken is impairing his swimming to the point that he is losing ground against the current. The others are moving away, and Harry is too weak to make himself heard by the bobbing figures ahead.

Every time Stephen kicks, he cries out. He's trying to make it on his arms alone, and Harry can see it isn't going to be enough. Everything his father could teach him won't get him through this. Goddammit, Harry thinks, why couldn't you see your son needed help? Why are you putting this on me?

There just isn't enough, Harry sees. Not enough life preservers, time, luck, able bodies. What we're going for here, he thinks to himself, is the best possible outcome, trying to do the best we can.

Harry wants to tell someone he's far overdue for a nap. He giggles and swallows some saltwater.

Still, it is not an easy thing — mentally or physically — to slip the life jacket over his head and hand it to the boy.

"Here," he says. Stephen shakes his head, swallowing Gulf water and coughing, but something makes him reach out for it anyhow. Harry summons the strength to help him slide it on.

Harry tells him, two or three ragged, breathless words at a time, that he will be alongside, that the old man is twice the swimmer he is. Just aim for the red roof, he says, and don't look back.

Harry wishes there were time to tell Stephen the story of his grandfather, the man who swam a river to get to America.

He stays above water for some seconds, long enough to see Stephen turn and follow the other bobbing forms in front of him. He looks back once, and Harry can swear that the face he sees there belongs to a sergeant who's been dead more than half a century. The sergeant, like Harry Stein himself, appears to be finally at peace.

THIRTY-TWO

Nov. 10, 1995
Saraw, N.C.

Dearest Harry,

We are home now.

It's been so long since I've written you a letter that I hardly remember how to start.

They let me out of the hospital last week, and Paul and Tran wanted me to stay with them in Atlanta for a while, or at least they said they did. But I'll recuperate better back here, in my very own house.

They want me to eat more, but there's not a thing in the world that I want right now. I wish you could see me; yesterday, I walked into the bathroom, turned around and there was this starved skeleton of an old hag. I made Hank take that mirror down.

The pneumonia seems to be gone. I'm not coughing up blood any more, although they insist that I keep taking these dreadful pills for two more weeks. My wrist has healed.

But you know, Harry, it isn't the same. I don't think it ever will be.

I'm resentful, Harry. This is supposed to help. The doctor, the psychiatrist they sent me to after they were able to move me from Florida up to the hospital in Atlanta, said it might. I told her about our letters on the third visit; she must have listened to me for an hour. I guess that's what they get paid to do.

The next time, she suggested that I write you one more letter. I didn't see how that made much sense, and I think I called her a quack. This morning, though, I got up at dawn, and I saw the first real frost, turning the dead grass from here to Kinlaw's Hell into a diamond field in the first light. And I turned around to call it to your attention. That's when I started thinking about doing what that psychiatrist suggested.

It's mid-morning now. I'm back in bed, sitting up and using the lap table. The light is playing on the wall we used to face together, and the naked pecan tree is making patterns on it with its brittle old branches.

It's a good day for writing.

Naomi swears we weren't in the water more than 15 minutes, but it seemed like hours. Nothing has ever frightened me so, Harry. I needed a lifetime worth of courage to keep going, although I'm not sure Naomi wouldn't have just carried me in on her back if it had come to that.

There wasn't time to think of anything for a while. I'd swallowed so much water that when I came to, I was vomiting it and everything else up. They said Naomi gave me mouth-to-mouth. They had to carry me up the hill to the motel — I think Hank did that — because the storm was coming back.

Lying across his shoulder like a sack of flour, I was looking backward, from where we'd just come. I saw Leigh standing, looking out at the waves. Tran was at her feet, where Stephen was lying, the life jacket still around him. Two men with a board were trying to move him. I wondered why Paul was still in the water, almost neck deep in it. Tran was calling to him, and I couldn't make out what she said at first. Finally, I understood.

Leave him, she was shouting. It's too late. You'll drown, too.

Hank wouldn't let me down. From his voice, I knew he was crying. You've got to come on, Momma, he said. There isn't anything we can do. Come on, Momma.

We rode out the lesser half of the storm in that motel. There were others in there who had lost family, and there were others there more beaten up than Stephen. The people inside made more noise than the hurricane, grief feeding on itself.

If it makes you feel any better, the doctor said he's pretty sure Stephen never would have made it to shore without that life jacket. Even with it, Paul had to help him in. He's still using a cane, but his hip will be fine.

We all blame ourselves, Harry. We can't help it. The doctor, the one who told me to write to you, says it's normal, it'll pass.

Stephen swears he's never going to the ocean again. He

wants to move to Colorado and live with Naomi's family, as far away from the beach as he can get.

He and I were in the same hospital, and one day he came to see me, hobbling down the hall on the crutches they'd just turned him loose with.

We talked some, about this and that. He's not much of a talker, and I've been a little terse of late. Finally, he just burst out crying, sitting in the chair beside my bed, and told me how sorry he was that he took that life jacket.

I told him what I think you probably would have told him, Harry, that you knew he wasn't going to make it without some help, and that you were too weak to make it anyway, even with the life jacket. "Why throw good money after bad?" you might have said. I told him you were a good man and a smart one, that you had figured all the angles. I told him what you always told me: Harry Stein doesn't make a play if he doesn't know how it will turn out (although we both know you broke that rule on occasion). The only way to pay Harry back, I told Stephen, was to live long and well with the life he gave you. We held on to each other for a while and then he left.

Someday, Harry, and although this just came to me, I know it just as well as I know I'm sitting here in this bed, Stephen will marry and have a son, and he'll name him Harry. Maybe not Harold Stein Flood, but Harry for sure. I know that just as sure as I knew there was another hurricane in my life.

Paul feels guilty about everything. I don't know if he'll ever get over this. But Harry, the only way he'd have taken it any worse would have been if Stephen had drowned. How could he have lived with that? We've all told him that it could have happened to anyone. Who could have predicted such a thing as that barge breaking loose? We tell him 12 people drowned on the island, and if the Sugar Beach Inn had been built a little more shoddy, it would have been a lot worse than that.

By the way, you'd get a laugh out of this: They're already talking about another link, a drawbridge, for the other side of the island, a back door out. And you know what they're talking about naming it? The Harry Stein

Memorial Bridge. They made so much of it in the papers and on TV. They interviewed Tran on CNN, and she did such a fine job of telling the whole world what you did. I don't suppose a state senator from North Carolina carries a lot of clout in Florida, but I have a few friends of friends, Harry. It could happen.

I took Paul aside before we left. Look, I told him, I've spent my whole life afraid of the sea, terrified. I don't want you to be like that. What I want you to do is take that insurance money and build yourself another cottage at the beach. Maybe not right here, but on some beach somewhere. I promised him I'd visit him just like always, that the water was just the water and not some curse or ghost out there to haunt us. Truth is, I'm less afraid of it now than I've ever been. It's done its worst with me and mine. It can have me, if it wants me. Paul's fearlessness, his love of danger and challenge, is what has made him what he is. He wouldn't be worth a hoot as a father or a husband or a man if he changed from that. Paul will get better, although it may take some more prodding to get him back to the beach. I might let someone else do the rest of the prodding, though; my heart's just not in it, Harry.

Hank punishes himself for not being a better swimmer. If he had been a better swimmer, there would have been one more life jacket, is how he figures it. I've told him, over and over, that you weren't going to make it, that I saw it in the look you gave me before I went over. That's my story, as they say, and I'm sticking to it.

I told him the last thing I saw Harry Stein do was laugh.

It was really fine of your family to let you be buried here, in the same cemetery with my parents, the same one I'll be in someday. I was glad Martin and Nancy came.

There were some in my little church, maybe, who tisk-tisked about a Jew in the Crowder family cemetery, but they're the same ones who disapproved of us living together in our terrible sin, and nobody has the nerve to criticize me to my face anymore. I'm too old and too mean.

One day, it will make me comfortable to look out my window and see your headstone, hard as it is now. I couldn't bear to think of you under some horizontal piece of rock, the kind people can step on or their dogs can go to the bathroom on, in some place far away. I didn't want you cremated in a vase in one of those little drawers. I'd have to visit you once or twice a year, no matter where you were, and it would make me sad all over again. Having you here every day will eventually make me immune to the pain.

Eventually.

And Naomi. Poor Naomi takes the blame, too.

She wishes she had been nicer to you. (I tell her she was as nice as could be expected, under the circumstances.) She wishes she hadn't kept you outside until almost dawn (as if a couple of hours' sleep one the way or the other could have changed things; as if, I'm sure, you weren't the one doing all the talking). She wishes she would have insisted on getting you to a hospital when she first saw you at Sugar Beach, because she knew you were at death's door. (Why not spend the last few days with your family, I told her, at a nice beach?)

Of course, while I'm trying to make everyone else feel normal and halfway good again, my own guilt is like a sack of bricks on my back. Why didn't I marry you, when you came back to me and made my life worth living? Why didn't I take better care of you?

I've always been too stubborn, too proud of sticking with something just because I decided to stick with it, as if changing for the better would be a sign of weakness. "I'm not going to make Harry Stein feel like he has to marry me because I'm pregnant, and that's it." "I'm going to have the baby, and that's it." "I'm not going to leave my husband just because he beats me and terrorizes the children, and that's it." "I'm not going to get married again, because the first one was such a disaster, and that's it." My life has been defined by "that's it."

After my parents died, my grandfather decreed that I would never be allowed anywhere near the ocean again. I was 14 and on a secret date before I ever returned to the beach. My grandfather's favorite expression, his response to any questioning of his authority, was "Because I said so." People thought he was a strong man because he never relented. They say my father was like that, too. Heredity? Environment? Surely there's something I can blame.

I realize that, as much as we talked and wrote, all those years, there are still things I never said.

I never said how hurt I really was, beneath all the pride, that you didn't somehow deduce my pregnancy, my need for you, my willingness to stand beside you no matter what anyone might say, in your family or mine. I never totally forgave you for that.

I never said how big a part that hurt pride played in my refusing to marry you when you came back.

I never told you how secretly, maliciously glad I was, in that dark little corner of my heart where selfishness blots out all else, when your marriage didn't work out.

I never admitted the grim martyr's pleasure I took in waiting out Henry Flood, no matter what it cost my children.

That psychiatrist — I told her some of this. I don't know why; I guess they're just good at drawing people out.

She told me it's never too late.

It's too late if Harry's dead, I snapped back.

But it's never too late for you, she said. She told me something that worked for her. She said that she just tried, every day, to improve a little bit. Maybe she would learn a new word, or she would read an article about something important, even if it bored her to death. Or she would make peace with someone, even if she thought the other person was wrong.

Nobody ever reaches perfection, she told me, but it gives you a sense of accomplishment, a feeling of forward motion, if you just keep pushing that rock up the hill, like Sisyphus. Except, she said, in real life, the rock doesn't roll back. In real life, you can push it a few inches forward, stop and rest, and then push it a few more inches.

Fair enough. So these are my few inches for this particular day.

If anything good has come out of this blackest month, it's Naomi and me. She stayed with me for a week, before they moved me to Atlanta. We talked and talked, more than we had since she was a little girl.

There was a time, before Henry Flood changed all that, when Naomi and I could sit there at the grill, between shifts, and talk with such ease. In the years before your return, the memories that got me through rough days were Harry Stein on the church steps in 1942 and my chats with Naomi in those innocent times. Damn Henry Flood. Damn forgiveness. This day, I'm not up to pushing the rock those few inches. I might never be strong enough for that.

Before Naomi went back to Colorado, we agreed to wipe the slate clean. We agreed that life was too short for us to get on each other's nerves anymore. We agreed, for the most part, to stop dwelling on the imperfections of the past and try to salvage what we have left.

It might work. It might not. I'm going to try my damndest, though, and I'm not going to sulk and fret. If I have to go out there uninvited, I'm going to visit Naomi and Thomas and Grace and Gary in the new year.

On the evening before she left, Naomi hugged me goodbye, and for the first time in 40 years, I didn't feel that tension, that holding back. And she told me she loved me. That might be what got me this far out of that black night you left us in.

You know what? I think I might be getting my Naomi back. Wouldn't that be something, Harry?

There is one more thing.

Roy McGinnis came and got me in Atlanta — talked Hank into letting him do it — and drove me all the way back to Saraw. He didn't say much, just drove until he got tired, then got us two rooms at a Hampton Inn, bought us dinner and breakfast the next morning, then took me home.

He's been up here to see me almost every day, even though most days I'm not much company. Those days, he just sits and holds his hat in his hands, says something once in a while, waits for me to cheer up. He usually does cheer me up, Harry.

Roy never was much to look at, and he isn't getting any better with age. Who among us is?

But he's been my friend. Just between you and me, I think he's had a crush on me for the last 50-some years, since we were in high school. He's been my protector more than once, and I'm ashamed to say I've usually taken him for granted. Now, him an old widower and me an old widow (truly a widow now, Harry), I finally told him how much his loyalty has meant to me. He just shrugged his big old shoulders and said that was what friends were for.

I'm going to let him keep coming around, Harry, just to see how things go. It might work out, it might not. Too soon to tell.

There's one thing we ought to get straight, though. There will never, ever be another time for me like that evening on the front porch of Crowders Presbyterian Church, Sept. 5, 1942. Everything else has been made of lesser stuff, even the second coming of Harry Stein. Some of it's been good, some of it's been bad, some of it's just been different. My weeks with you, my early days with Naomi, nothing came along to match that. It's horrible to say such things, when you've given birth to three other children, by another man, and that's why no living soul is going to see this letter. But it's true.

The key from here on out, if you listen to that doctor I had in Atlanta, is to make the best out of the material we have left. The idea of pushing forward a little bit every day, that's growing on me.

Maybe I'll even take swimming lessons.

I don't believe in omens, Harry, and, God help me, I'm not even sure about Him sometimes. Before I finished this letter, though, I took a little nap. When I woke up, the radio was on this station that neither Hank nor I have ever listened to, to my knowledge.

And you know what was playing?

"Deep in the Heart of Texas."

I clapped four times, and said goodbye.